Magi
Mayhem

Slate R. Raven

Dedication

This book is dedicated to my friends and *few* family members; those who stayed by my side and had my back, despite how difficult it was to do it. You have my undying gratitude and love!

Chapter One

Jessica stood glancing at her watch, wondering how much time she had to get ready before she went to her favorite tavern in the area. Rushing into the lake house, she stripped down and pulled on the clothes she'd bought at the mall back in Chicago. While she stood in the bathroom drinking a cup of cold Southern Comfort, she sighed and began to curl her bangs.

When she finally finished her necessary beautification ritual, she spared no time to even glance in the mirror. Jess wasn't a very patient person, so she swiftly swiped her keys off the countertop and walked purposefully out of the house toward her forest green Ford Explorer baring vanity plates that were far out of date. She'd purchased them back when she was working as a CPA and was so proud that her plates announced it. However, now she was no longer working in the world of numbers and reports, making her plates in dire need of retirement; Jessica was always dilatory when it came to getting things done, another reason her divorce had taken her so long to get finalized.

Loading her purse and person with little tricks and illusions from the back of her truck, Jessica was ready to go to Badgers. She often played practical jokes on drunken people in the bars—it was her form of entertainment. It gave her the ability to practice her trade while amusing Rick and Nancy, the owners of the Badger's Paw. Their bar was their second home. Everyone in the place knew and loved them immediately. Both truly enjoyed their work, and thus, they had earned in full measure their bar's mantra, "Best Bar in Wisconsin!"

Jessica's tricks frequently came in handy when fending off unwanted attention from some of the more undesirable men that would constantly hit on her—as though the drinks they had consumed miraculously made them more attractive to her instead of making them slur their words and spew spittle across her table. The part that upset her was that only the most undesirable types made passes at her; the others she had to pursue on her own. A few flashy illusions, a wintry stare, and a few elegant insults would leave the drunkards stumbling away, their faces burning with embarrassment. Half of the time, they would walk away never fully

4

understanding that they had been disparaged in any way, just shot down once more.

Jess never used to shoot men down in such a distinct style, deciding that sleeping with them would get them out of her life much quicker. However, her friend Bane had explained the need for such directness, what with all the diseases that were out there and Jessica's habitual disregarding of safe sex practices.

Bane was a friend she had since she was in high school, with a mysterious past that continued to haunt him. With his long brown hair, black leather, jeans, and T-shirt, most people underestimated him, a mistake on every occasion. He was not only highly intelligent, but Bane was also street smart, often a rare combination. He knew how to read people and judge their reactions before anything ever transpired, and was often right. As a good friend, he was pleased to help educate Jessica on the ways of the darker minds. His philosophy was that the more she knew, the better prepared for problems she would be when they arose.

Her drive to the bar was a short and uneventful one, with only the ancient barns and the empty road to keep her company. When driving the distance to Badgers, Jessica often imagined she was the last person on earth, racing toward an unknown fate. With no cars passing through that area, it was a thought that bore much fruit in her imagination. Jessica never considered herself a very creative type of person; that is until she went into the entertainment venue for a career. It was there that she unlocked much of her sparse potential.

Pulling into the parking lot of the delightful Badgers, Jessica brought her truck to a halt. Considering the bar's appeal, the place looked rather barren from outside. Only three motorcycles and two other vehicles bedecked the lot out front. Jess smiled coyly as she spied the hottest looking bike she'd ever seen—a Harley Davidson in spectacular condition. The tank had a beautiful picture painted across its side; the artist depicted a beautiful woman kneeling while wearing a skimpy leather string bikini, with feathery white wings spread outward. "Angel" was printed across the top of the tank in flowing script style.

In an instant, Jessica knew her old friend Bane had perched himself atop a barstool to tell Rick and Nancy the tales of his latest adventures. No matter where he traveled, Bane never had to look for trouble; it seemed to always know exactly where to find him. She stepped up to the inner door and flung it open, her excitement building. It had been many long months since she'd seen her old friends. When she walked through the door, she shouted a greeting but was quickly silenced by everyone in the bar.

Being something of a spoiled brat, she tilted her head to the side, not being one who takes to being shushed lightly. Jessica was about to slap Bane on the arm when she saw what they were watching. The television was on, tuned to a news program that told the tale of the nineteenth child abduction and mutilation. While their bodies were intact, their little delicate heads were torn to pieces. Out of respect for the families, the media had refrained from displaying the horrifying crime scene photos. The nation was on "full alert"; as they believed the sickening transgressions were all linked to the same suspect.

Throughout the United States, children were being plucked right out of their beds. No commotion or forced entry was found at any of the scenes. Every child abducted in that fashion was likely to be found in the same condition as the other bodies. Jessica had heard a little of the tragic story but was generally too self-involved to watch the news or read the papers. Her nerves kicked into overdrive. She needed a drink more than ever after that terrible report.

"Pour ya a pitcher?" Rick asked as the news shifted to another topic.

"Hell yeah! Hey, Nancy, how's it going?" she beamed, through the dark thoughts that seemed to smother the bar.

"Not too bad; we just got back from camping this Sunday."

"How did the weather hold up for you?"

"Actually not bad. Rained on the first night, but hell, what are ya gonna do?" Nancy smiled, which was her predisposition to do. Nancy had a kind face, the type that put a person at ease the moment she engaged someone in conversation. For a pretty woman in her mid-thirties, she was very dedicated to her work.

Rick was pouring Jessica a pitcher of Miller Lite, her usual, and looking over the bar with a pride-filled smile. He too was in his thirties and a handsome gentleman often found wearing colorful Hawaiian shirts. Something about a person in that type of wardrobe ameliorated most people's tensions.

"Hey, how did your tour go? How's the master of the box doing? Learn any new tricks?" Rick inquired, knowing that he had just made an invitation to a small show.

"Oh, sure, say hello to Rick and Nancy, but ignore your old pal, Bane. I see how you are," interrupted Bane with a sarcastic, smug look draped over his face.

Jessica blushed and was about to object when Bane came over, sweeping her up into his arms in a tight, yet gentle bear hug. He spun her around, then returned her feet to the floor, whispering softly, "I've missed you."

Bane took a moment to take inventory of her, looking for any changes in appearance. However, time left Jessica untouched, save for perhaps a bit more childlike wonder in her misty green eyes. She had maintained her slim, athletic build for as long as he had known her, with just a subtle bulge of cellulite around her stomach. It was clear that Jessica had held onto her easygoing smile and congenial personality. She wore a heart-shaped pendant with a blue gemstone in the center; she called it her good luck charm.

"Where's Carrie anyway? You two are usually attached at the hip."

"Convention in Dallas, but she's coming up here in three days." A sadness touched his eyes. "I believe she's most likely having an affair."

"Bane, no! Are you sure?"

"Almost positive. Normally she would ask me to join her on a trip. This time she insisted on going alone, but when I called her the other night at around three a.m., I heard a man in her room. Carrie got off the phone quicker than I've ever known her to do. For the moment, I'm just pretending I don't know and see where that leads us. I also sent a few people I know to keep an eye on her while she was away. It was just to ensure her safety while we were apart. Now they don't want to tell me what they know over the phone."

"I'm so sorry. She doesn't deserve a good guy like you," Jessica stated, reeling from the terrible news. "You've always treated her like she was a goddess, and this is how she repays you?"

"You gonna be in town that long? Or are ya going to jet off to new exotic locations?" he probed diligently, doing his best to change the subject.

"Nope, no travel plans for a month. We don't have any shows scheduled for a month from next Thursday. What's the convention for anyway?" Jess asked, sliding back onto a stool at the bar. Normally she'd have gone directly to the table, but she wanted to chat with everyone.

"You ask way too many questions," he shot back. Whenever they talked, she usually ran at least a hundred questions by him. "She got another

7

promotion; she's now the purchasing manager at work—pays good money, but the hours are god-awful."

"That's awesome! What happened to her boss? I thought he'd hold that job until he was ninety-five!"

Bane chuckled, though even to his own ears it sounded forced. "He came into some large finances and has retired to enjoy the fruits of his labors. More to the point, he's off hunting, fishing, and barbecuing to his heart's content."

"Then, when she gets here, the first round is on her, now that she can afford it." Jessica suppressed a smirk, knowing that Bane would take that as a challenge.

"Hey— I make good money, ya know. Sure, I'm not a famous magician's assistant, but we're more than comfortable. Carrie doesn't work because she has to, ya know!" Bane scowled.

Jessica had a knack for picking fights with Bane, and mostly about the dumbest topics. She knew exactly what buttons to push to elicit an irritated response from him and used that knowledge at her every opportunity. They both had very strong personalities, and she tested him every chance that she got. Even a minor victory over Bane was a massive triumph, as he was frequently right, and that was a trait that really bothered Jessica. Bane never surrendered when he thought he was justified, and fought that much harder when he was wrong.

"Uh, Ms. Braun, I believe your pitcher has arrived, and my glass looks conspicuously empty. What's wrong with that picture?" Bane questioned as Rick delivered Jess's order.

"Oh! Can't have Bane with an empty glass, now can we? "I may have to suffer Bane's wrath!" Jessica stated in mock horror before snickering.

"Damn straight!" They both laughed. Nothing that he could conceive of would cause him to harm Jessica in any way, so the threat of his wrath was nothing more than a joke between them. However, to people, he didn't know or like, that wrath was exceedingly real. In addition to the veracity of his vengeance, it was usually quite violent as well. His temper was white-hot, and his fuse was shorter than a Lilliputian. Not that he enjoyed brutality per se, but he wasn't averse to using violence when the need arose. After all, he was an amazing warrior; his instincts would simply take over, vanquishing foe after foe.

Beers were poured, while Jessica slid a five-dollar bill into the jukebox, basically commandeering the music selection for eighteen songs. As those songs came to a conclusion, she would always pay to have another run of the jukebox, making certain she monopolized the tunes all night. Mr. Fuzz, the cat that thought he was the king of the bar, lounged lazily in the center of the pool table, glancing around at his loyal subjects. He waited for someone to walk by and give him a good scratch behind the ears on the way to the bathroom. Though the cat would leap on just about any surface in the bar, he never set a paw on the bar, as though he knew that would be taboo for him.

It wasn't very brightly lit, but enough light existed to allow people to see where they were going without too much trouble. It created an atmosphere of familiarity.

A man entered the bar and headed toward the two booths where a touch game separated the tables. He glanced over at the dartboard but didn't spare a second glance at the raised platform that the bands used when they played live. Not finding what he was looking for, he walked near the pool table, which was by the two bathrooms; behind the billiards table was the doorway to the courtyard out-back. Just to the right of the back door were more games, which were apparently what he was looking for since it was there that he stopped wandering around.

Jessica slid back into her seat. "So what's going on with those murdered children?"

Bane shook his head despondently, "Man, it's really messed up. Some psycho is out there snagging kids and tearing their little heads apart. That's not even the worst of it; the freak is stealing their brains. No traces have been recovered from the scene; lately, the children are found right in their rooms, completely mutilated. I can't even imagine how horrible the parents must feel walking into their child's bedroom to wake them up, only to discover that kind of carnage."

"Oh my god!" Jessica rubbed her forearms.

"Yeah, it's pretty crazy. If I ever get my hands on that bastard, I'm gonna tear him apart. I'll make a career out of tormenting that son-of-a-bitch!" Bane grumbled for a moment, then stopped and stared at her intently. "Hey, I thought you only rubbed your forearms when I mentioned something scary from my past? I see we're expanding our horizons. Well, you needn't worry if the killer changes MO's again and starts hunting adults for their brains; you'd have nothing he'd value."

She shook her head. "You always did know how to soften the blow of any news," Jessica snickered. "You and that screwball sense of humor of yours."

9

"Yes, well, someone's gotta do it. It may as well be me." Bane grinned before taking a large swallow of his beer.

"Nice outfit by the way; planning on scaring people out of their wits today?"

"Hey, be careful, or I'll have to 'Jess slap' ya!" Bane returned with a gleeful grin. She always hated it when he substituted her name with the word "bitch." However, the term was so completely accurate for her, when she was in a bad mood or acting like a spoiled brat; Bane did make that substitution, just to annoy her.

"You wouldn't dare."

"And just what's wrong with what I'm wearing?" he demanded, acting as though he were truly offended.

"Well, your spiked fingerless gloves for one thing. The spikes are half an inch long!"

"Ha! You're just jealous. I've got the personality combined with the strength of character to pull this outfit off, and you don't."

Jessica wasn't really complaining about his clothing; it was just another thing she'd do to goad him into an argument. In fact, she found the way he dressed quite provocative, stirring urges in her she had been repressing for years. Bane often dressed in jeans, leather, and whatever wicked-looking adornments he could add to his ensemble. He was right when he stated that she could never pull off dressing the way he did; it just didn't fit her temperament.

Shadows in the bar grew deeper and darker as the sun fell from the sky, landing out of view of the planet. Though it was an energetic building, as the shadows expanded, the cozier it appeared to become. The man who had walked in and gone to the machines came forward, standing directly behind Bane. Glancing around nervously as though he were waiting for some unseen force to arrive, the man simply stood there. Bane caught a glimpse of the man behind him and kept a close eye on him; people standing around him for no reason always made him uneasy. Without warning, the man whipped out a .44 Desert Eagle handgun and pointed it over Bane's shoulder at Rick.

"Give me all the money in the register, and no one will get hurt," the man commanded.

Jessica ignited a piece of flash paper, causing a distraction. Making a very large mistake, the thief glanced in her direction, giving Bane a chance to take action. His instincts were honed to a razor's edge, making them just as powerful of a weapon as those that he often carried. Combining his instincts with his skills and other equipment, Bane became a walking battalion all unto himself.

Bane swiftly brought his right arm up, batting the gun skyward. The weapon discharged; the smell of gunpowder filled the air. Pieces of the ceiling crashed down atop the bar as the bullet rocketed through the drywall. With a serpentine and nimble attack that would leave a crocodile cringing, Bane took advantage of the weapon's direction; he slammed his elbow into the robber's solar plexus, knocking the wind out of his foe. He leaped onto the foot of his enemy as he stood up. Everyone else was rather stunned by the sudden attack; all stood in awe as Bane throttled the man. He quickly slapped the bottom edge of his hand into the man's throat. Bane's gloves impaled the robber's face with each impact, drawing out blood from each new hole the spikes created with a distinct slurping constituent.

Bringing his knee up into the man's bloody face, Bane shattered the felon's jaw like a bag of eggshells. The gun fell from the man's listless hand, as Bane finished the fight with a vicious snap kick to the man's groin. The power of the blow could be felt throughout the bar, seeing as the man was briefly lifted off the ground from the sheer force of the strike. Pain enslaved the man and left him rolling around across the tile.

Jessica scooped up the weapon from the floor, holding it like it was going to bite her, and handed it to Bane. After checking the weapon, he aimed it at the groaning figure on the ground. When he lost his temper, all hell often broke loose; this instance was no exception to the rule. It took all his self-control not to empty the clip into the bleeding mass.

"I'll call the cops!" Nancy announced as she hurried to the cordless phone.

He placed his right foot across the neck of the robber to stop him from rolling back and forth. Bane had targeted the crook's head with the muzzle of the large-caliber semi-automatic. A fellow patron of the bar put a restraining arm on Bane, only to find his hand broken before he knew what happened. Bane appeared to keep his eyes on his quarry for the milliseconds that it took for him to disable, in his mind, his unannounced attacker. The injured bar goer cradled his hurt hand against his other arm and backed away from Bane rapidly.

"Bane?" Jessica asked in a trembling voice. "Bane? Are you okay?"

In the grips of bloodlust, Bane didn't seem to hear a word she had said. His eyes flashed dangerously, and a chilling smile crossed his face; his

11

breathing was ragged and heavy. Jess was very disconcerted by what she was seeing. She had long known that Bane had a problem containing his temper, but had never borne witness to his rage prior to that day. Rick was standing close by, wondering if there was anything he could do to defuse the situation. A guttural snarl escaped Bane's lips, with his fury battling his common sense and winning.

"They're on their way!" Nancy shouted reassuringly from across the room. "Is . . . he . . . um—you know . . . alright?"

"I don't know. I've never seen him like this before," Jess answered with worry lines creasing her forehead. A fearful shiver bounced off the inside of her skin throughout her entire body. "From what I've heard, this isn't his usual reaction after a fight; he's usually quite exhilarated and cheerful. Carrie's told me about more than a few of them. He doesn't look good, almost animalistic."

Rick popped the top off a beer bottle and slid it over to where Bane was standing. As though that sound consisted of angels singing, Bane blinked several times, shook his head, and plucked the beverage from the bar. Less than three seconds later, the bottle was empty, and Bane looked as though he had conquered his rage, at least for the moment. Ejecting the clip from the gun and pulling the slide back on the weapon, ensuring that it was empty, Bane placed it on the bar.

"That was fucking awesome!" Jess roared, deciding everything was well again.

Bane snorted in amusement, shrugged casually, then stated in candid modesty, "No big deal. The guy was a total amateur; biggest threat he posed was if I fell down laughing at him. He really jacked out the hearing in my ear; it's still ringing."

Both Rick and Nancy were having a hard time thinking of something to say at that point. Everything happened too fast to take in the situation in its fullest measure. When the police arrived moments later, they scooped up the bleeding thief and hauled him to their car. It took almost forty minutes for the cops to get statements from everyone and leave. Most of that time was spent interviewing and, in part, harassing Bane. His dark past was something that the police were acutely aware of and were happy to exploit, all in the name of justice. Bane paid them little attention, answering their questions with a monosyllabic response each time. He was more than used to their mistreatment— it tended to amuse him. The more entertained Bane became, the angrier the police got.

Being the kind and fun-loving people that everyone knew them to be, Nancy and Rick bought Bane and Jessica a pitcher for their assistance in foiling the robbery, adding only that Bane was handy to have around, which won them a sly, triumphant smile and a wink.

"Smooth move, that flashy thing. You magicians always carry that crap around with you?" Bane asked after pounding down a few glasses of beer.

"Of course! It's damn helpful, isn't it?"

"In this instance, I'd have to say most definitely. You'll have to teach me that one."

"Sorry, magicians never reveal their secrets," Jessica answered mysteriously.

"Alright, that I'll give you. However, you're not a magician, you're an assistant, so that means you can tell me," countered Bane, knowing that he wouldn't get an answer no matter what he said.

"I'll be one soon enough. Besides, if everyone could do it, why would they pay to see me perform on stage?"

"How about seeing you in those skimpy outfits?"

"Nah, I won't have to wear those when I'm the magician. Besides, I'm getting fat, and those outfits don't hide very much."

"Got an answer for everything, don't ya?" he prompted grimly.

"Not everything, but close enough. You buy a place up here yet, or will you be staying at the lake house with me?"

"Jess, Jess, Jess." He shook his head slowly from side to side. "Of course, I'm staying at the lake house with you. You've got a keg on tap over there. Actually, I was planning on grabbing a motel room for a couple of weeks. We're renovating an old house we bought, but it won't be ready for a while. If you don't mind, I'll crash out at your place for the duration. Once my new place is completed, it'll be the perfect party house. You'll love it. I've got a dungeon being built into the back part of the house. I can't wait until it's finally completed."

"No problem. You can call Carrie from there and let her know where to find you. It'll be like old times!" Jessica glowed happily. "In addition, it'll give me some company while I'm up here. No one is planning on visiting until the end of the month. I'd get pretty bored without anyone to talk to."

"Your family isn't up here?" Bane asked puzzled. "The weather is so beautiful, and the forecast claims it'll be like this all week."

13

"Devon may come up with his wife Erika this weekend, but they're heading back on Sunday. Unlike some people, they have real jobs, with normal hours."

"Ah, so you now fit into the category of working irregular hours," chided Bane, who for years was accused of not having a real job because he set his own work schedule. A nasty noise emanated from the jukebox. "Oh shit, Jess! You played that country music garbage again! Why do you insist on torturing me with that foul gurgling crap?"

"You love this song; you just won't admit it!" announced Jessica in her defense.

"Yeah, I love it about as much as I love being hit by an eighteen-wheeler doing ninety miles an hour," Bane stated bitterly.

Jessica had a very eclectic taste when it came to music, everything from chart-topping pop hits to country. Bane was content with classic rock, and most specifically Fleetwood Mac. She often claimed to have an open perspective when it came to the melodies she listened to; it was more evidence of the fact that Jessica couldn't make up her mind. Dreading the knowledge of Jessica's tendency to play several country songs in a row, Bane ordered several shots of whiskey to dull the ear-bleeding noise that would soon ensue.

"So that's what happened to your face!"

"Like the hamburger says to the fat man...bite me," chuckled Bane.

"Where did your last joy ride take you this time?"

"I was in sin city, baby, Las Vegas! Figured it was about time I rode my bike down there, and what a blast I had. I was there a few times before, but never on my bike, and couldn't stay long due to complications." Jessica knew that his complications were usually violent, or involved with the police in some way.

"How much dough did you drop on the tables?"

"Nope, not this time. I took the casinos there for over ninety grand! Gotta love shooting craps. After all, life is a gamble. Why not dance with lady luck in more than just the normal methods? "

"You won over ninety thousand dollars? " Jessica asked incredulously. "Where's mine?"

"Win your own money; you make a good living. Besides, I put my winnings into a college fund for my nephews. With all the money I've been putting into that thing, they'll be able to attend wherever they want to, with no thought to cost for anything."

14

"I can see you're worried about them. Is it because of the psycho out there?"

Bane nodded his head. "If that freak touches a single hair on their heads, he'll never be dead enough. The problem, as I see it, is this guy has no central location from which he strikes. He's hit all over the country. I have no idea how he moves so fast. The third attack happened in New York; the fourth happened in Nevada. Those attacks were less than two hours apart. I'd say that there's more than one hunter out there killing children, but the feds don't think that's likely."

"Do you think it's supernatural?" Jessica asked, more than a little skeptical.

"Hell if I know. I believe that there are tons of things out there," he waved a hand in a wide arc indicating the entire world, "that defy rational explanation. I don't know if I believe some monster is out there with powers of flight, with salivating jaws waiting to rip open kids for the fun of it. My God! It sounds like something right out of a horror movie!"

Jessica reached out a hand, rubbing his back reassuringly. She cared deeply for her friend Bane and hated to see him so uncertain because, for him, that was a very uncommon trait. Bane turned to her, flashing her a grateful smile before drinking down the last of his beverage. With a grandiose gesture and more flair than he usually put into his statements, Bane ordered a round of drinks for everyone in the bar, pausing only briefly to add that he was buying. A small cheer lit through the Badger's Paw; those sitting within earshot of him were happy to take him up on his offer. He withdrew two hundred dollars from his wallet and placed it on the bar.

"Keep the change. You guys earned it," Bane stated as both Rick and Nancy came to collect for the drinks. He knew that the total wouldn't amount to anywhere near two hundred dollars, but he was always accused of over tipping and enjoyed the title in abundance. Of course, neither Rick nor Nancy was a fool, so they quickly swept up the bills and began filling the drinks for the free round bought by Bane.

"So how's the rectal raider doing? He found himself a new lover yet, or is he still deciding whether or not to come out of the closet?"

"Brendon?"

"Yeah, Mr. Brendon 'take it in the rear for a beer' Duck, is he out of the closet officially yet?"

"You know, Bane, I don't know that he'll ever be fully out of the closet. He's just too much of a coward to give it serious thought. Besides, his

15

mother is bipolar. Think of what it could do to her? Shit, he knew that he was horrible in bed, so he'd watch pornographic videos in an effort to improve, not that it ever helped him in the least. In the end, he just bought butt sex videos, so he could pleasure himself." Jessica shrugged. "I can't believe I married a man who was that terrible in the sack. My father seemed so certain we belonged together, so I guess I figured it would get better."

"Well, he was a fool. He married a wonderful girl like you and still wanted to have sex with men. I don't understand that, but then again, I'm a total homophobe, so I'll never truly understand that whole same-gender sex thing," Bane explained. "I'm glad you went back to your maiden name; it's much better if you ask me."

"Sometimes, I'm sorry that I told you about that. He really was a nice guy—"

Bane interrupted with a grin, "Did you say he was a really nice gay?"

"Bane! Behave yourself!" Jessica blurted. "Sometimes two people simply don't belong together; this was just one of those instances."

"An anal entry man and a spoiled brat— no, they never belong together. Just because Mister Brendon Duck likes to do men doesn't mean he should've married you to hide that fact. What kind of asshole does that to a person?" Bane paused momentarily. "I guess the kind of shithead that wants to be beaten and whipped by his newest male lover."

"He's got a new roommate, Roger something or other."

"Do you think they're doing the colon clogging dance together?"

"Probably. That Roger guy seems exactly like Brendon's type."

"What? Male and willing to take one up the rear?"

"Oh geez, Bane, give the poor guy a break. You know something? You are a homophobe."

"Maybe, maybe not, but I know it's damnation in the eyes of God, and who am I to argue with the creator of the world?"

"According to you on your less than modest days, you are the creator of the world."

"Hell no! I'm not taking credit for this planet! Not a chance. This place is too screwed up. Man, I wish I were in Illinois. We could be shooting pool at Gators. Oh well, here is what I propose…We finish this pitcher, and maybe one more, then head back to the house. I need a place to grab a shower, clean off some of this road dust."

"Sounds like a good plan to me."

16

As the darkness descended upon the unsuspecting populace, children were put to bed, and parents enjoyed the long-awaited solitude. The closet door was open just a crack, but it was enough to send the little boy sliding down under his covers for protection. Fear of the closet monster was universal; every child, no matter whom, had an adverse feeling when the door wasn't sealed tightly. Unfortunately for the young lad, the door slowly crept open just a bit further; the glittering cobalt blue light was barely perceivable against the shadowy backdrop of the closet.

From within the depths of the dank cabinet crept a man wearing a top hat, long black cape, and a tuxedo. His thin mustache raised into a sneer as he tiptoed toward the bed, making no more sound than a mouse scurrying across the floor. Lupine fangs protruded from the man's mouth as he reached the edge of the bed. Waving a small wand with white tips at either end, the blankets disappeared, leaving the child unprotected and paralyzed with fear. He tried to scream, attempted to summon his parents to come and save him from the terrifying man looming above him, but no noise escaped his trembling lips.

The magician could smell the innocence in the child, like a spilled perfume bottle. He could feel the surge of adrenaline in the child's veins and could hear the pounding of his victim's little heart.

Swoosh. Lub-lub-dub. Lub-lub-dub.

In a flash, the salivating savage jaws began to rend the skull of the small child.

Lub-lub-dub. Lub-lub-dub.

No commotion could be heard, save for the snapping of bone and the slurping of blood. Chunks of the kid's brain were being devoured at an alarming velocity. The wicked man's eyes began to glow a soft yellow color, his muscles bulging underneath his dapper clothing. Despite the horrible carnage that was taking place, not a single drop of blood marred any fraction of the apparel worn by the horrible monster.

Footsteps from the hallway caused the creature - like man to take notice of his surroundings. Rearing his head back in utter glee, the man twirled around, causing his cape to flutter in a flamboyant flourish. In that instant, he rolled under the bed and disappeared, accompanied only by that strange, yet ominous, blue glittering light that brought him through the closet. The bedroom door opened slowly, in an attempt not to wake their slumbering child. His mother poked her head into the room only to discover her worst nightmares had come true.

The sheets were soaked in the spattered blood of her only offspring. A horror-bidden shriek pierced the night, shattering the solace and serenity found when the day had come to a conclusion. Racing to the bedside, tears cascading down her face, the four-year-old boy's mother cradled her mutilated child to her breast. His father sprinted to her side, not sure what all the pandemonium was about. Not until he saw the bloodbath did his heart sink to its fullest extent. He let out a heartbreaking groan of dismay, knowing that his little boy had become the latest victim of the psychopathic murderer.

It wasn't until one in the morning that the police were summoned to investigate the grisly crime scene. Once again they were left with no clues as to how the man had gained entry into the home, nor did they find any evidence as to how it was pulled off with such anonymity. They had checked all the doors and windows in the room. Both the closet and bedroom door squealed in protest as they swung on rusty hinges. The two windows scraped abysmally loud, as they hadn't been lubricated in a very long time. Yet, neither parent heard a single sound that would lead them to believe someone had entered the room of their beloved offspring. Who would be next?

Chapter Two

Federal agent Linsey Phillips boldly walked forward, her badge hanging from the pocket of her gray suit coat. She entered the crime scene and pulled on a pair of latex gloves. Local police gave her a wide berth, for the look upon her face was grim and determined. She had been flying all across the country as she spearheaded the investigation into the string of child murders. Whether it was the gruesome manner in which the children were being killed or jet lag combined with lack of sleep that made her so cranky, it didn't seem to matter.

"What have we got?" she asked the medical examiner.

"From what I understand, we've got the same issue that has been seen everywhere else."

"I didn't ask what you've read of the other crimes," she snapped. "I asked what you know of this crime scene."

"Sorry, ma'am. Cranial trauma from the very top of the skull is massive—sundered straight down the center of the front and back of the head. No remnants of brain tissue can be located, but that will have to be confirmed during the autopsy. Additionally, we'll be looking for signs of saliva, DNA fragments, basically anything foreign inside the skull. Signs of struggle are minimal, no tissue under the nails, and the body seems unusually rigid," he reported diligently.

Phillips turned to the forensics team leader. "Any signs of forced entry?"

"Not a single shred. The parents were in the living room where they could view the child's door from down the hallway. We've dusted for prints, and we've got layers upon layers of the family's prints. Not even a partial or smudge from anyone else." Before Pamela could say anything else, the forensics woman nodded. "I know. We'll dust it again and go over the entire house with a fine-toothed comb."

Using one of her latex-gloved hands, Phillips pulled up the dust ruffle surrounding the bed, taking note that there were blood splatters across much of the Star Wars figures printed across the sheets. Leaning down to look under the bed, she saw a silk handkerchief of varying colors. Poking her head back up, she asked if the room had been thoroughly photographed.

When she was informed that it had been, Pamela pulled the silk cloth out from under the bed. Quickly, a local officer handed her a clear evidence bag into which she could place the item.

"What do you make of that?" he asked; his eyes and the nod of his head indicated the bag.

"I want this thing identified. I want to know who made it, where it came from, what stores sell them, and everything else that can be learned from it. Get on that right away," she ordered as she clicked open her cellphone and walked out of the room.

"Sir, we've found another one of those damned handkerchiefs. It's definitely connected to the other crimes."

"We've got another crime in Minnesota. Sounds like this bastard has struck twice in one night. How he moves so fast is something we need to figure out— and soon. Understood?"

"Yes, sir. I'll take the jet to Minnesota right now. Can you ask Mary to call ahead and have it fueled and ready to go?"

"No problem, and . . . Ms. Phillips?"

"Yes, sir?"

"Good work."

"Thank you, sir," she stated before hitting the end button on the call. Pamela clicked the phone to lock and slid it back into her coat pocket. As she exited the home, she stopped to tell one of the local police where to send all the information that they gathered. He nodded, writing down her instructions in his notebook. Without giving him a second glance, she got into a car and drove toward the airport.

They had analyzed the silk cloth left at the other scenes and had come up with no answers, at least none that gave them any leads. It was made of standard silk and was commonly used in magicians' acts for various tricks. The problem was they were very common and could be bought over the Internet, as well as any magic shop. Tracking down the origins of any of those would be more than a little time-consuming. Already they had twenty-five agents working overtime trying to track down every handkerchief bulk order across the country, with little results coming from their hard work.

After long hours on a government-owned jet, Pamela was in an even worse mood than before. She spent that time studying crime scene photos, pouring over the case files repeatedly, searching for some connection between the children. However, she wasn't having any luck locating any pattern, save for the way the crimes were carried out. At first, the crimes were considered abductions, but the killer had discarded that method after the ninth child. It was that change that disturbed her the most, as most serial killers had been monogamous to their preferred style of murder.

The best minds at the Federal Bureau of Investigation were having great difficulty understanding what prompted the shift in the assassin's methods. With the shift came a greater possibility of catching him in the act; however, it also meant that he was very adaptable. Their main problem stemmed from not knowing when or where he would strike again. The murderer seemed to move on immeasurably swift wings of darkness, and no paradigms could be deciphered to try to put a stop to the crime before it happened.

As the jet landed, a car rolled forward to meet Pamela Phillips at the ramp. The valet stepped out of the car, helped her with her luggage and moved out of her path. She simply nodded to him before getting inside and driving off. Pamela used her phone to alert her boss that she had landed and was en-route to the latest crime scene. He explained that it was a rather grisly scene, not that the others were a pretty sight to behold, but something about this particular crime was worse than the others. So far the serial killer hadn't slain anyone older than thirteen years of age.

The nation lived in fear, fretting that their beloved sons or daughters might be the next on the heinous killer's death list. Parents nationwide were outraged, demanding more action, more information and added protection for their kids. Though the terror they felt was universal, no one even trusted their own neighbors anymore. Everyone was a suspect, as far as the world was concerned, even the simple task of putting their children to bed at night almost felt like saying goodbye. Many fathers had taken to sleeping in the room with their children, in an effort to keep them safe.

When Pamela arrived at the home, she strode in without bothering to report to the senior officer on the scene. Without pausing to acknowledge anyone in her path, she marched into the bedroom, her eyes turning into large saucers. A grown man was pinned to the wall, by methods hard to discern from where she stood. His entrails dangled down across the action figures and toy trucks, several of which had been placed within the man's stomach as though it were some new action figure playground. In the two beds were the remains of the little boys who had once shared the room. Neither could have been older than four years old, but both were savagely mutilated from the neck up. On the wall was an adorable photo of the twin boys hugging each other inside a large cardboard box.

The forensic technicians looked up; seeing a federal agent, they diligently went back to work without interrupting her train of thought. She was absolutely astounded to see the brutality with which the father had been disposed. Someone had literally torn his tongue out of his head and left it on the dresser, while his jaw was hanging from a coat rack. One of his arms was hanging on by only a few pieces of bloody skin, stretched taut against the weight of the meaty appendage. His right foot was missing entirely; Phillips glanced around the room to see if it had been put on display elsewhere but couldn't locate it.

"Where's the man's foot?" she asked crisply.

"No sign of it. House has been thoroughly tossed, and it isn't on the premises. The killer must have taken it with him. Wait until you see what the bastard did to the dog; it's in the closet," he stated grimly, with a cheerless shake of his head.

"What breed of dog?"

"Doberman Pincher— a big sucker too. Its head is, like that guy's foot . . . missing. The legs were severed and stabbed into its back. This guy's a real wacko if you ask my opinion."

"I didn't," Phillips barked impersonally.

Wandering around the room, she saw that they had already bagged a handkerchief similar to the ones left at the other crime scenes. As she drew closer to the mangled corpse of the father, she still couldn't see what was holding him up. Once again, she adorned her latex gloves and began moving body parts aside to get a better look. Flashbulbs caused a strobe effect on the room, making things even more difficult to see. Removing a flashlight from her purse, Pamela eyed the back of the body with great intrigue.

"What the hell's keeping this victim on the wall?" she asked anyone in the room.

"Some sort of adhesive we think— no cords, wires, nails. Nothing visible can be found. We'll know more once we pull the body down," a technician answered quickly.

"Alright, when will you be doing that? " she demanded in exasperation.

"That's the next thing we're going to work on, ma'am. We've been dusting the room thoroughly, but haven't found anything of interest. The perv must be wearing gloves, rubber or leather because there aren't any fibers left behind from cloth gloves."

"I want to know what is holding this guy up there, so get to work on that now. I've got other duties to perform, and I don't have a lot of time to

22

spend waiting on futile efforts looking for prints you don't think exist," she ordered acidly. "You can go back to dusting after you've pried the man off the wall and analyzed what is binding him to it."

"Ma'am, our procedures are—" He never finished his sentence.

"I don't give a damn about your procedures! I gave you an order, and you will follow it, or you can leave the crime scene. I'll simply find someone who is more cooperative to assist me. Do I make myself clear, lieutenant? " She snarled, her face turning an ugly shade of red.

"Err . . . uh . . . yes, ma'am," he stammered, and if looks could kill, she'd be the next victim in the room. Pamela shrugged off the glare as inconsequential; to her, the technician was less than a bug on the windshield. The entire world was watching with a great deal of anticipation the recent series of killings, and she didn't have time to mince words with underlings.

"Check the blood in this closet comprehensively. If the dog happened to bite the killer, we may get a sample."

"Yes, ma'am. Should we do that now before we get the victim down?" the man inquired, slightly baiting her with his question.

"Are you questioning my orders? " she shouted.

"No, just asking for clarification."

"You can inspect the closet any time after I leave. I want to know what is holding that large man to that wall! Are you incompetent or just being irritating on purpose?"

He saw no need to answer that question. No matter how he responded, he knew that she wouldn't like his reply. Any statement he made would only serve to infuriate her further, which in the end could cost him his job. She was, after all, a high-ranking member of the FBI and obviously not a person to be trifled with. Normally he would've made a snide remark or sarcastic answer, but prudence had caused him to hold his tongue—a feat that had eluded the man hanging on the wall. The technician half-wondered if Agent Phillips had been here before and the man smarted off to her.

After forty minutes of working diligently, they were able to pry the corpse off the baby blue painted walls. Unfortunately, it took most of the skin and clothing off the large man's body as it was removed from its precarious position, meaning it would take longer to determine what type of adhesive was used in keeping him suspended above the ground. The forensic technicians were absolutely baffled as to what could hold a man that size up so far from the floor, not to mention how large the man was and the ordeal they had trying to pull the remains down.

Three hours passed, with an impatient Pamela Phillips watching their every move, and at long last, the forensic technicians discovered that there were no traces of adhesive on the wall. What held the man suspended off the floor was another mystery that needed to be solved. Not a single trace of chemicals of any type was used on the wall or the corpse, other than the paint that coated the entire room. Pamela was completely incensed by their report and demanded that they perform a more comprehensive examination of the affected area, and she commanded it to be done at least four more times to confirm the results.

"He wasn't held there by magic, dammit! I want to know how he was stuck there." Pamela had to report to her boss that they had yet one more mystery to solve. In addition, she needed to tell him that even a parent in the room with one's children didn't seem to dissuade the killer in any way. This was a call she wasn't anxious to make since she was the person stuck on the hook for the entire investigation and its lack of results thus far. She refused to fail; it wasn't in her nature. The simple fact of the matter was Agent Phillips was floundering contemptibly. She hadn't slept much in the past few weeks; every time Pamela closed her eyes she was haunted by the images of the butchered children for whom she sought out justice.

Though to the outside world she appeared to be cold-hearted, uncaring, and, in general, a real mega-bitch, she was in actuality a very sensitive woman. Pamela took murders rather personally, and when someone chose to slay the utmost innocent, she got exceedingly involved in the cases. Her every waking thought would be about how she could capture the killer and deliver the bastard to justice. It was clear that her brisk, cool, and often brusque manner irritated and angered her fellow law enforcement agents. She wasn't in the game to make friends; she was there to catch and build solid cases against the murderers.

When Pamela wanted something, be it information, action, or silence, she demanded it right away. Delays in getting what she desired only served to provoke her and bring out her standoffish attitude. Phillips's impatience was what had cost her promotions and favorable reviews on many occasions. However, she didn't care about her ranking and standing among her peers at work, so long as she was permitted to continue serving the constituency by incarcerating criminals. Pamela's superiors respected her dedication, drive, and determination, but noted more than once in her personnel jacket that her interpersonal communication skills left much to be desired.

Two hours had passed before the technicians were able to confirm their analysis four times, and yet it still left the enigma as to what fastened the man on the wall. Pamela was seething; she nearly threw a temper-tantrum in the middle of the children's bedroom. By luck only, she was able to contain her anger until she got into her car. Then she screamed and berated her subordinates for being incompetent fools. Of course, in her vehicle, they weren't near enough to overhear her malicious, vile comments about their skills.

She answered a call. "I don't know, sir. This is getting even more bizarre with each killing. A man who was easily over two hundred pounds, closing in on two hundred and fifty, was held to the wall by some method that we have yet to figure out. No chemicals were found on the surface, and there was no other evidence of wires or cables holding the man in place. Apparently, the man was the children's father, standing watch over his twin boys against the killer, but it didn't do much good. The strange part was the fact that the man's skull wasn't ravaged like the children's heads were."

"Why do you think the father's head was left alone and only the children were attacked like that?" her boss asked in confusion.

Beats the hell out of me. He was severely mangled but not in the fashion that the killer has disposed of the other victims. Even their household pet was slaughtered violently, but again dissimilarly than all the others. We've got a real problem here. If the media gets out the news that even parents can't ward off the murderer, we'll have a full-scale panic on our hands."

"Already we have the militias and gun nuts arming themselves and claiming it's some government experiment gone horribly wrong. Smith and Wesson have made record sales in the last four weeks that beat all their sales for the previous two years. Everyone is getting gun-crazy, and I can't say I blame them. My wife sleeps with my Ithaca shotgun next to her, and the children are sleeping in our room on the floor," he sighed softly. "Keep me informed and keep up the good work. I know it's little conciliation, but I'm aware of the hard hours you've put into this. You're a damn fine agent. Just don't go overboard. I can't afford to have you burn yourself out on this case. On the other hand, there isn't anyone I'd rather have working this particular one."

"Thank you, sir. I'll keep you posted. Could you please put me through to my assistant? I want to get some things clear with her before I board the bureau jet."

"No problem. Good hunting, Agent Phillips," he said as he transferred the call to her administrative assistant Mary Rosenberg.

"Ms. Phillips?" Mary asked timidly.

Yes, it's me. Have the reports I asked for come in yet?"

"They have in fact— just got here ten minutes ago. Would you like me to fax them to your jet? I've got you booked at the Holiday Inn, suite ten-thirteen. I've taken the liberty of Federal Expressing the photos and hard copies of the documents of those reports to that location. Is there anything else I can do for you today?" Mary was very efficient and an extremely competent woman, if she weren't, she'd never have lasted for as long as she had with Pamela as her supervisor.

"Just make certain the jet gets refueled after each landing. Also, this latest crime scene," she paused as a shiver trickled down her spine. "I want some of our best forensic teams over there. I don't trust these local screw-ups. See if we can get Ryan to close off the scene to the local authorities as soon as possible. I don't want them tampering with the evidence."

Mary took notes as they spoke. "That shouldn't be a problem. I'll have the teams on the first plane out. Ryan is looking over my shoulder now. He said and I quote, 'I'll have that place shut down tighter than a frog's watertight ass.' One more thing, I did program your iPhone to contact me directly with one touch of an app. I've kept my phone on ever since you left the office. Don't hesitate to call me anytime you need anything at all. Just hit the blue concentric circled icon and I'll be on the line."

"Thanks, Mary. You're the best."

"Nope, I work for the best. Try to get some rest, Lin. I can hear how tired you are."

With that done, Pamela Phillips was on her way to the turbojet, which would fly her to Chicago where she had reservations at a hotel.

Carrie drove down the empty streets, passing by the house she and Bane were having renovated. She saw only work vehicles and large equipment on the lawn and driveway. So she drove past her friend Jessica's house to see if she was up at the lake. There, she noticed her husband's motorcycle parked out front. Pulling onto the grass, parking her car, Carrie hefted her bag and walked toward the front door. She knocked on the door several times. Not getting an answer, she strode around the back across the wraparound deck. It was there that she found Bane and Jess drinking beers, watching the waves of the lake dance and splash against the shore.

"Hey, there you guys are!" Carrie shouted with a broad smile hiding her irritation of having to look for them. Bane had forgotten to leave Carrie a message about where he was staying.

"Carrie!" Bane responded racing over to greet her with a large hug, one that masked his suspicions of her adultery. "How was the conference? Did ya learn a lot?"

"Same stuff I already knew, but it was fun anyway. I drove by the house. Looks like the workers aren't done with it yet. Good thing I checked over here; otherwise, I'd have assumed you were still out on the road. Speaking of which, did you have a good ride?"

"Of course! Don't I always? The interstate was a tad clogged through Ohio, but other than that, it was a piece of cake," Bane explained.

"Any tickets this time?" Carrie asked shrewdly.

"Nope, no police problems until I got back up here. I'll explain that later." Bane moved aside allowing Jessica to get closer to Carrie for a hug and greeting.

"TNT!" Carrie shouted with honest excitement in her voice, using Jessica's nickname. Bane had given her that nickname years earlier to counter the lame ones that her accounting friends tried to come up with. TNT stood for dynamite, an easy definition of her personality traits. Additionally, everyone called her "The Bomb," a slang term that meant she was explosive and full of energy. "My God! You look great!"

"That's what working in the world of illusion does for you," Bane snickered.

Jessica looked at Carrie after their embrace, seeing her sandy brown hair had grown down past her shoulders. Carrie was only an inch shy of five feet tall and had managed to put on over seventy pounds and completely destroying her figure over the many months that Jess was on the road. Traditionally, Carrie wore shorts with a pair of boots that matched her comfortable shirts, whereas Jessica was completely addicted to anything with a designer label. Bane watched the two with an amused grin seeping onto his lips; his eyes alight with the energy they seemed to absorb from one another.

27

"You look really pretty today! Your hair's getting so long." Jessica lied good-naturedly.

"Yeah, but not as long as Bane's, the asshole," Carrie laughed.

"Nope, my brother moved me out while I was on tour. But I guess I still get mail sent there. Forwarding has stopped as of last month," Jessica replied. "The shows have been really draining lately; we're working on some of the most difficult illusions we've ever attempted. On the bright side, though, they are awesome!"

"We gonna talk shop all day, or are we going to do some drinking? " Bane suggested with a satiric expression, holding his empty plastic cup upside down in the process.

Both women turned to look at him, and with a laugh, they said in unison, "Shut up!"

Again they shared a giggle and were joined by Bane's hearty laughter. He never took their statements personally; he knew they always meant them with a great deal of affection. To an outside party, the comments shot back and forth among the three might sound like they were bitter enemies, but they knew better. An example that always sprang to Carrie's mind was one night at the Badger's Paw, Bane was inserting the word "bitch" in place of Jess's name whenever it came up. A drunken man strutted over and asked if Bane had some sort of problem and if he needed a lesson in respect.

While Bane was at the ready to show the man how to "mind his own damn business" Jessica was quick to diffuse the situation by explaining it was an inside joke. It mollified the man to some extent, but he walked away glaring at Bane just the same. Carrie had to hold Bane's hand to ensure he wouldn't follow the man and beat him to a bloody pulp, assuring him that the man meant well. Also, she mentioned that Bane himself would've gone ballistic if someone said something like that to either of them. He was quick to respond with the logic that someone else wouldn't have intended it as an inside joke.

"I'll go refill our cups and the pitcher. Why don't you guys go uncover the boat? We can go out for a late-night boat ride and stare at the stars for a while," proposed Bane diplomatically.

"Deal," Jess stated quickly.

"You got it, baby!" Carrie said giving him a quick kiss on the lips before he turned toward the sliding glass door.

I wonder if she kisses her new lover with more fervor when they part, Bane thought irritably.

So late at night, the water's surface was so level; it was like wet asphalt under the midnight sky. The cherry-red boat appeared to change into a dark bloody maroon color beneath the blue and red light seated at the front of the boat. In the back stemmed a long pole with a white light attached at the very tip, showing the front and aft of the vessel to any others on the water. Methodically the engine hummed as they churned through the thick greasy looking surface of the lake; they often searched out the darkest area to admire the stars in all their brilliance.

Jessica's boat had an ancient tape cassette player covered by a piece of hard plastic to keep it dry. When the tape came to an end, static-filled the speakers, as no radio stations seemed powerful enough to come in through the aerial. Something genuinely strange occurred on their boat ride this time when Bane's tape of Fleetwood Mac came to conclusion. Jessica's voice sailed through the radio.

"I hope Bane flips the tape. Oh . . . there's a great spot for us to anchor! Geez, what's taking him so long," the radio stated softly.

Everyone stopped and looked at the radio. Then Carrie and Bane stared at Jessica in surprise. "What did you say?" Bane asked as his brow crinkled into confusion.

"Why are they staring at me? And what the hell is the radio picking up on? "I didn't say anything!" Jessica protested.

"But we heard you, Jess," Carrie stated, her hands knotting up in nervous tension.

"Bane's ass looks really hot in those black jeans. Wow! Check him out as he's bending over to look for the anchor! Oh, my God! It's being heard over the radio!"

"Well, thank you very much, Jess." Bane smiled with an immodest grin.

Carrie looked askew at Jessica but said nothing. She knew that even if Jess wanted Bane, she wouldn't do anything about it; nor would Bane for that matter. Jessica looked completely stunned, not to mention severely mortified. She didn't know how her thoughts traveled through the radio, but she was mainly concerned that it might be being broadcast across the country. Of course, Bane took full advantage of the situation.

Whatever you do, don't think of your full name." He grinned.

"Like that dumb trick is going to make me think Jessica Amanda Braun. Shit! That bastard! He did it to me again!" the radio shrieked.

"Shut up!" Jessica shouted.

29

Oh, this is too strange! What the hell's going on? I'm going to flip the tape myself. Jessica thought out loud through the radio before she turned the tape over and placed it on play.

"That was messed up! How'd you do that?" Bane asked, thinking that Jess had pulled another one of her magic tricks on them.

She had, after all, once placed a device in his gas tank on his Harley so that whenever he drove over seventy miles per hour, it would shout out, "Hey slow down, you maniac!" As a consequence, he nearly dropped his bike when he hit that speed and stared down at his gas tank in amazement. It was a trick she only played once after he explained the near-tragic results that it could have had on him and his beloved motorcycle, also adding that under no circumstances should anyone ever play around with a man's bike; it was sacrilege, as far as he was concerned.

"I didn't do anything!" Jessica insisted.

"Come on. That stuff doesn't happen by itself, ya know." Carrie grinned suspiciously.

"I'm telling you I had nothing to do with that!" Jessica shouted, her face had been drained of all of its color, and a cold sweat broke out on her forehead. Carrie moved over to give Jess a hug and try to placate her a bit.

"It's okay. Everything will be fine—just some strange anomaly with the radio. We believe you, alright?" Carrie stated in her most gentle voice.

"Yeah, it's cool. Don't worry about a thing, dear; you got the mighty Bane hangin' with you. Nothing is going to mess with you while I'm around," he said with as much bravado as he could manage to muster. Bane puffed out his chest and bowed his arms outward to make himself look larger. Carrie and Jess both laughed. He always knew how to make them feel better despite the reasons they felt bad.

"Carrie, I didn't mean to think that about Bane—" Jess began.

"Relax, Jess, his ass *does* look good in those jeans. Appreciating a view and doing something about it are two different things entirely. You've been without a real man for a long time, and let's face it; Bane's hot. So, of course, you're going to look," Carrie explained, trying to keep Jess from freaking out.

"I . . . " For the first time since Bane and Carrie had known her, Jessica seemed utterly speechless. Searching for the right words, Jess simply blushed and faced the water, using the fact that she was driving the boat as an excuse not to look at Bane, not that she was going anywhere now that the anchor was in the water. She knew that for weeks to come he'd harass her about her private thoughts, which were broadcast over the radio. He never was the type of person to allow a good joke to go untold, despite any reasons to do so.

"Hey, Jess, I'm thinking of bending over to pick up my cigarettes. Better get a good look while you can," Bane joked, amused by his own humor, as he often was.

"Screw you," Jessica said, shaking her head in dismay at how fast the jokes had begun.

"Bane, leave her alone. She's had a rough night," Carrie admonished him.

"But I'm eye candy now!" he protested with a gleeful laugh. "I think I better go out and buy a few more pairs of these black jeans, seeing as my ass looks so great in them."

"Bane! Cut it out. It's not funny. How would you like it if your every thought was revealed to the world?"

"What the hell would I care? I pretty much say what's on my mind anyway. Besides, at least you weren't calling me an asshole or anything worse."

"Eject the tape again, and we'll see to that," Jessica growled.

Bane and Carrie both laughed; it was the first joke Jess had made since she was so thoroughly humiliated. They rode in silence for much of the trip, Jessica due to her nimiety, Carrie because she was enjoying the stars in the sky. Bane was thinking up a plethora of new jokes to force Jess to blush an assortment of new shades of red. After all, red was Bane's favorite color, and he liked it on all things, especially his friends' faces.

At long last, Jessica shattered the window of silence with the hammer of her words. "Have either of you ever walked in your sleep?"

"I have a couple of times. First was when I was a young kid at summer camp. I woke up outside my cabin in the woods. Freaked me out something fierce, but I managed to find my way back without too much trouble." Bane paused between stories for dramatic effect. "The second time was at my old house on Galloway. I used to sleep in the nude, and when I woke up, I was outside at the bottom of the long brick driveway. That wasn't the worst of it! We had one of those doors that locks itself after it closed. So I was forced to ring the doorbell, standing buck naked, praying that it was my father who answered the door. Luckily my dad did open the door. He was more than a little surprised to see me there naked but was too tired to ask me any questions."

Jessica and Carrie were laughing throughout the second story, giggling like hysterical schoolgirls. Bane continued, "Needless to say, from that night on, I slept in a pair of shorts or sweat pants. I wasn't about to go through that again."

"But those were the only times?" Jessica asked.

"Well, my parents told me stories of a few other events, but those I don't remember at all. I guess they put me back to bed before I woke," Bane answered. "Why? What's up?"

"Just curious."

"Bullshit. I know you better than that; you had a reason in mind. Sure, you ask more questions than anyone I know, but that one had a purpose. That was far out of left field. What's going on?"

"I've got a bad case of somnambulism...."

"Somnambulism?" Carrie asked, her vocabulary being severely limited.

"Large word for sleepwalking, dear," Bane commented, quickly wondering how he managed to stay married to a woman with so few mental cogs functioning.

"How often are you walking in your sleep?" Carrie asked.

"Three to four times a week. I wake up in places in my house or hotel room that I know I didn't go to sleep in. Most of the time, I wake up in a closet, or when I'm home, I come to underneath the dining room table or under my bed. It's starting to scare the hell out of me!" Jessica blurted out.

"Well, you've got a super guardian now. You know what a light sleeper Bane is. If you start walking around, he'll wake up and keep an eye on you. I think you might want to go see a doctor, though. They have medicine that might help you out. They've done a ton of research on sleep disorders, and I'd be willing to bet that sleepwalking is among that list," Carrie offered.

"Or we could just tie you to your bed, although I suspect you might enjoy that too much." Bane grinned, turning to Carrie. "Especially if she could look at my ass while I tied her feet to the bed. Then she'd have erotic dreams of my ass all night."

"Don't even think about it!" she shouted again.

"Relax, Jess. It was just a joke. Although maybe I'll tune in W-J-E-S-S on the radio tonight. Perhaps I'll hear what a woman like you dreams about in the still of the night."

"Bane, I'd have to kill you!"

"You'd have to try, you mean. Many have attempted, but since I'm here to make fun of you ladies, obviously they all failed."

32

"We're glad about that," Carrie stated honestly for the most part. "Who would keep all those freaky drunks away from us at the bars if you weren't around?"

"Not to mention the cute ones I may be interested in," Jess added despondently.

"Hey, I can't help it if my standards for men that you date are higher than yours. You may believe any man with a penis and a pulse will suffice. However, I firmly believe that the man who should win your heart should be able to scoop the stars from the sky as a gift for you, a person who could write an epic poem about the wonders that are you, and then be able to go out and kick the kidneys out of anyone who may have wronged you."

"Bane, if I wait for that man to come along, I'll be alone for a very long time. I do have urges, you know."

"Yeah, so I've heard. My ass being as cute as it is, you must have plenty of urges. I guess you're getting a bit horny." Bane grinned again.

Her brow furrowed. "Hey, are you calling me a slut?"

"Not while I'm around, you're not!" he bantered back in the same playful tone she used.

"So you think I'm a slut when you're not around to get rid of the men? " Jessica demanded irrationally, deciding that she was offended, even when they were all just teasing a moment ago.

"Did I mention that you look really nice in that shirt today?" he replied, avoiding the question.

"Sometimes you can be the sweetest man in the world—"

"Hey, I am not! Saying stuff like that could ruin my reputation," Bane interrupted.

Continuing as though Bane had said nothing, Jess interrupted, " But other times you're a real asshole, ya know that?"

"You tell me that part on a regular basis. How could I possibly forget?"

"Your memory sucks. You forget everything," Jess taunted, though clearly still angry.

"I only forget trivial things; the important ones are stuck in my head forever, your highness," Bane responded, accenting the last two words into a verbal slam.

"Okay, you two, no more fighting, or I'll have to kick both of your asses." Carrie thought for a moment. "Hey how about a magic trick to lighten the mood?"

Jessica was happy to comply since Carrie had asked for it; if it had been Bane, she'd have told him to drop dead. Jessica had a very petulant way about her, even when she was the one to take offense during a game she started. She wasn't one who could take it as well as she dished it out. She pulled out an ordinary quarter from her purse and showed it to Bane since Bane was the most skeptical of the three. After he verified that it was a normal coin, he started to give it back to Jess. She shook her head, handing him a permanent marker, commanding him to write something across the face of the coin; however, it had to be something original to prove that Jessica wouldn't know it ahead of time. He wrote, "Jess wants to squeeze my ass" in small block letters around the face of the coin. Once his assignment was complete, he again tried to give the coin back to Jess.

"No. Place the quarter in your leather vest pocket, then turn and face away from me." She smiled, knowing this trick would baffle their senses. "Now, what I'm going to do is tap you on your back. All the while, Carrie will be watching me. The quarter will magically jump from your pocket into the palm of my hand. Passing through the leather, your body, and into my possession. All I have to do is say my magic words . . . Retoe, Baltoe, Wren!" With those words spoken, Jess patted Bane on the back three times.

Jessica opened her palm, showing its contents to Carrie, who gasped with delight seeing a marked-up quarter. Bane turned around looked at the coin, then checked his vest pocket, and sure enough, the quarter was gone. Being a total skeptic, Bane scooped the coin from Jess's hand and examined it; it had all the markings he had written on it.

"Now that was cool! How'd you marked-up to do that? " Bane exclaimed, losing his cool temporarily.

"I told you the other day; a magician never reveals her secrets." She smiled graciously, I'm glad you liked that trick; I've been waiting to test it out on you for weeks. One more trick I set up this afternoon while you were sleeping, I know you're just going to love!"

"Really? Let's see this magic at work! You're quite talented, you know that?"

Carrie nodded in agreement. "Yeah, show us more. We are your biggest fans, after all. Can't disappoint your fan club, you know."

"Retoe, Baltoe, Wren!" Jessica shouted as her hands arched toward the sky.

When they followed her gesture upward, they saw an enormous red dragon flying toward them, flames puffing out its nose and mouth. The dragon's eyes glowed a purple hue, as its bluish forked tongue flickered out of its gaping maw. Swooping lower, before ascending higher into the sky, the dragon allowed them to get a better look at it before it flew up so high it left their line of sight. Suddenly, it shimmered and mingled with the rambunctious stars in the sky.

Completely in awe of Jessica's growing powers of illusion, neither Bane nor Carrie spoke. Instead, they stared at the spot that the dragon disappeared, and then shifted their slack-jawed gaze to Jessica. Under such scrutiny, Jess felt a bit subconscious, one thing from her line of work that she had yet to overcome. While she loved attention, she preferred that it be subtle and intimate attention, rather than overwhelming gawking. She averted her gaze, not looking at either of them in the eye, but the sardonic grin that was painted across her lips showed she was pleased at how completely awestruck her friends were.

"I'm totally amazed! That was absolutely magnificent! Hey, now that you are that skilled, can you make my monster-in-law disappear? You wouldn't have to make her reappear," Bane submitted.

"Yeah, I'm thoroughly impressed. This guy must be teaching you fast and well. What's his name again?" Carrie asked.

"The Resplendent Roberts. He's a wonderful teacher, mentor, and basically a really great guy. In a year, he said I'd be ready for my own show," she stated enthusiastically.

After an hour and a half of staring at the stars, watching the moon play hide and seek with the clouds, they drove the boat back to the dock. Carrie and Jessica were growing ever more sleepy with each passing moment. Bane was basically nocturnal. He slept most of the day while staying up almost all night long. He had long ago made his money as a vigilante, hunting down murderers, rapists, and child molesters for a price.

Night was the time when most criminals took to the streets, feeling that the cover of darkness and the abundant shadows provided them with some anonymity. However, it was in those dark places that most people feared to enter where Bane boldly stepped forward to capture his prey. Bane was generally fearless when it came to physical conflict. His training in several forms of martial arts, coupled with his experience in street fighting, gave him well-earned confidence in his abilities. He often carried himself with that same self-assurance, which caused most people to give him a wide berth.

Bane was one of the few citizens in the country who was authorized on a federal level to carry a concealed weapon in any state he chose. Normally, he opted for his Ruger, 9-millimeter semiautomatic handgun. It was easy to conceal, giving him ten rounds in the magazine. He often kept one bullet in the chamber; which offered him eleven shots if the need arose. At least twelve hours of his week were spent at the firing range, improving his skills. A minimum of one hour a day was devoted to practicing his martial arts, working out, and stretching to hone his talents even further.

In addition to his handgun, Bane was never without at least three knives. One was a throwing knife, perfectly balanced, contained within a forearm sheath. Another could be found in his back pocket; usually, it was an oriental butterfly knife. The third was carried in his boot, a new-aged switchblade. He never drew any of his weapons unless he truly intended on using them, but once one of them was drawn, his foe was about to feel the full force of his power. Bane always believed that no one ever won a fight, but he refused to be vanquished by anyone.

The boat pulled into the lift next to the other speedboat, and Jessica was quick to cut the motor and begin pulling the candy apple-colored boat from the water. Carrie, being short, had a difficult time getting out of the boat if it was fully raised, so she quickly leaped out before it got too high. Since there were no storm clouds sailing through the atmosphere, Jessica decided to leave the cover off the boat for the night. She opted for going up to the house and getting as much sleep as she could. Carrie slept on the Futon, Jessica on the bed by the door, whereas Bane set up his blankets on the floor where he often slept when at the lake house. Not only did it provide him with a flat surface to sleep, but it also kept him sleeping lightly, aware of his surroundings at all times.

While the two women drifted off into deep slumber, Bane had an interesting thought. Marching upstairs, he picked up the old portable radio with headphones and brought them downstairs. Perhaps if the radio anomaly was more than a fluke, he could eavesdrop on Jessica's dreams. Sleepwalking was often due to something that terrified a person in one's dreams, and thus the person literally got up in an effort to escape the fear he/she felt. If he could find out what was wrong with her dreams, perhaps he could help her end her sleepwalking adventures. After he plugged in the earbud to the radio and the radio to the electrical outlet, Bane located a station that was full of static. Now all he had to do was wait for Jessica to enter REM sleep.

Tropical winds blew lightly against her mid-section, her purple and black bikini showing off her gorgeous curves. The warm rays of the sun-stroked her tanned skin, glistening mystically off her well-oiled body. A blue drink with several pieces of fruit speared by a tiny pink umbrella was just within arm's reach; half of the beverage had already been consumed. Golden grains of sand stretched for miles in either direction; only palm trees provided shade for those who wanted it. No one else occupied the beach; she was alone, listening to her favorite music on her Walkman. The radio expounded dutifully. So far Bane found nothing horrifying about her dream, nothing that would cause her to walk in her sleep.*

Chaotic, dark clouds rolled in rapidly, far too fast to be a natural weather pattern. Pulling off her sunglasses, she looked up at the sky and began to tremble in fear. It was as though she knew something was coming, something terrible that she couldn't prevent. Suddenly, she was somewhere else entirely. She was standing in a bedroom, a child's room by the look of it. Pop culture musical icon posters hung on the wall; Pokémon cards were in a plastic carrying case on a small desk. Talking toys and an old computer with video games strewn across the floor identified the room as a juvenile's dwelling.

Stammering in gibberish, she tried to wake the slumbering child, attempting to warn the little girl to run, that danger was close at hand. However, she had no voice, at least not one that the child could hear. Jessica began stirring restlessly in her bed; her hands flailed back and forth. Her feet kicked at an unseen assailant, and she began murmuring in her sleep.

From under the little girl's bed came a blue shimmering light, and from below, a man wearing a dark cape, top hat, and a magician's outfit rolled out into view. She screamed, but no sound escaped her taut lips, white with terror. It was as though the man couldn't see her since he passed right by her and proceeded to silence the child. Once the child was quiet, he sank a taloned claw into the very center of the top of the head. Long canine fangs erupted from his mouth as he sank them into her brain. The skull creaked and cracked as he fed on her grey matter; blood gushed down across her face, which was locked in eternal panic.

A sound reminiscent of the last few sips from a soda sipped through a straw echoed out of the now empty skull of the young child. Not a single drop of blood spattered the man's nectarous clothing, a feat that sent a series of chills down from the top of her neck to her tail bone. The door to the bedroom began to open slowly on well-oiled hinges, but the man waved a wand in that direction, and an eleven-ton anvil appeared out of thin air; it was an effective way to bar entry into the room. Out of his vest pocket, the killer produced a silk handkerchief and placed it on the end of the bed.

With his work complete, the man seemed to glide toward the closet. The door opened for him as though it were an automated door, activated by motion sensors. It closed behind him, only slightly ajar, but from the crack under the door, a blue shimmering light flashed out brightly.

Bane was so entranced listening to the tragic nightmare that he completely forgot to keep a watchful eye on Jessica, who was no longer in her bed. Tearing the earbuds out of his ears, he leaped to his feet, scanning the room for where she might have gone. The back door was still securely locked, so she hadn't left the house. With his exceptional hearing, Bane detected a faint sound of sniffling coming from the closet where the floatation devices for the boat were kept. He opened the door, and there he saw Jess curled up in fetal position. She had pulled the inner tubes down over her as if they could shield her from danger.

Without waking her, Bane gently lifted her off the ground and placed her back in bed. He sat there on the edge of the bed, stroking her hair and watching her like a mother panther protecting her young. From that moment until she woke later that morning, he kept an eye on her, noticing that she didn't show any indications that her nightmare had returned.

Chapter Three

Grime occupied every corner of the small area; filth seemed to have made itself at home. Gloom filled the place; desperation clung to the walls, sheets, and just about everything else that was trapped inside the dank cell. The potent aroma of urine overpowered the three occupants of the tiny jail cell. A single light covered by a metal grate provided barely enough illumination to see the insects crawling across the floors. Every portion of the bars was greasy and sticky. What type of stains they consisted of was open to speculation.

He didn't know why he'd been put there; he was a straight-arrow type of person. Never having been in a great deal of trouble, this experience was beyond his comprehension. Certainly, there had been a case of mistaken identity, but no one from his family was in town to clear up the misunderstanding. That wasn't what bothered him the most. What really had him concerned was the way one of his cellmates was staring at him; a look of desire was melting in his eyes, giving him terrifying thoughts of a sexual advance coming toward him later in the night.

The man was not only looking at him like he was a piece of meat, but he towered over him. Devon knew that he stood very little chance of fending off any attack made by the large man. His other cellmate looked like he was a Hell's Angel; his long stringy hair and multiple tattoos heralded him as a biker. The biker's eyes were a deep green color, especially in contrast to how bloodshot the whites were. He seemed completely unaware and disinterested in his whole jailhouse situation, simply kicking back on the bottom bunk, lying quietly, and observing everything that went on around him.

After four hours of trying to appear to be sleeping, keeping one eye open, hoping that the strange man would keep his distance, Devon's hopes were dashed when the large man walked over to Devon's bunk. "Suck my dick, or I'll break your neck."

"Uh, no way!" Devon shouted, his hands balling into fists, knowing that a brutal beating was on its way. He had no intention of making it easy on the guy, even if he was destined to lose. Tossing off his covers, he stood up, his back toward the wall. The larger man's sledgehammer hands slammed into Devon's face repeatedly, each blow feeling like a freight train was smashing him into tiny pieces. Blood flowed like a river from Devon's nose; he was certain that it was broken. He returned several punches, but they didn't seem to have much effect on his much more burly opponent.

"You're gonna suck my dick, or I'm gonna do you up the ass, pretty boy!"

"Leave him alone," the biker muttered softly, but with such conviction it made the large man stop and gawk at him.

Ignoring the biker, the large man returned to brutalizing Devon with enthusiasm. Once again, the biker spoke softly, "I said, leave him alone."

However, as the big man drew back his arm for another devastating blow, his wrist was caught by the biker in an iron grip. He moved so quickly and quietly neither Devon nor his attacker heard the tattooed man approach. The biker twisted back hard on the large guy's wrist, using his left elbow to break the man's forearm. Sidestepping to his right, he spun the big bully around to face him. Two lightning fast snap kicks to the man's midsection, followed by blindingly rapid punches to the face left the man gasping for mercy.

"Next time I tell you to do something, do it. Leave the guy alone; he doesn't belong in a place like this. Look at him." The biker pushed the man's face in Devon's direction. "He looks like a bright, clean-cut man. He was whining earlier to the guard that it was a mistaken identity thing; he doesn't need this crap from you. Now, for the duration of his, or your stay . . . leave him the hell alone!"

The large man groaned and weakly nodded his head; it indicated he understood and would obey the biker's command. Devon was doing his best to stop the bleeding, using the pillowcase as a bandage. He thanked the biker for his assistance but kept coughing on the blood as it drained down the back of his throat.

"Name is Thunder. You're Devon Braun. I heard you telling the guard that, even though he called you Devon Matthews. No need to thank me, it was kinda good exercise. I needed a good workout after such a long day." He smiled softly; everything he did seemed quiet and casual.

"Thunder?" Devon said before he was beset by another coughing fit. Once he regained his composure again, he tried again. "Thunder? Is that your real name?"

Thunder scowled grumpily, as though the question was an invasion of epic proportions. Settling back onto his bunk, he looked up at the battered man he had just rescued. From what Devon could tell, Thunder was sizing him up, to see what type of person he was; the scrutiny was less than comforting, but there was little he could do about it.

"I didn't mean to offend you, seriously. It's just I knew a girl named Sky, a child of two hippies, who never grew up," apologized Devon quickly.

"It's the only name I answer to. My birth name hasn't been used by anyone but the cops and the newspapers. You want to get along with me, then Thunder is the name. Oh, and don't worry about sleeping tonight. As of now, you're under my personal protection; no one will mess with you without going through me. Of course, I'm getting out day after tomorrow; after that, you're on your own."

"Thank you very—"

"Think nothing of it, chief. It's just my nature. I'm going to grab some Z's. You have any problems or need anything, just give a shout," Thunder offered.

"What about him?" Devon asked, pointing to the unconscious man lying on the floor.

"What about him?" Thunder asked. "He'll wake up with enough pain that he won't want to do anything but sleep."

With nothing left to do, no gratitude being accepted by Thunder, Devon decided to try to get some sleep, despite his bone-chilling surroundings. He had rarely gotten into any trouble in his life, and never had any of it landed him in Cook County Correctional Center. This case of mistaken identity would never have happened if he didn't leave his wallet at home. If only his wife, Erika, hadn't had her flight home canceled. She was forced to book a flight for the next day. His sister was up at the lake house, and for some reason, she wasn't answering her cell. He left a message, but by the time she got it, Erika would already be there to straighten out the entire identity fiasco.

So he'd be stuck enduring a night in jail, which would probably make an interesting anecdote once the whole thing was over. Devon pinched his eyelids closed as tightly as possible; trying to picture he was home in bed with the television on too loud. He might have actually been able to convince himself of it, if not for the putrid smell and the uncomfortable bunk in which he laid. I can survive one night in here, especially with that biker guy looking out for me, he thought, trying to give himself some comfort, what little there was to be had.

***

41

"I think that he has a right to know, but you know his temper," she stated plainly through her tears.

"We can't tell him, not yet. Let him settle into his new house. Once that's over, we'll break the news to him," her father answered.

"Dad, he'll never forgive us if we don't tell him. He'll miss the funeral, not to mention he'll probably redirect his anger at us for not keeping him informed." She sobbed uncontrollably for a few minutes before being able to continue. "They were his nephews! My sweet grandchildren— gone! My dear daughter is gone forever! I'll never look upon her beautiful face again. It's all so senseless, not to mention tragic."

Her father hugged her, as they wept over the loss of their family members. The deranged serial killer had struck again, and he had taken the lives of her grandchildren—two boys whose innocence couldn't be measured by current technology, or theology. They were incredibly bright, even for their young age; that was not even mentioning how well behaved they were. Even at their crabbiest moments, they were still very polite and humble. Born only a year and a half apart, they were very close, always watching out for each other.

Holding his daughter in his arms, her father stated, "Okay, but let me or your mother tell him. He's our favorite grandchild, and maybe we'll be able to soften the blow. I know he's your son, but he'll hear your grief. Hearing that may push him over the edge, and we don't want that."

"I don't know."

"Trust me. I know how he gets. He's very protective of our family. If he hears how heartbroken you are, he'll lose it. We'll get through this; we just have to trust in the Lord now. Lean on him, and he'll ease our sorrow."

***

Pamela Phillips arrived in Chicago late at night, as her jet had to travel around a severe thunderstorm. By the time the jet landed at O'Hare International Airport, she had already gotten a call telling her to get to Illinois fast. Another crime scene had been discovered, near Elgin; two young boys were slaughtered in their beds. She would arrive on the scene much quicker than she had at the others since she was already in the area when the call came in. Perhaps getting a fresher look at the victims and their surroundings would provide her with a better lead than the ones she had gotten from the other scenes.

"I'm on my way. I should be there in less than thirty minutes," Pamela chirped into the phone as she hung up and raced to the car they had waiting for her on the runway. Her carry-on bag didn't seem to slow her in any way, knowing that her other bags would be transported to the hotel while she was doing her job. From what she was told, the children hadn't been dead for longer than a half-hour. She prayed that she would glean some new lead to help her catch the killer; however, Pamela wasn't a very religious person. So when she prayed, she didn't truly believe that her prayers would be answered.

She was rapidly growing beyond fatigued, but couldn't resist the morbid attraction that the crime scenes engendered deep within her. Pamela had a penetrating need to catch child killers and bring them before Lady Justice. Though she knew that justice was blind, Pamela still felt that, although ultimately corrupt, the system could work the way it was intended. No possibility of sleep would arise if Pamela didn't check out the latest massacre. Knowing fully that the images would haunt her; she needed a break in the case in order to capture the serial killer.

At least forty squad cars with their lights flashing hypnotically, even clashing with each other, were parked out front of the modest home. The eerie glow cast off the lights gave the home a much more macabre visage than the house could have ever shed amidst the rays of sunlight. It was normally a quiet neighborhood where parents with children settled and supported each other as their kids grew up. However, the tranquility of the small community had been violated, possibly forever, with one single act of heinous destruction by a psychopathic monster.

Pamela had to walk over a block to get anywhere near the house where the gruesome murders had occurred. With her badge securely fastened onto the front of her coat, she passed right by the officers keeping gawkers away from the area. Of course, their secondary and more pressing duties were to maintain a large area cornered off for when the press arrived, which they believed would be any possible second. Passing through the open door, she noticed the smears of blood on the doorframe, as though someone used blood as paint.

"Where is the commander of this crime scene?" she shouted unceremoniously.

"Right here. I'm Detective Gregory Rose, homicide division. We've got a really nasty one here."

Detective Rose paused, then took a breath to continue his report. "The two children are still in their beds, and the room was sealed off. We had orders not to enter the room until after you arrived. I don't like being kept away from a case in my jurisdiction, so maybe now that you're here we can get some work done. We've already begun our preliminary work on the parents' corpses."

"I'll go through first. Once I'm done, you can send in your forensics teams. This is—"

"Bullshit," Greg stated brazenly. "This is pure bullshit! We're not from some hick 'Podunk town' police department. Our department is competent and skilled at solving murders. I thought we could cooperate."

"We will cooperate, detective, after I do the original walkthrough. This killer has traveled and killed across state lines, making this now a federal case. Feel fortunate that we're sharing any information at all." Seeing his scowl deepen, Pamela held up a hand trying to pause his angry retort. "Look, I've been up for more hours straight than I care to count. I want your help— I need your help, but we're going to do this my way. It's my ass on the line out here, detective, and we're both really pissed off about this killer, so cut me a little slack, alright?"

The detective nodded in acquiescence, realizing she could toss his entire force out of the area and call in a federal team to work the scene. He was able to see that she truly cared about the victims and the cops investigating the crimes. However, she was a determined woman and a formidable one at that; pushing her buttons would only bring about more trouble.

"It's your show, Agent Phillips. Just tell us what you need us to do, and we'll get it done. We want this bastard caught, and from what my superiors said, you're the one with the most leads so far."

Most leads? I wish I had even one good lead to follow! But, if the bureau wants the local police to believe I have leads, I'm not going to screw that up, Pamela thought silently as she ascended the steps, carefully avoiding damaging any evidence on the way up.

When she entered the room, she was struck by a wave of vertigo; the room spun around, twisted and turned in her vision. For a moment, Pamela thought she might vomit, but she managed to swallow the bile back down. One set of bunk beds stood to the right side of the closet; crimson stains flowed over the Power Ranger sheets. A hockey poster was spattered by fresh blood, and it still dripped reluctantly down the wall, giving the wolf mascot an appearance of having eaten some carrion recently.

A picture frame stood empty by their bedside, an occurrence that hadn't happened before. The killer had thus far only stolen body parts, never physical property. Because of the young age of the victims, their heads were not merely split open; their skulls were practically torn to shreds. Blue curtains blew gently in the soft wind, wafting in through the open screened window. A bouquet of flowers was in a strange vase near that window. When Pamela investigated further, she saw that they were trick flowers used by common magicians as a quick illusion. Underneath the flowers, like a doily for the vase, was that same telltale handkerchief.

The hole through the center of the mattress and supports was at least three feet in diameter. Peering through the hole, Pamela could see it went clear through to the bottom of the bed, as though a large drill bored its way up to the top bunk. The closet door was wide open, and obscure amounts of glitter could be detected clinging to the nape of the carpeting. Drawing a knife from its sheath, Pamela quickly cut and bagged a sample of the carpet. Slowly the glitter remaining on the floor began to dissipate into nothingness.

"Detective! Call in your best forensic people now; this scene is filled with evidence and potential leads! Let's get it all recorded and bagged," Pamela ordered, scanning the walls and floor of the closet.

"Here they are," Gregory Rose stated from the doorway, which he had been standing in, waiting for her to allow them entry into the room. Four men entered the room with briefcases, latex gloves, accompanied with intelligence behind their eyes. Pamela was clearly impressed with their efficiency, professionalism, and work ethic.

"Also, I want to know what picture was in that frame. Talk to any and all family members to find out, but we need that information. Get the medical examiner in here to confirm what we already know about the children. I'll take a cursory examination of the rest of the house. My office will tell you where to send your results and reports. After that, I'm going to the hotel to try to sleep, despite the horrors I've seen in the past forty-eight hours," Pamela rattled off her orders to the detective who seemed to be taking notes as she spoke.

"No problem. I'll see that it's done properly. We'll keep you up to date; I promise you that, Agent Phillips," Detective Rose answered, closing his notebook.

Marching through the crime scene, Pamela took notice of the way the place was kept. The house was furnished in ultra-yuppie style, everything in its proper place. Pamela looked over the couch with a floral pattern covering the pillows, and a large chair, looking as though it was made for someone weightily challenged. The kitchen opened up directly into the family room, where the carpeting held the pools of blood on top of the bristling fibers. As she expected and would've been furious to see not preserved, the landline was lying off the hook.

Smudged with the father's blood, the handset glowed softly from the digital display on the handset. The bodies of the parents were given a simple once-over because she knew that she'd be returning to the house before too long. Since she was feeling weaker by the moment, Pamela left the house. Once she hit the outside air, a chill bounced between each vertebra in her spine. Again that acidity returned to the back of her throat. Swallowing it back down once more, Pamela rushed off to her car.

She sped away with red lights flashing, hastily making her way to her hotel. Pamela checked into her hotel with a speed that surprised her; again her assistant worked minor miracles. She went to her room, secured the deadbolt, placed her handgun under a pillow, and without changing out of her clothes, climbed under the covers, instantly falling into a fitful slumber.

***

"What? " Bane shouted through clenched teeth. His fury was so profound that it terrified both Jessica and Carrie. Whoever called him was giving him some very bad news, the type that was sending him over the edge. He asked many questions in rapid-fire succession, as his mind became a whirlwind: "When did this happen? Who did it? Any leads? Who's heading up the investigation? Give me the number so I can contact them."

Silent tears flowed down his face unbidden, a sight so rarely seen by either woman that they began to sob slightly themselves without even knowing why. His eyes looked like coins with a black hole in the center, so steely grey were the irises that they looked to be made of dense metal. His eyeballs bulged slightly from their sockets. Dark circles deepened under his eyes, and his jaw locked into a vicious scowl. Breathing through his nose, Bane's nostrils flared outward, making him look even more menacing if that were possible.

"Alright, I'll be down for the funeral if I can make it." The pause from Bane was longer than any pause he gave the person on the other end of the phone before. "Okay, I'll try. I love you too, Grandma. May the Lord comfort you too, in this time of tragedy."

Carrie looked over at him, examining his features. "What's going on?"

He waved her question away with his left hand, continuing talking into the phone. "I see. I'll talk to you soon."

Bane slid the phone back onto its cradle and stared out the window, trying to bring himself under control. "My nephews were mutilated by that fucking serial killer—both of them! My sister and brother-in-law were slaughtered as well. That son-of-a-whore is going to pay for this! Oh, yes, he will pay! He'll pay in blood. When his blood has been spilled, then I'll have a part of what he took from me."

He continued mumbling strange, outrageous, and insidious plans for what he planned to do to the killer once he was caught. The images he described terrified both ladies to their very core, knowing he was capable of doing everything he was saying, now that someone messed with his family. Bane's hands furled and unfurled from tightly balled fists, over and over. At their tightest fist, the knuckles in his fingers cracked inadvertently. Standing there, quivering in silent rage, Bane went over a mental checklist of the contacts he needed to speak with to start tracking his new enemy.

"Honey, I'm so sorry." Carrie wept, having loved those children as if they were her own.

"Bane, dear, it'll all be alright. I know it's hard to see right now, but you'll get through this; we'll help you through it." Solemn tears flowed down Jessica's face; she was genuinely concerned for him. However, she couldn't help but feel dread over how dark Bane's mood would become. He was the person who cheered them up when things got rough, and on a purely selfish level, she wanted that comfort for herself.

"This is what I need from you, Jess. It's very important, so don't forget. I want you to leave the station on the radio where it is and begin taping the moment before you go to sleep. Your dreams have some sort of connection or vision of this bastard. You might be able to help me track him."

"You listened to my dreams? " Jess shouted, angry at the invasion of privacy; not once did she give a thought to his current emotional pain. When it came to her feelings, no one else's really mattered. It was a flaw that those who cared about her tried their best to overlook.

"I was trying to help with the sleepwalking. Now, will you please trust me and give me your word of honor that you'll send me all the tapes unedited?" Bane pleaded, trying to remain calm in the face of her outrage. "I'm asking as a personal favor from me to you."

"You have my word. Just so you know, you can always count on me."

Bane nodded solemnly. "I do know that, Jess, which is why I was confident in my request to you. Be careful. I want to come back here and find you safe and sound. Understand?"

Jessica nodded. As she blinked back the tears in her eyes, she gave Bane one last lingering hug before she released him.

"When are we going back?" Carrie asked, her eyes bloodshot from the trauma.

"Pack some things; we're leaving right away. I'll need your iPhone Max with a charged battery for the ride back. I'm taking my Harley. You meet me at our house down there. Then we'll go to my parent's house. I need to see how they are holding up. They are going to need our strength, especially with my nephew's mother viciously slaughtered."

"Even now you're still going to hold that grudge? " Carrie asked, shocked beyond belief.

"Let's not do this shit now! We can save this argument for another day. Right now, we got to get rolling." Pulling out a semiautomatic handgun from a bag, Bane handed it to Jess. "Take this and keep it with you, just in case. Don't be afraid to use it if you have the need."

"I will. Everything will be fine with me while you're gone."

Bane loaded up on weapons and pulled on his black leather trench coat. He already had spare ammunition and clothing in his saddlebags on his bike. Without another word, he strode straight to the Harley and started it. With the sound of what appeared to be an earthquake coming from his motorcycle, Bane raced out onto the street and headed for Illinois, knowing Carrie would follow when she was done packing her belongings.

Chapter Four

The sound of thunder roared loudly as Bane pulled into the driveway. The police began trying to bring him to a halt, only to be brushed away by his cold nature. With the front door open wide, he strode in with purpose and fury boiling in his blood. He took notice of the smears of blood along the doorjamb. Suddenly, he came face to face with a comely woman with the most frigid eyes he'd ever seen. She glared at him for a few moments, assessing whom she was dealing with. Strangely, she felt an aura of courage and self-confidence in the way he carried himself.

"Who the hell are you, and what are you doing in the middle of my crime scene? " Pamela demanded impatiently.

"I'm Bane Bloodworth. My nephews and sister were the ones who were killed. I came here to see who's in charge and what's going on. I assume from your posture and attitude, that you're the person running the show." He stated with basic certainty.

"Since you're here, I guess you could be of some use to me after all. The rest of your family is so terribly distressed that they had little information to provide. I should warn you before we go into that room—it's very grizzly. However, you look like a man who can handle what lies inside. Brace yourself; it's going to be difficult, no matter how tough you think you are."

Bane looked at her impassively, *it's got nothing to do with a matter of what I think, lady.*

They walked into the room, and Bane looked around; he was forced to blink back the tears several times to keep them from spilling over his eyelids. Pamela looked at Bane, crunching her forehead, knowing how hard it must be for him to see that type of carnage. Bane toured the room slowly, taking mental photographs of the entire area for himself, to process later. Perspiration broke out across his brow; beads of sweat rolled unchecked down his face. He knelt down by the side of the bunk bed and said a quick prayer for his fallen nephews.

Upon rising, he turned and looked at Agent Phillips. "How can I help?"

"That frame right there . . . do you happen to know what picture was in it before tonight?"

He wiped a hand across his left eye to keep a tear from rolling down his cheek." It was a picture of the boys and me. We were all wearing leather vests. They looked adorable. It was the only time they wore them; my sister, God rest her soul, took hours of pleasure feeling superior to anyone beneath her husband's pay grade. In her mind that included anyone who rode motorcycles, she wasn't very knowledgeable about people in general. She formed opinions, based on the media and never changed it. She made it near impossible to have a relationship with my own nephews. I can't believe they're gone."

"I have a few more questions for you. First, I need to check on the forensics team though."

Pulling out his wife's cell, he dialed a number and waited for the person to answer the line. In a whisper, he said, "Tom, it's Bane. I need a big favor." Bane looked around to make certain no one was nearby. "My nephews were slaughtered, and I need to get full clearance for working with this crime."

"I think I can get that arranged. Give me an hour, and I'll have it all worked out. You'll be temporarily assigned to an unnamed agency, as a freelance investigator. Where can I have a messenger sent with your credentials? Where will you be?" Tom asked quickly, knowing Bane's determination; not to mention all the favors he owed to Bane.

"Send them to my house. I'll be there in an hour to grab a shower. I've been riding like a maniac to get to this crime scene. Look, man, I appreciate your help. I really do."

"Think nothing of it. You saved my life three times before I even entered law enforcement and many more times since then. I owe you more than I could ever repay. If there's anything else you need, just say the word."

"Tom, those credentials will allow me to carry a weapon openly, right?"

"You already had that privilege, remember? But yes, you'll have full law enforcement prerogatives. Good luck, and, Bane...I'm really sorry for your loss."

"Thanks, Tom. It means a lot to me. I'll talk to you soon." He turned off the phone and walked out into the dining room, where Pamela Phillips was discussing things with the forensic team leader. As he entered, Bane saw his brother-in-law literally shredded, lying in each place setting at the table. His head was severed into two pieces, and each side was looking at the other. Hanging from the chandelier was a silk tie, given to him for Father's Day.

Bane moved backward several steps, the shock of the gruesome scene setting in. When he saw his nephews, he was vaguely aware of the condition they would be in, so Bane was able to steel himself against the horrific tragedy. He knew in an instant that his sister must also be dead; what condition her body would be in was what worried Bane. Turning away from the dining room, and his brother-in-law's corpse, he finally saw what happened to his sister.

Her entrails were pulled out of her, wrapped around her neck, suspending her from the ceiling. Bane couldn't see what was holding the entrails in place, but looking into his sister's body through the holes torn in her, caused bile to rise in Bane's throat. At one time, they had been pretty close emotionally, but over the years, they'd lost touch. His lifestyle was beyond her comprehension. She never really understood him, nor the things he was interested in. Additionally, she didn't even bother trying to show any interest in what he was into, which was what caused the large rift in their relationship.

When she got married and had children, she always looked down her nose at Bane, as though she were somehow better than he was. While she was a bright woman, her intelligence in no way compared to Bane's. Bane was thoroughly tested in his youth and was found to be a genius, with an IQ well over 180. He tried hard to care about the things she was interested in, even though to him they seemed mundane and exhaustively uninteresting. Bane made the pretense of interest in her activities, while she simply rolled her eyes when he discussed the things he did and wanted to do.

Finally, using the college education she had gotten at Ball State University, she became a teacher's aide, then a teacher in her own right. At least then she did something interesting and worthwhile. She worked with mentally stunted students. The only problem that stemmed from that is it brought her delusions of superiority to soaring new heights. Especially when she claimed that she had become a better parent due to her studies, which was blatantly not true, despite Bane's dark side. That he got on his own; no parenting could've prevented that. So ever larger the rift grew, it was between them to the day her life was brutally snuffed out.

Still, though they hadn't spoken in many years, the pain of her death was sharp and piercing. His heart thundered against his chest, raising his pulse by leaps and bounds. Suddenly, Bane's world was spinning, as though

51

he were in a drunken stupor; he staggered until he bumped into a wall. A detective walked over to him, demanding to know what he was doing on the scene. However, Bane was so out of control that he couldn't make sense of the words the man was saying.

Pamela Phillips entered the room, hearing the nasty comments the detective was spewing at Bane, due to his refusal to answer him.

"Leave him alone, detective."

"What?"

"I mean, back off! He's a family member of the victims, here providing us with some additional information. If this were your family, I doubt you'd be able to provide information, nor hold it together the way this man has! Go on about your other duties now!"

"Yes, ma'am," the detective answered skeptically.

"Bane? Are you alright?" Pamela asked with genuine concern. When she got no response, she led him through the house and outside; hoping the fresh air would do him some good. His breathing started to slow, deep breaths in through his nose and out through his mouth.

"Bane?"

"Yeah."

"Feeling any better? I'm sorry you had to see all of that. You really shouldn't have been inside that house. I don't think I mentioned my name yet; I'm agent Pamela Phillips, Federal Bureau of Investigation."

"I'm special agent Bane Bloodworth, of . . . another agency, if you take my meaning," he stated numbly.

"You're in law enforcement?" She stared at him quizzically. Pamela wasn't a fan of the black operations agencies that ran as law enforcement. This was mainly because she never knew what their legal limitations were; their jurisdiction fell, and most importantly where they ranked among other agents.

"Yeah. I know I don't look the part, but that's the whole idea. Look. I need to go home and grab a shower to get the smell of the long road trip off me. Then I need to go see my family. Is there some way I can contact you to find out what you've learned?"

Pamela handed him her card as he returned her cell phone. "I'll keep you up to date— I promise."

"Thanks. I'll be in touch." Bane turned on his heel and hopped on his Harley. Starting it, he gunned the engine, and then shifted it into gear, driving off toward his house. He knew that by the time he got there, Carrie would be home waiting for him. He could almost picture the look of sympathy that she would surely wear when he walked through the door.

Bane arrived at his house just as the messenger pulled into the driveway. A small shoebox-sized package was pulled from the van. Bane signed for the parcel and went inside to get cleaned up. Carrie immediately rushed to his side, hugging him tightly and rubbing his back. "Sweetie, I'm so sorry. Are you okay?"

"I . . . I saw the bodies," was the only statement Bane could muster. Pulling a knife from one of the sheaths on his belt, he opened the box. Contained within was an identification wallet, the latest iPhone fully encrypted, a shoulder rig that would carry two equal weight firearms comfortably, several clip holders that could be attached to his belt, a portable red scrolling light for his car, and a stack of business cards with the phone numbers to his iPhone and a landline voicemail set up for his use. Additionally, there was a note from his friend Tom. Bane read the note, leaving it on the table in the kitchen. "I'm going to take a quick shower, then head over to my parents' house. Do you want to go with me, or would you rather stay here?"

"I'll go with you; the family needs us right now," Carrie answered simply, suddenly longing for the touch of her boyfriend. Her husband was a better lover and strictly fantastic in the bed. Her boyfriend Carl was much more feminine and his approach reflected it. If only he were as gifted in the bedroom as Bane, he'd be the perfect man for her.

Bane shrugged off his coat draping it over the back of a chair; he slid off his boots and socks. He padded his way down the hall to the bathroom where he stripped down and ran the warm water. When the temperature was just right, he got inside and slid the glass doors shut. The steaming hot water sluiced across his body, draining away the tension in his muscles. No matter how warm the shower was, it wouldn't burn away the images he had witnessed earlier in the day. Bane's heart ached, but his lust for vengeance greatly outweighed the pain.

As he was toweling off, Carrie came in and asked him what he was planning to wear so she could get it out of the drawers for him. She wanted to do anything she could to make things easier on her husband. Carrie could instinctively feel the agony he was silently enduring. They had been married for so long she could almost read his mind. He told her the outfit he wanted, and she quickly went to retrieve it for him.

She got back just in time to hear him recording the outgoing message for his new landline voicemail. "You've reached the voicemail of special agent Bane Bloodworth, verify your name and number which we've already logged. Please leave a brief message as to why you called. If you need assistance using another language please press 8 now, where you will be transferred to the nearest enrollment for language learning classes!"

Bane dressed in black leather pants, a dark blue pullover, his motorcycle boots, and a sturdy black leather belt. He began pulling his guns out of their display case after he strapped the shoulder holster on. Two nine-millimeter Ruger semi-automatic firearms were placed into the holsters; along with a .44 Desert Eagle he shoved onto a belt holster, at his right hip. Bane began filling the clip holders with ammunition, two for his .44, and the other four for his Rugers. Onto both of his forearms, Bane fastened a knife in a black sheath; into his right boot, he slid a .25 caliber semiautomatic. Into his left boot, he shoved a small sapper, used to club people over the head.

His black leather vest seemed to camouflage the fact he was packing a pair of guns beneath it. When he shrugged into his trench coat, Bane grabbed the credentials, putting them into his inside pocket. In his left-hand pocket, he carried the cell phone; in his right-hand pocket he carried a spare powered battery. Carrie handed him a business card holder, which she filled with his new cards, kissing him gently on his forehead. Without even thinking about it, Bane pulled on his leather driving gloves, which were so tight they were like having a second skin.

"We'll take two cars to my parents' house. I may have to leave if Agent Phillips calls."

"How will she know what your new numbers are?" Carrie asked, picking up on what Bane had missed.

"Good point. I'll give Tom a call en-route and he can let her know how to reach me, besides I'm certain she'll want to check up on me a bit; this will just save everyone time."

Bane and Carrie arrived at his parents' home, finding a group of cars filling the driveway, forcing them to park in the street. Bane recognized many of the vehicles belonging to his family. He realized too late that the entire family would be there to support his grief-stricken parents. Not that he didn't want to see his relatives; he actually missed them all greatly. The problem was whenever he saw his mother or father shed a tear, he most often seemed to follow, which was one thing that didn't go along well with his tough guy exterior.

Entering the code to the garage door's keypad, Bane waited for the door to rise. Passing between the two cars, Carrie and Bane made it to the door that led to the interior of the house. The decor inside was an elegant cross between country and rustic, with numerous knickknacks to fill any empty space. Considering how many cars were parked out front, Bane found it odd that there was no sound of voices. No sobbing could be detected, and suddenly Bane feared the worst—something happened to the family.

He dropped a hand to his hip, allowing it to come to rest on the handle of the .44 Desert Eagle. The cool metal gave him a feeling of reassurance, bringing his anxiety down a few notches. Bane motioned for Carrie to stay by the door until he signaled to her that all was well. She silently slid her hand closer to the slender knife, which was concealed at the small of her back. He slowly walked down the hallway toward the bedrooms. None of the three rooms had any occupants, nor did the bathrooms in the master bedroom or in the hall. The cold finger of fear traced its path along his back. Moving cautiously but much more swiftly, he checked the living room, then the dining room; once again, he found no signs of his family.

Bane was about to pull his weapon from the holster as he entered the kitchen but chose to remain calm despite the pit in the center of his stomach. Looking through the second door to the kitchen, he saw that Carrie was still standing by the garage door; she shot him a questioning look, which he answered with a simple shrug. Continuing his search, he moved into the laundry room, for it held the only access to the basement. Down the steps he went, taking each step with great care not to make too much noise announcing his presence.

For the basement, he had chosen to pull out his gun; if something were amiss, the basement would hold the most danger. The darkness and shadows clung to that room, like a tattoo. A small workstation had been set up in one corner with the rest being used for storage. One area had a workout bench and barbells where his father got his exercise. Pangs of fear wrenched at his heart as he approached the wooden panel that led to the crawlspace. Picking up a flashlight in one hand, while aiming at the door with his gun, Bane flung the door open.

Nothing but insulation, old pipes, cobwebs, and insects were contained within. Cursing himself for a fool, Bane raced up the stairs looking to make sure Carrie was all right. Again she flashed him an inquisitive look; he holstered his gun and waved her over. He strode purposefully to the family room, which had a set of French doors that led into the backyard. Through the windows, he could see his family standing outside near a manmade pond. His mother was staring at the waterfall with his uncle's arm around her shoulder. His father was sitting on a beautifully crafted oak bench talking with Bane's grandparents.

Bane opened the door, and all eyes turned to look in his direction. "We got here as soon as we could."

Both Bane's mother and father raced over and embraced him; neither of them even feigning an attempt of letting go for a while. Carrie went to greet the rest of the family, her eyes already red-rimmed with tears. All three of them stood weeping over their loss and taking comfort in the family they had left. When his parents finally released him from their grip, they stood back a step and looked at him.

"What in the world are you carrying under your coat?" His mother sniffled, trying to regain her composure with little success.

"I've been assigned to the government agency on a temporary basis, Mom. You felt my firearms, in their shoulder holsters." Before his father's skepticism reared from his grief, Bane pulled out his identification and business cards. "I called in a few favors and got some credentials so I might investigate these things further. We'll get this guy, somehow, someway, but he'll pay for what he's done to our family!"

"Do you really think that's a good idea?" his mother asked through the deeply worried fabric draped over her face.

"Why wouldn't it be?"

"Well, you might see things that were —" She broke off into sobs.

"You may see photographs of what happened to your sister and nephews," his father finished for her.

Bane wiped several tears away with a gloved hand, his face pale as a ghost. "I was already at the crime scene. I saw it all. I made all the identifications so no one else has to, and I seriously advise no one look at the remains."

"Oh my God! Are you all right? " his parents asked in unison.

"No, but I will be, in time. It was beyond horrible."

"You know your sister loved you very much," Bane's mother stated through her tears.

"I know, Mom, and I loved her too, even if we didn't get along well. Our years of silence were the only way we knew how to maintain that love.

We were too different; we never saw eye to eye and fought too much when we talked, but deep down, we still loved each other."

In turn, each of Bane's family came over and hugged him, offering their sympathy as well as their support. Through their tears, they each showed in their eyes a great deal of pride in him. The emotional pain he felt grew worse the longer he remained; he prayed for a distraction, for something to happen that would allow him to exit without causing a scene. He wanted to be of help to the family but he lost all of his will to fight against his flooding emotions. His cloak of bravery was easily removed when in the presence of his family, for they knew how deeply his mental agony was.

The Lord in heaven answered his prayers as his phone rang. He clicked it to the open screen and stated, "Bane Bloodworth."

"We've got a development. Can we meet to discuss it?" Pamela Phillips asked markedly softer than usual.

"Sure. I can be at your hotel in forty minutes, or we can meet at a restaurant of some sort."

"You know, I checked your credentials after you left. I'm sure you can understand why. From what your superior officer said, I'm surprised you don't have a big red 'S' painted on your shirt. I look forward to having your assistance in this case, but let's make one thing clear— I'm the senior officer on this case. As long as you agree to that, I'll conveniently forget that you have an emotional attachment to the case."

"Your terms are accepted. I'm honored to work with you, agent Phillips. Where should we meet?"

"I'm nearer to you now. I'm calling from a Denny's on Rand and Dundee Road. Do you know where that is?" she asked.

"Yeah, I'll be there in ten minutes. See ya then." Bane pocketed his phone and apologized to the family, but he had to leave. Explaining briefly why and where he was going, Bane hugged each relative again and then left.

"I'm taking the Hummer, sweetie. I'll call you when I'm done. Get in touch with Jessica; I'm going to need her help. As soon as the funeral is over, we're going to Wisconsin again and staying with her." He didn't wait for an answer; he just got into the truck and drove away as swiftly as possible with his emergency beacon flashing brightly.

***

The sun slid down behind the horizon, tossing off the purple cloak of twilight. Devon, Erika, and their guest arrived at the lake house just as the gentle shadows crept out of the cracks and crevices in the broken asphalt streets. They began unloading their bags, luggage, and coolers from the winter blue truck, hauling it into the house. Not expecting any company, Jessica climbed the steps from the basement; the handgun Bane had left her gripped tightly between both hands. As she opened the door slowly, she leaped forward, weapon aimed in front of her. Devon stood there stunned as he stared down the barrel of a 9 mm Beretta.

"Jesus Christ! Jess, what the hell are you doing? " Devon shouted, out of terror.

Jessica lowered the gun, flicking the safety on. "Sorry. I wasn't expecting you up here for another few days. You scared me."

"Scared you? I nearly crapped my pants! Where on earth did you get a gun?" he grilled her angrily. "No, let me guess. Bane gave it to you."

"It's not like you think. He was worried about me. Later I'll fill you in on the whole story. Do you need some help getting the truck unloaded?"

"No, Thunder and I have it covered."

"Thunder? Who's that?"

"He's a guy I met in county jail. Geez, you don't check your voicemail often, do you?"

"I got your messages, but they didn't say anything about anyone named Thunder. Your last one said Erika came and got you out so I didn't have to worry about it." Jess grabbed Devon's arm and led him into the family room. "You're bringing criminals into our house now?"

"You bring Bane here," Devon stated plainly. Though he liked Bane, he also was wary of him and his dark past. "Besides, Thunder's okay. He saved me while we were inside, and he's actually pretty cool once you get to know him."

"What was he in jail for?" Jess asked skeptically.

"Assault and battery. He got nailed in a barroom brawl, not unlike your friend, Bane, I might add," Devon said with a note of reproach coating his words like milk over cereal.

Jessica couldn't help but wish that Bane was still staying at the lake house. He had proven, time and again, that he could handle just about any situation. With him around, she wouldn't have cared if Devon brought a mass murderer into the house for the weekend because Bane always saw to it that she was safe.

"Well, you guys are sleeping upstairs. The basement is already set up for Carrie, Bane, and me. Where's Erika anyway?" Jess stated calmly.

"She's helping Thunder unpack, which is what I have to do too. Why don't you pour a pitcher from the keg? We'll introduce you to Thunder, and we'll all sit and chat."

Jess was hesitant. She had already been drinking a bit already but decided that she might as well try to get along with this newfound friend of Devon's. Once the pitcher was poured, Jess returned to see Erika, Devon and a biker sitting around the dinner table.

"Thunder, this is my sister, Jessica. Jess, this is Thunder."

"Nice to meet you," Jess said warmly. She looked him over and realized he was rather attractive. He reminded her of Bane in several ways, though she couldn't see his butt. She hoped it would be as nice as Bane's.

"It's a pleasure to meet you as well. Dev has told me a lot of nice things about you. It's cool to see he isn't a liar." Thunder smiled, and it sent a warm tingle through Jess's body.

Thunder took the pitcher from Jess's hands and began pouring everyone a tall plastic cup of beer. He waited for her to sit before he took a seat as well; very gentlemen-like, Jessica noted, another feature that reminded her of Bane. They both looked rough and uncouth with their outward appearances but had the virtues of chivalry and etiquette hidden underneath. Though it wasn't obvious to anyone else in the room, Thunder checked Jessica out thoroughly. It was clear that he liked what he saw.

"Are Carrie and Bane coming back up? I haven't seen them in ages!" Erika asked excitedly.

"I hope so. Bane's nephews, sister, and brother-in-law were murdered. They went to attend the funeral," Jessica reported sadly.

"Oh my god! How awful!" Erika exclaimed.

Erika was a pretty woman, with a warm heart; it often took people a while to realize that because she was so terribly shy. Even Bane, king of the extroverts had a hard time getting Erika to drop her shields and open up to him. However, he was very patient and kind to her until she felt more comfortable around him. When Bane stuck up for Devon and his friends at a bar, Erika saw him as more than just a ruffian. Devon had won a few games of pool, and his opponents decided they had been hustled; Bane simply stepped forward and stated that Devon and his friends were under his protection, and any problems that arose would go through him.

"Bane? I know of a guy named Bane. Mean son-of-a-bitch— he's like a whirlwind of misery to anyone who pisses him off, which I hear isn't hard to do. The dude has a temper quicker than a rabbit on caffeine pills. Plus the guy has so many connections, it's freakin' scary," Thunder continued, "he's one character I wouldn't want to be on the wrong side of if you know what I mean."

"Know his last name?" Jessica suppressed a grin, thinking that description sounded a lot like her friend, plus Bane wasn't a common name unless you lived inside a comic book.

"Bloodworth. Bane Bloodworth is that guy's name. I've never crossed paths with him, but I know a couple of people who have. Some came out for the better, most of them for the worse because of it . . . one that didn't come out of it at all." His haunted expression made Jessica shiver.

Devon let out a chuckle, Erika giggled, and Jessica smiled charmingly. "He's the one who'll be coming up here. He's one of my best friends in the world, even if he's a little overprotective of me. I think you two will get along just fine," she paused for dramatic effect. "As long as you don't try to hurt me or any of his friends," Jessica stated ominously.

"Wouldn't dream of it, Jessica. Wow, The honorable Bane Bloodworth! This should be an interesting weekend," Thunder mused quietly. *I just hope I survive this interesting weekend.*

"You mean that you've actually heard of him?" Devon asked with a measure of surprise.

"Hell yeah! That dude is infamous! In more than just the circle I run with, too. He leaves no stone unturned when it comes to contacts and favors owed. From what I understand, he has so many favors owed to him, from over the years, he could probably start a small war if he chose to," Thunder reported, then gave Jess a skeptical glance. "And you're saying he's a good friend of yours?"

"Yes, he's been my friend since we went to high school together. That's when he assumed the role of my big brother, not that I ever asked him to, but it was just his way." She shrugged slightly, smiling as brightly as ever. "Though we tend to fight a lot, there is a lot of love in our relationship, which is how we can remain friends through all the turmoil."

"That's a very good ally to have watching out for you—better than a guardian angel or a personal security guard. I imagine even when he's not around, his presence is still felt. I'd even go so far as to bet that he has friends watching out for you when he can't be there to do it himself," Thunder claimed.

"I wonder what he's going to do about his family being murdered?" Erika wondered out loud to no one in particular. Jessica suddenly fell silent, knowing Bane would never want her to mention her recent nightmares to anyone, especially if it would lead him to the killer. She knew he'd want his hands on that guy first.

Chapter Five

V oices mingled with each other discordantly, sounding more like a thousand geese honking than people speaking. Their chaos did little to compare to the decor of the restaurant: purples, blues, reds, yellows, and pinks were splashed across the seats in a haphazard pattern, which nearly made one's eyes hurt simply by looking at it. While the walls were painted a pastel purple, it did little to tone down the terrible seat covers. It was a new look for the place, as it once had a dull countenance, which was suitable for most adults. Apparently, the franchise wanted to attract children and their parents more than it wanted single adults to frequent their establishment.

After taking a tentative sip from his mug, Bane looked over at Pamela. "Agent Phillips, what is this new development you spoke of earlier on the phone?"

"Tell you what, let's drop the agent stuff. My name is Pamela. If you don't mind, I'll call you Bane," she stated with a hint of a smile playing about her lips. "We've gotten several sobbing calls from the parents of the victims so far, almost exactly in order, I should mention. They were very upset, and from what I've heard, they have every right to be disturbed. Small doll heads were sent to them, but the spooky aspect of it is, the heads look exactly like the child, or children, they lost."

"How were they delivered?"

"Federal Express. We're already trying to track that angle down now. The sender has already gotten three-quarters of the way through the mourning families so far. "Pamela stated.

"Wait a second." Bane pulled out his iPhone and called his wife. "Listen, if any packages arrive at my parent's house through Federal Express or any other messenger service, I want you to intercept it and keep it for me. Don't open it! Don't let the family get to it! Just hold it for me and call me right away. Alright?"

She agreed without asking questions, after hearing the tone of voice he used. He was very serious about whatever might be inside the package. Bane turned back to Pamela. "Sorry about that. I just didn't want my parents to go through that horror if they got one of those packages. Now, let me ask you this: was there any note or anything with the heads?"

"Yes, a simple five-word note was left in each box. 'For the one I took.' Like it was any consolation to those people!" Pamela answered sourly.

"The doll heads— how big are they, and exactly how identical are they to the children that were slaughtered?" Bane asked, trying to understand the purpose behind the madness.

"I'm having all of the ones that have been received thus far sent to my hotel. They've already been through forensic testing, so I can get a better idea of what we're dealing with. However, from what information I do have, they are exact matches to the children, down to birthmarks, scars, dimples, and average facial expression. The eyes inside the dolls are the type that move when the doll is shifted from side to side, standard gravity eyes used in many common baby dolls. So the eyes follow you when you change the direction you're holding it.

"Another thing the forensics team determined was that the hair on the doll heads was genetically identical to the real child's hair. As of yet, we've found no signs that any hair had been extracted from any of the crime scenes though. The overall size of the heads are about the size of a standard baseball, but much heavier, as though there was some type of weight inserted inside," Agent Phillips reported.

"Okay, so have any of the heads been cracked open to see what's delivering the weight inside? How would the killer know the natural state of the child's face to create an exact duplicate, unless he photographed them from several angles before killing them?" He paused, almost having said that he knew that the killer hadn't done that. Bane wasn't quite ready to tell Pamela about Jessica and her psychic dreams over the radio.

"One of them was opened, which is how we knew about the eyes. Here is where this thing gets even stranger: The heads are hollow, save for the addition of the eyes and the roots of the hair. Forensics sent that head to the medical examiner, who swears that the hair is actually living and growing from the roots, which were healthy."

"Okay, so how heavy are these things? I'm sure they were weighed, especially once they discovered nothing inside to add extra heft."

"Six pounds exactly, not one ounce more or less. Each and every head was exactly the same weight," Pamela stated as though she were using sagely wisdom. "I don't mean to sound condescending, but you ask some really good questions. Most of this I wouldn't have thought to bring up unless asked."

"Thanks and no insult was taken by that. I appreciate a compliment anytime I receive one. Anyway, I need to ask about the adult victims? Were their heads duplicated in doll form?"

"I don't think so. I'll make a call and find out. Why don't you flag down our waitress and see if we can get our coffee refilled." Her remark caused Bane to look down at his mug. Much to his surprise, it was totally empty; he hadn't even remembered drinking that much of it.

Their cups were filled while Pamela was on the phone. The moment she got off, she stared at Bane with wide-eyed amazement. "You're good. You've even asked questions that I wasn't prepared for. The answer is, no. We believe it is because none of the adults lost their skulls in the way the children did."

"Were the bodies of these parents ever found outside the children's bedroom? As I understand it, the killer simply destroyed anyone who got in his way. He didn't even search the house to slaughter anyone else, did he?" Bane asked, thinking of his family.

"No, the only instance it happened in was . . . " She let her voice trail off; they both knew where and with whom that exception had been made.

"So the question remains, why did he deviate from his standard practice? He's done it three times now. First, he abducted the children from their homes before mutilating them. Then, he started doing it right in their bedrooms. Now, he left the confines of the bedroom to maul the parents of his victims, for no obvious reason. Not to mention he stole a picture from its frame when he's never stolen property before. Seems to me those changes could be very crucial to catching him. All we have to do is figure out the connection between the changes."

"Not as easy as you make it sounds. However, you're right; we need to remain optimistic about catching the killer. He's got an agenda; that much is certain, but what that plan is, we haven't deciphered." Pamela frowned deeply. "Bane, I sense that you're holding something back, and I'd like to know what it is."

"I don't know what you mean? Look, I'm playing catch up here, trying to learn all about what has happened so I can help make sense of this." Bane waved a hand encompassing the planet in a grand sweep. "I've been given permission by my superiors to investigate this, which is a rare thing, indeed. Once the memorial for my family is over, I'll return to Wisconsin. You can continue to reach me as you have been. I've other things I must work on; it's part of the deal I made to be allowed to work this case. So I'd appreciate any information you'll pass along."

Pamela studied his face carefully, and then sighed softly. "Alright, I'll keep you up to date with each murder, and if I need your help—"

"I'll come running; don't worry about that. I want this bastard just as much as you do. Even though you're the one that the world is watching, I'd still bet that I want him more than you; after all, that son-of-a-bitch killed my family!" Bane interrupted.

"Bane, I really am sorry for your loss, but I'm glad to have you working with me on this case. Something that I can't quite put my finger on tells me, that together, we'll catch him. I'll be in touch frequently, even if it's just for us to bounce ideas and questions off each other," Pamela stated with a touch of relief in her voice. "It'll be nice to have someone else to share the workload with, and to talk to about this case."

The waitress came back, dropped off the check and disappeared to wait on her other tables. Bane left a twenty-dollar tip, as Pamela took the check up to the register. They walked out of the restaurant, heading to their respective vehicles. Pamela stopped, turned around and watched Bane get into his Hummer. She was certain that he was, in fact, holding something back, but it wasn't the time to push him. He lost his family and would surely put up a fight if she pressured him.

Bane called his wife from the truck, "Carrie, did any packages arrive?"

Her voice trembled. "Yes, actually, sounds like two pieces are inside. I can hear them rolling around. It's taking all my willpower to keep your mother from opening the package. What is so important about this particular parcel?"

"Sweetheart, just tell her not to open that box. It's very important. If she does, she'll freak out— big time. I'll explain it all later. When is the memorial service?"

"Today, in about two hours. Since the bodies are being held by the police, they wanted to get the memorial service done as quickly as possible. I think that was Grandma's idea; she's really holding everyone together. You know your grandparents are amazing people; they are the literal pillars of strength you always hear about."

" Grandma and Grandpa are the best people I know. No one on earth is like 'em; I wouldn't be the person I am today if not for them. I'm on my way over there now; I'll take the box. We'll go to the memorial service and head back to Wisconsin. I want to check on Jessica; her dreams may be the key to unraveling this entire mystery. No wonder she's walking in her sleep," Bane explained.

Still sobbing lightly, Carrie answered, "Okay, just hurry alright. I feel safer when you're around, ya know?"

"No worries, babe. I'm on my way. I'll be there in less than ten. Just keep that box closed!" Bane comforted, as he flipped on the red flashing beacon so that he could pass through stoplights and clogged traffic. "I love you. Bye."

"Love you too." Shortly after she hung up she was on the phone with her secret boyfriend, letting him know it would be a while before she could see him. It took her twenty minutes to explain the situation and the reasons why Bane would become so suspicious if she disappeared for a sexual rendezvous. Her boyfriend wasn't the brightest man in the world, which is exactly why she liked him; Carrie always felt inferior around Bane, due to his intelligence.

The memorial service lasted two hours, and the funeral home was filled with the pungent scent of marigolds, roses, lilies, and carnations. A wide arrangement of flowers adorned the wood-paneled room. Three large pictures displayed images of the family members that had been slain brutally. Rows of mourners were stifling their sobs as the minister delivered a moving and beautiful eulogy. Even Bane's eyes leaked his sorrow while thinking of all the time lost for his loved ones, remembering all the things that the children would never experience: they'd never know the pleasure of their first kiss, first love, winning a hockey game, learning to drive, and oh so much more.

He wept over not forgiving his sister for her transgressions against him. Now she wouldn't have the opportunity to forgive him for whatever slights or wrongdoings she perceived. Despite the fact that they loved each other, they never came to terms about their argument, mainly because they were either too proud or bullheaded to apologize. Now it was too late; it was all too late— she was gone. Though she was dead, as the procession passed by the pictures of the fallen, he stood for a moment by the photograph of his sister, and whispered, "I forgive you anyway."

When the people exited the funeral home, Bane hugged his family. "Mom, I've got to go. I'd really like to stick around and offer comfort and support. The problem is I won't be able to catch their killer from your house."

She wept openly and held him tightly against her. "Please be careful. I love you."

"I love you too, Mom." When she finally released him, his father was right there to take over, hugging him tightly. For a moment, Bane found it difficult to breathe from the intensity of his grip.

"Bane, I don't know how you got those credentials. Just don't get into any trouble, okay? Call home often to make sure we all know you're all right," his father urged. Bane noticed his bloodshot eyes that were filled with tears.

"Don't worry, Dad; it's all legit. I'll stay in touch. One thing is for certain; I'll catch this bastard!"

"That sounds dangerous, Bane. Maybe you shouldn't—"

"I know, but believe me. I've spent my entire life as a warrior. Finally, it is all for a good cause. At last, all those years of what you thought was a waste of time will become an asset. The Lord is with me, and he's going to standby you throughout this painful time," Bane assured.

Walking past his uncle, aunt, and grandparents, Bane stopped and said, "Take care of them; they're going to need a lot of support."

"You know we will. Bane, I know you've heard this before, but be careful."

***

Leaves from the trees decided that they would have an early fall season, drawing back their drapes of green to reveal a fiery crimson color. A myriad of colors danced among the trees, in a spectacular show that only Mother Nature could provide. None of the foliage had fallen from the trees, clinging tightly to the branches. Boating season was far from over; wave runners, pontoon boats, and skiers filled the lake. Jessica raced along on her SeaDoo, a fast wave runner, as Thunder, Devon, and Erika sliced through the water in the electric-blue speedboat.

Slowly the sun began to descend, and after a certain time of night, no wakes were permitted. So all water treading vehicles would be forced to travel an unhurried rate or risk an unfriendly encounter with the police that monitored the lake. They had exceedingly fast boats that could catch up to just about any law-breaker on the water. In addition to their boats, they employed the use of wave runners to patrol the lake. Mainly their duties required only passing out tickets for those who broke the lake laws.

Jessica sped past her brother and friends, challenging them to a race she was assured to win. After all, the only time she competed was when she was certain that she would win. Since time was growing short for allowing their boats to create a wake, Devon pushed the throttle down and did his best to catch up to his older sister. As the waves pounded the boat, it bobbed up and down in the water, whereas Jessica leaped the waves on her SeaDoo and continued doing well over forty miles per hour. Winning the race with ease; she came upon the slow wake zone buoy; Jess let off on the accelerator and moved the wave runner onto the lift attached to the dock.

Shortly after Jessica had the SeaDoo raised out of the water, Devon pulled into the dock. Thunder bounded out of the boat and turned the knob on an electric lift, bringing it up and securing it. Erika landed on the dock and took the life jacket from Jess, tossing it into the boat for it to dry out. Since the forecast called for continued sunshine, they left the boat uncovered. Devon was the last to leave the boat, and then they all walked up toward the house together.

Jessica glanced down at the tape player when she entered through the back door beneath the wooden deck. It was taking all of her willpower to keep from listening to the tape from her dreams of the previous night. When she was honest with herself, Jess feared what the audiocassette might contain. She removed the tape and inserted a fresh one; she was planning on taking a nap before she went to the Badger's Paw. Jessica told Devon to fill a few pitchers of beer so that they wouldn't come down and disturb her while she slept.

So far, she had two tapes to give to Bane; this nap would provide her with a third. Her somnambulism hadn't ceased; she always ended up waking in a place that would provide her some protection. Lately, she hid under her bed or in a small closet; sometimes she found herself in the laundry room behind the dryer. If it continued much longer, she figured she would need to seek out professional help. No matter where she awoke, Jessica came out of her slumber deeply terrified but with no memory of her nightmares.

Jess hit record on the radio and slumped down under her covers, bunching her pillows under her head. Her eyelids, feeling deep and heavy, lowered wearily until they were finally closed. She let out a gentle, exhausted sigh before her breathing became rhythmic and steady. Not much time passed before Jessica's body curled into a fetal position, and she was fast asleep. Within twenty minutes, she was deep in REM sleep, where dreams took place.

Devon was engaged in an attempt to drink Thunder under the table, and having a hard time of it. Thunder seemed very able to hold his liquor, and he also seemed skilled at the quarters game that they played. By bouncing a quarter off a table into a shot glass, the player forces his opponent to drink. As long as the player makes the shot into the cup, the player is permitted to continue with his turn. Should the player miss, he is allotted an extra shot by calling for a "chance," where if he misses, he is the one who must drink.

Erika was busying herself on the couch, reading a good novel, and sipping wine from a glass. She was a sight to behold, with her legs tucked sweetly underneath her. Her hair glistened from having just gotten out of the shower, yet her makeup was applied with a perfect and delicate hand. So entranced in the novel, a bomb blast would've had an arduous time tearing her attention from the book.

"Devon, can I ask you something?" Thunder said as he bounced the quarter into the Las Vegas souvenir shot glass.

"Sure. What's up?"

"Is your sister seeing anyone at the moment?" he asked with a grin, pulling the edges of his mouth upward.

"No, she's on the road a lot. Not to mention, I think she has a crush on her friend Bane. She uses him as a template by which all prospects are judged. Both Erika and Jessica say Bane wears sexy like a second skin." Devon paused a moment, the thought finally coming to him. Not that he didn't know the answer, he asked, "Why do you ask?"

"Well, obviously she's a beautiful woman. She also seems to have a very good sense of humor; Jess is highly intelligent and extremely desirable," Thunder stated as he missed his shot, his concentration moving from the game to the woman sleeping downstairs.

"So what? You're asking my permission to ask her out?"

"Sort of, Devon; it's a point of honor, so to speak."

"Thunder, you don't need my permission. You really saved my butt the other day. I owe you a great deal, so if it makes you happy . . . you've got my blessing. However, I'm not the one you need to worry about. She's not easy to impress, has a mind of her own with a will to match. Just tread softly and move slowly, and you've got a chance," Devon answered while making several shots into the shot glass. Not even allowing himself to think about the other person Thunder would have to convince of his value.

***

Blue glittering light poured out from one of the many beds in the room, fighting the darkness that suffocated the expanse. Oozing out from the tiny space between the bed and the floor, the magician stood to his full height. Looking around the room, his eyes filled with an immeasurable appetite. Over forty beds were filled with slumbering children, and he knew that with each child consumed, his magical powers would continue to grow and develop. He pulled out a cliché magician's wand and waved it at the doors, which locked immediately.

Another flick of his wand and an orange wave crossed the room; it landed on each bed and remained there. Once that was done, he circled the room like a shark looking over his prey. Seeing a pretty little girl with bouncy red curls in her hair slumbering peacefully, the magician opened his mouth, and two lupine fangs emerged. Fire flickered and flared within his eyes, quite literally; the heat was even faintly detected near his eyelids. At the tips of his gloves, silver talons tore through the fabric, but he didn't seem to mind.

Gently running a taloned finger across to the young girl's cheek, a glistening red line of blood appeared like a trail behind the silver talon. So light was the touch and so sharp was the talon that the little girl didn't even stir in her bed. Her bed had lost the orange glow that embraced the rest of the cots. Glancing in both directions, the magician saw that nothing had changed, and he plunged his fangs deep inside the girl's skull. His taloned hands ruptured her skull to allow him to eat more efficiently.

Without a sound, he devoured her brain, practically inhaling his meal. When he stepped away, her blood poured out of her open head, soaking the pristine pillowcase. Not a single drop of blood vitiated his clothes, face, or hands. He moved to the next bed, where an eight-year-old boy slept, undisturbed by what happened just a few feet from him, his sable skin ablaze with the orange light until the magician stood directly over his head.

Again the killer feasted on the child, ripping apart his afro-covered head. The magician repeated the process on thirteen children, in less than five minutes, until he approached a twelve-year-old boy who was strapped down to his bed. Tilting his head to one side, the killer studied the child, wondering what would cause them to restrain him. He spat on the restraints through the orange, and the straps began to dissolve as if being eaten by acid.

Leaving the glow and child intact, the magician moved on, dining on several of the little girls in the room. He could feel his muscles bulging, and

70

the power within him surging through his veins. Through all of the mutilations, the magician remained completely free of any spatters of blood. Even with all of the destruction he caused, his top hat never budged an inch. His quaint mustache remained perfectly combed, and there wasn't even a wrinkle in his clothing.

Thirty-nine children were mangled beyond recognition, and a half an hour hadn't yet passed. One child, the one who was restrained, still lived. For some reason, the magician had chosen to spare the child, save him until the end. Something about his nature gave the killer a special appetite for him. Instead of just munching on the kid's brain, he ate the child completely; leaving no trace of the youth, save for the blood all over the sheets.

Glancing down at his pocket watch, he realized that the orderlies would be making their rounds. He knew that his time was running short, so with a flourish from his cape that he found so charming, the killer slid into one of the open closets. Closing the door, the telltale blue glittering light peeked out through the crack near the floor, and he was gone.

***

While driving through the crisp night air, Bane kept the windows rolled down to help him remain alert. He was overly tired, having been unable to sleep much since the memorial service for his dead family members. Over and over in his mind, he replayed the scene of his nephews' heads shredded beyond recognition and was haunted by the images of his sister and brother-in-law torn to pieces for no reason that he could fathom. His trip toward Wisconsin wasn't a particularly long one, only a little over an hour, but it felt like it took much longer than that. Attached to the back of his Hummer was a trailer that carried two motorcycles; one of them was the Harley he rode on a regular basis, and the other was a modified cycle that had several neat tricks added on to it. It was solid ebony in color; not a single piece of the bike gave off any type of reflection, as though the paint itself absorbed light. Two slots along its tailpipe were set up to carry a shotgun and an assault rifle, while his saddlebags were filled with ammunition. Underneath the seat was a set of explosives that would detonate if anyone attempted to steal his bike. The engine was not the standard for most motorcycles; it was a modified racing engine with nitrous injectors for additional speed. Special tires were installed to allow it to travel with ease over rough and smooth terrain.

If Bane ever considered selling that motorcycle, which he wouldn't, it would've gone for a minimum of four hundred fifty thousand dollars. It was designed, styled, and created by the top three bike designers in the world. That motorcycle stood alone, a complete original; no other bike in the world was quite like it. When Bane rode it, he felt a little like James Bond. With the simple touch of a button, he could cause his exhaust to spray out resembling a thick fog. The fog itself had unique properties: it was greasy, sticky, and clung to whatever it touched. Any windshield hit by the exhaust spray would be hard pressed to clean it off.

Bane often theorized that if he had some caltrops or oil slicks, he could literally play James Bond on the roadways, not that it would be difficult for him to pick up some caltrops, and distribute them by hand, seeing as he would be on his motorcycle. On each side of the handlebars, a thin, round blade was concealed for emergency use. His only wish was that he had thought to secure a slot on the opposite side of the bike for his favorite sword, an oriental katana. As he drove down the road, it was that exact thought that started rolling through his mind—how he could conceal a katana on that motorcycle.

Carrie had stayed behind at his parents' house; she would follow the next day. She was mentally and emotionally exhausted from the memorial service, not to mention that she wanted to keep an eye on his parents and make certain they were doing all right. Their home would seem so empty without anyone around. They lived alone; however, after such a traumatic event, it would seem so shallow and cold. Carrie loved his parents like they were her own, especially since her real mother was such a bitch; they hadn't spoken in eight years, and Carrie liked it that way.

Bane made a few calls to assign some men to watch out for Carrie while she was still at his parents' house. The men owed him several favors and, thus, were happy to keep a close eye on his wife for him. Additionally, it would be a fantastic way to ensure she didn't sneak off to sleep with her lover.

The only reason Bane didn't stay the night was he was very anxious to listen to the tapes of Jessica's dreams. To his way of thinking, they may provide him with invaluable clues, and perhaps a way to lay a trap for the man killing the children nationwide. He turned the corner near Badgers and decided he had time for a quick drink before going to Jessica's lake house. He had an uncommon attraction to that bar, as though he were a metal shaving, and it was a powerful magnet. Getting out of the truck, Bane closed his coat tighter around him to keep his weapons from showing. The bar didn't need to see he was now openly carrying a gun on his right hip.

When he walked in, Nancy immediately spotted him and circled the bar to give him a warm hug. The news had already told the tale of the death of his family members, and her compassion was that of legends. Rick came over as well; not being the type to hug another man, he clapped a hand on Bane's shoulder as a sign of support. They offered him a double shot of Captain Morgan's Spiced Rum on the house, which he gladly accepted. It had been a long, hard, traumatic day, and he felt he needed a chance to unwind before he went to see his friend Jess, last thing he wanted to do was to bring his stress into her life.

"How are you holding up?" Rick asked compassionately.

"I'll manage. I can say one thing for sure; the killer made a fatal mistake."

"Really? The news didn't say anything about it. What mistake was that?" Nancy asked.

"He fucked with my family and pissed me off. Now he's got me to deal with as well as the Federal Bureau of Investigation," Bane answered grimly.

Both Rick and Nancy smiled at his response; they knew his irrepressible nature would continue to surface no matter what life threw his way. The proof was his latest comment; it was just what they had come to expect from Bane, and he had never let them down before. He slid a hand into his pocket, withdrawing a large plastic bag filled with "Marlboro miles." They collected them, and since he did not, he saved the miles for them in between visits. Bane was brought up to believe that a guest should never arrive empty-handed.

Mr. Fuzz even seemed rather saddened by the loss Bane suffered; despite his allergies to cats, Mr. Fuzz usually rubbed up against him. This visit, however, the cat remained a respectful distance from Bane, raising its paw in a strange feline salute. Several of the regulars nodded a grim, respectful welcome to Bane when he sat down to drink his alcohol, which he responded to in kind. The crash of billiards balls filled the bar, and it reminded Bane of the package he had yet to open in the back of his truck. Downing the double shot of Rum, Bane dropped a fifty-dollar tip on the edge of the bar and walked out without another word.

Ten minutes later, he arrived at the lake house and pulled onto the lawn, since the driveway was filled to capacity. Knowing that Devon and Erika were inside, Bane decided to come in through the basement back door

73

not to disturb their sleep. Midnight winds slipped off the lake like a silk camisole gliding down to a bedroom floor. He carried the package from the truck to the back door and tried the knob, finding it locked. A quick few jiggles with his lock picks, and the back door swung open. Striding into the darkness of the room, Bane set the box down on the Ping-Pong table and looked around to see where Jessica was.

The radio was taping, so he knew she was sleeping, but he didn't find Jessica in her bed. Instead, she was curled into a fetal position inside the closet underneath an inflatable raft, his gun clutched tightly in her hands. He stepped on the firearm gently so he didn't crush her fingers, but with enough force that she couldn't swing the gun up out of fear. Stooping over her, he ran his hand over her forehead, pulling the hair out of Jess's face. Her eyes fluttered for a moment, then went wide with terror.

"Shh, don't worry, dear; it's just me. Are you okay?" Bane reassured Jessica, who had just awoken from a nightmare under terrifying circumstances.

"Bane? What . . . what's going on? What time is it?" Jessica asked, her mind still groggy from its deep slumber.

"It's a little past one in the morning. Are you okay?" he whispered again.

"Yeah, I'm fine," she lied.

"Let's get you back to bed, shall we?" Bane didn't bother to pay attention to her protests that she could do it on her own; he simply scooped her up into his arms and carried her to the bed. After he tucked her in and calmed her down, a telltale creak gave away to the fact that someone was trying to sneak downstairs. He drew his Ruger, flipped off the safety, and waited for the person to come around the corner. He assumed it might be Devon coming to get something to drink or to investigate the noise he heard when found Jess. Somewhat startled, Bane saw it wasn't Devon or Erika; it was a strange biker wielding a knife. Bane rolled forward and came up standing two feet from the intruder, gun pointed at his head.

"Don't make a single move! You invaded the wrong house, asshole! Now drop the blade, put your hands in the air or kiss your ass goodbye!" Bane snarled menacingly.

Thunder complied instantly, knowing the advantage wasn't his at that point. Jessica sat straight up in her bed, hearing the commotion.

"Bane, wait! He's a guest of Devon's! Please don't shoot him," Jess called out.

"Turn on the lights, Jess. I want a better look at this guy," Bane commanded.

Thunder's brow broke out in a cold sweat. "You're Bane Bloodworth?"

"That's right. Who the hell are you?" Bane asked.

"I'm Thunder, a friend of Devon's. We have some mutual friends back in Chicago—Chains, Diversity, Mad Dog, Ben Wagner, Johnathan Scotts, and Thor. I've got to admit, it's an honor to meet you, even if you nearly killed me in the process," he answered reverently.

"Well, if you're a friend of Devon's, you're alright in my book." Bane holstered his gun and held out a hand in greeting. "Nice to meet you."

Thunder gripped Bane's forearm, as Bane did the same; it was considered a warrior's handshake. Thunder drew a breath. "I heard a noise and worried that Jess might need some help, so I came to see what was going on."

"Honorable deed, well met. Although, if she were truly in trouble, you'd have given your position away; next time step along the outside of the steps, not the middle. They have more support and won't creak when you put your weight on it," Bane informed, pleased to hear that Thunder was willing to protect his dearest friend.

"I'll keep that in mind for future reference. I bet you have a lot of tricks like that you could teach me."

"More than a few, I'm sure. In time, perhaps I will when I get to know you better. For now, I suggest you go back to bed. Jess is as safe as she could ever be since I'll be sleeping down here with her tonight."

Thunder raised an eyebrow in wonder. Bane shook his head. "Not that way. I sleep on the floor next to her. The beds aren't that comfortable, and I'm a married man."

"Goodnight, everyone," Thunder said as he started up the stairs.

"Hey, Thunder." Thunder paused on the steps as Bane called out to him. "You forgot your blade, man."

Bane handed him his knife, making certain that he returned it to him hilt first, a disported expression passing over his face, as he noted several weaknesses Thunder tried hard to hide. However, Bane was a shrewd judge of people and noted more things about a person than their personality. Bane was well trained to seek out a person's flaws and utilize them to his advantage. Thunder had a weak left leg, but covered it by a strong stance—the weaker his position, the more aggressive his posture.

Pulling blankets off the loft bed, and pillows to match, he laid them out on the floor near Jess's bed. He sank down onto his makeshift bed and closed his eyes, hoping for sleep to overcome his senses. After twelve minutes, darkness descended over his consciousness, and he was in the land of dreams, for better or worse . . .

Chapter Six

The blade sliced swiftly through the translucent bindings holding the thick cardboard box closed. As the flaps opened, two doll heads rolled around the bottom of the package as if they were alive. Along with the heads was a photocopy of the picture that had been stolen from the frame in Bane's nephew's room. Bane's face was circled in red marker, with a thick slash through the center. Instead of the handsome appearance of his nephews, the picture depicted what they looked like after their slaughter.

Reaching a steady hand inside the box, Bane removed the doll heads and placed them on the Ping-Pong table for further inspection. Next, he grabbed the photocopy and examined the front of it tenaciously. When he flipped the paper over, he saw crisp, black letters handwritten across the backside of the page. His normally well-tanned face suddenly became drained of all color as he stared at the words that the killer had written. Bane began shaking in fury, wanting nothing more than to get his hands on the magician.

Bane—

You don't know me; however, I gathered a great deal of knowledge about you, when I saw those two scrumptious morsels, I had no choice but to feast upon them. Then I noticed the picture in the frame by their bed and recognized you instantly. While I knew that you would hunt for me after finding out your nephews were killed, I decided to make the game at it more *interesting by slaughtering their parents as well. I'm certain that you'll be coming for me; however, you must realize how futile that effort will turn out to be. Not to be arrogant, but you will be no match for me. Keep your nose out of this for your own safety, as well as those you care about! Heed my warning for I'll only give you this one chance to walk away.*

The note wasn't signed, but Bane was fairly certain that twisted, maniacal murderer was implied. Using all of his restraint to keep from crumpling the page, Bane placed the paper on the table as well. He picked up the doll head of his eldest nephew; the eyes followed him wherever he held it. The resemblance was undeniable; it was an exact copy of the little boy's face and head. Holding it in his hand, he felt it move as though there were something alive within the doll head.

Jessica came up behind him so softly that when she put a compassionate hand on his shoulder, he nearly jumped. Her eyes grew wide when she looked upon the faces of the doll heads. Jess hadn't been told yet about the little "gifts" the killer sent the victims' families. She began chewing on her lower lip, desperately trying to come up with some words of comfort, but they refused to rise inside her mind. Bane turned to look at her and saw that Jessica's eyes were bloodshot from another rough night of restless sleep. Jess was touched to see the concern on his face for her, considering the emotional agony he must have been feeling.

"What the hell's going on, Bane?" Jessica asked through her fear.

"I'll explain in just a little bit, but first I have to call agent Phillips to give her an update. She's the person heading up this investigation."

Yanking out his phone, Bane pulled up the contact screen for Pamela. "Pamela, it's me, Bane. I think we have something here that might make a pretty good lead if it pans out."

"Really? What exactly is it?" she asked skeptically since none of the other leads had brought them any closer to catching the killer.

"He wrote me a note and left it with the doll heads of my nephews. He bade me not to stay involved in the case." Bane scoffed at the very idea. "Which isn't gonna happen. I'll get this monster, somehow."

"The killer struck again, this time at an orphanage. Thirty-nine children with their skulls torn asunder and the fortieth was completely consumed."

"Completely consumed? You mean, as in the killer ate the entire body of the child?"

"That's exactly what I mean. The child's name was Evan Roberts. He had been restrained, due to several unsuccessful suicide attempts. We've got the lab boys investigating the straps, which appear to have been eaten through with some type of corrosive chemical," Agent Phillips reported with great sorrow filling her voice. "One more thing. Can you fax me the note and send a messenger to me the original? I'll have the lab boys take a look see if they can come up with anything worthwhile."

"No problem. I'll fax it from an office supply store in town. Then I'll get the original sent out to you. You should have it by the end of the day. I'm going to hang onto the doll heads for a while before I send them to the lab. In the meantime, I'll pursue another lead I discovered."

"What lead? I knew you were holding something back!" Pamela stated triumphantly.

"I can't say right now. It may jeopardize my contact. Don't worry. Whatever I find out I will share with you."

"I suppose that's fair, but I will want to know more about this lead later."

"Alright. Well, I've gotta go. I'll get back to you soon. Later," Bane said, hitting the end button on the screen.

Turning to look at Jessica, he asked her where the tapes she recorded were located. Without saying anything, Jess walked to the stack of cassettes and handed them to Bane. She had a strange look in her eye, a cross between being embarrassed and frightened. Instantly, Bane felt sorry for having to put her in such a difficult position; a person's dreams were private, as well as personal. The fact that she was dreaming of the killer was the only reason he would invade her privacy unless it was to help her.

Bane would scan a copy of the picture and warning into his iPhone. That way he could email a copy to agent Phillips and have a messenger deliver the original to her, and he'd still retain a copy for his own investigation. Bane looked over at Jessica, who was watching him intently, her cheeks a bright red color. She then looked at the doll heads, as they moved so that they were staring at her. When she glanced at their eyes, they appeared to be alive.

"Bane? Did you see that?"

"See what?"

"Those doll heads just rolled over to look at me!" Jessica spouted, assuming that he'd think she was insane or imagining things.

Instead of a condescending attitude, he said, "You're a magician's assistant and know quite a bit about illusions. Plus, you've spent quite a bit of time researching the occult. I was wondering if I could impose on you once more. I'd like you to examine those doll heads and give me your impression of them. Perhaps you can find a purpose for them that I might normally overlook."

"It's no imposition, Bane. You know I'll help you in any way I can. But I have a favor I need to ask of you."

"Name it, and it's done," Bane said confidently.

"Okay, it's two-fold. First, you have to promise me, no matter what is on the tapes, if it doesn't have to do with the killings, you won't say anything to anyone about them. Secondly, I don't want you making fun of me for my dreams. I mean . . . I can't control them; it'd be a low blow to my psyche for you to tease me over them," Jessica said uncomfortably.

"Jess," Bane began taking her in his arms in a hug, "you've got nothing to worry about. You're one of my best friends in the entire world, and I'll never judge you. You are doing me an incredible favor by allowing me to listen to your dreams; they're very personal and private. I respect that and appreciate your faith in me to allow me to hear them."

She kissed his cheek and walked over to the table to begin investigating the doll heads. Jess didn't really want to make eye contact with Bane once he started listening to the tapes. Bane placed the earbuds into his ears, minimizing the risk of anyone else hearing the contents of the ancient cassettes.

The room was dark with an air pressure that was thick enough to be chewed on. Her breaths were coming in rapid succession as she wandered through the bleak shadows. She began to run, but it was so murky there was no way for her to tell if she was making any ground. Like a ray of sunshine, a hand reached out to her, taking hold of it tightly; it lifted her from the gloom and into a beautiful meadow, grass so green that it offset the delightful red roses that filled the field.

When she looked up into the face of her hero that had rescued her from the darkness, it was her longtime friend Bane. She looked down at his left hand; no wedding ring adorned his fingers. She looked deeply into his eyes, and there she saw the love he held for her back in their high school days. He kissed her passionately as he took her into his arms. Bane's hands caressed her soft hair and drew her closer to him. In a whisper, he proclaimed, "our love will never die; it has always existed, on one level or another." Suddenly, their bodies melted into each other as their clothing disappeared; then they were making love feverishly.

Hours passed, and their passion continued to flourish, and the longer their sexual exploits continued, the more erotic things became. Her preferences, likes, and dislikes were made evident, and he satisfied each desire she had. His proficiency in making love amazed her beyond all her realizations.

Bane actually blushed, an occurrence that was as rare as a sighting of a unicorn or an honest politician. He had a crush on Jessica in high school, but since he was married, he had never thought of any other woman sexually. However, if he were to be with another woman, it would be with someone exactly like Jessica. He was surprised to find that Jessica's subconscious had considered him as a lover, though her conscious mind never had. Certainly, she found him physically attractive, as he was a very handsome man, but Jess never showed any signs of wanting him in that way.

After the marathon of sex, the world twisted and shifted in her mind. Instantly, she was somewhere else, watching like a ghost unable to influence her surroundings. Jessica hovered over a gruesome scene, watching the magician rip open children's heads and devour the contents contained within. Never once did a drop of blood spill from the kid's body onto the killer; he was very cautious not to soil his clothing. She felt a great deal of contempt for the magician, as he looked like the typical stereotype of a stage magician from the fifties. It was absurd.

One by one, the four children who huddled together in the same room for mutual protection were killed and feasted upon. A small kitten got tangled up in between the murderer's feet and paid for it with its life. A swift gesture from his wand turned the feline inside out, taking several moments for the cat to die its painful death. With the door to the closet standing wide open, the magician stepped inside, spoke several guttural words, and blue sparkling lights enveloped him. Seconds later, the man was gone, leaving only destruction in his trail.

A single, unadorned hand reached out and pulled her out of her horrifying ordeal; a simple touch startled her, for it was the only thing that she could feel around her. He smiled at her with an expression that melted her heart in an instant. Jessica flung herself into his arms sobbing softly, clinging to him as though he was her life jacket in a turbulent ocean storm. Bane was the only thing keeping her afloat in a tumultuous tide of emotions. Their passion began to wash over them like a tsunami, and the lovemaking was even more intense than it had been prior to the alarming dream of the magician.

Bane listened to the other cassettes, and only the first three had any sexual content including him. The rest appeared to focus mainly on the killer and his activities. It was no puzzle to Bane why she always sought out a place of hiding while she slept. Her terror of what she witnessed was evident in her every slumbering thought. Jess's dreams radiated fear and disgust that Bane could physically feel as he listened to every detail of her nightmares. He knew that if he mentioned the tapes where they had sex to anyone, it would be misconstrued.

Carrie would understand; Bane was sure of that— it was just her nature to have total faith in her friend and husband, despite the fact she was already having an illicit affair with some new guy. Even if Jessica really did want to have a sexual relationship with Bane, she would never act on it. Jess loved Carrie dearly and would never hurt her in that way.

Jess pulled the earbuds from his ears, tilting her head to one side with a demure smile bouncing on her lips. "Was there anything . . . I should be embarrassed about?"

"You haven't listened to these tapes?" Bane asked, his brow wrinkling in cynicism.

She shook her head vigorously. "No, I didn't really want to know what was on them, either good or bad. Bane, how far does this range go? I mean, does this transmit my dreams across state lines?"

"To be honest, I didn't really check. I will the next time I go somewhere though. How's that sound?"

"Wonderful," came her doleful response.

"Did you notice anything about the doll heads?"

"It's strange; they have real hair. It appears to be still growing, but at a very slow rate of speed. The eyes are spooky. I've seen them in normal dolls,

82

but these give me the creeps. They're very heavy for a doll head. Is there some sort of lead ball in the center? Or worse, is there a huge ball of colored wax on the interior?" Jess reported yet questioned like a professional.

"The inside of the heads are empty. We don't know what is giving them the weight they seem to have. What I meant was, anything that would trigger your occult study instincts? This guy we're chasing is a magician or at least dresses like one."

"I'll look through some of my old books and see if there is anything I can dig up." Jess looked around the room, noticing for the first time that something was strange. "Where's Carrie? I'd have thought you'd bring her back with you."

"She'll be back up here soon; I'd imagine a few hours from now. So what's for breakfast?" Bane asked charmingly.

"You want me to make breakfast? Do I look like a French maid?" Jessica asked with a hint of real scorn tarnishing her sarcasm.

"Well, if we got you one of those cute little outfits . . . " Bane never finished the sentence as Jess quickly, yet playfully, smacked him on the arm.

"Actually I was thinking of making some eggs for myself, so I guess I could make some for you too." She exaggerated her exacerbation. "How's scrambled sound? I can add some cheese to them if you want."

"That's why I love you, Jess. You're so good to me. Oh! I almost forgot. In the back of my truck is a present Carrie and I bought you for your birthday. I know it's late for the last one and too early for the next one, but you were on the road when we got it. Carrie was at a jewelry store and saw the perfect gift for you to wear out when you go to all those award shows and stuff." Bane smiled. "Well, I picked up the tab, but she was the one who chose the gift. I'll tell you what. While you're making the food, I'll run out and grab it for you."

"You didn't have to buy me anything," Jessica countered while her mind had other thoughts. *All right! I love gifts! Those two are so awesome.*

Bane climbed the steps ahead of Jessica and went out the front door to the house, while she started setting up the pans for cooking breakfast. He didn't even notice Devon wandering around the house half asleep when he went upstairs. At the back of his truck, Bane opened a small compartment in the side panel that was not only well concealed but locked up tightly. Pulling out the gift-wrapped box, Bane locked the cabinet and made it invisible once more.

Entering the house, he took notice of Devon, whose hair was standing straight up in the front and scuffed on the right side. "Hey, Dev, how's it going? Long time, no see."

"Hiya, Bane. How's life treating you?"

"Like a dog's chew toy, but that's how it goes, I guess. You just wake up? You're usually up long before I am," Bane returned.

"Yeah, Erika and I were up late last night after I got done playing quarters with Thunder." Devon left no room for the imagination as to why they were still awake late into the night with the tone of voice he used.

"How is Erika? I haven't seen her in a while either."

"She's doing great. You'll see her later when she wakes up."

"Cool."

"I'll introduce you to Thunder when he gets out of the shower. He's a great guy; I think you'll like him," Devon offered.

"We've already met. I nearly shot him when he came downstairs holding a knife." Devon frowned at the mention of violence, so Bane was quick to explain, "I didn't know he was your guest at the time. I thought he was a robber or killer."

"I suppose it's good to know we're safe while you're around." Devon smiled.

"You know it." Bane turned and faced Jessica and unceremoniously handed her the gift. He was never really good at the emotional part of his life; it always left him uncomfortable. Though he loved her dearly, he still felt weird giving her gifts without Carrie around, mainly because Carrie was the one who would give the gift and explain all about it.

"This is for me? Can I open it?" Jessica asked, knowing the answers to both questions.

"Yeah, and of course you can open it. Why would I give you a gift you couldn't open?" Bane asked, being a smart-ass.

"Maybe I should wait for Carrie to get here. She might want to see my reaction," Jessica mused, all the while hoping Bane would force her to open it right away.

"Come on. Just open it. I want to see what they got you for your birthday!" Devon injected into the conversation, without knowing he had assisted Jess.

Pulling off the golden ribbon that was wound around the box so she could get to the paper beneath, Jess looked around at Devon then at Bane. She smiled brightly as the elegant wrapping paper was removed. Staring

84

down that the oak box that bore the name Yadegar's of Beverly Hills, she gasped in shock, knowing that anything, even a pair of the cheapest earrings, bought at that store cost a small fortune. Her eyes grew wide as she stared at Bane in amazement.

Without even opening the box, Jess proclaimed, "I can't accept this! It must have cost you an arm and a leg."

"You're worth it. Carrie and I both agreed that we wanted you to have this. You'll look stunning at the next red carpet affair you attend. Besides, I have enough money to burn. Why not spend that money on the people I love?" Bane protested self-consciously.

"But—" Jessica was about to redouble her position again when Devon interrupted her.

"Damn, Jess, why not look inside and see if you like it. Then you can you put up a fight! It's a gift, for crying out loud! It'd be rude not to even look at it before turning it down. Besides, look at how uncomfortable you're making Bane."

"Didn't think anyone noticed. Am I that easy to read?" Bane wondered aloud.

"Not usually, but in this instance hell yeah. The fact is, you're often the most guarded person I've ever met." Devon smiled back.

When Jessica opened the ornately decorated box, she saw the most beautiful diamond necklace she'd ever seen. The red felt that lined the interior allowed the gems to glitter with an inner glow. The necklace itself had to have at least fifty diamonds going all the way around its surface, with platinum backing holding them in place. Each diamond was two full carats, which was especially costly. If she had to guess at the amount paid for such a necklace, she would have estimated it at well over two hundred fifty thousand dollars.

"Th . . . there's no way I can accept this! For your last birthday, I sent you a CD player! This is way too much. You shouldn't spend that much money on me," Jessica stammered in shock.

"You go to more high-class social events than Carrie or me. All of the women there wear stuff like that, so now you can too. Please, Jess, Carrie will kill me if you don't accept it." When Jessica looked skeptical, he continued, "Really, she will. Remember it was her idea. Besides, for her birthday I bought her a lake house and am having it remodeled to her specifications. That costs a hell of a lot more than that necklace. As an added bonus I had a small alteration made to it. If you look along this area here, you'll see the shallow spot that will cover your pendant so you don't have to remove it to wear this necklace! As I said, I had the money to burn "

Devon finally moved so he could look at what was inside the box since the lid blocked his view. When he did see it, he let out an appreciative whistle. Just staring at the necklace, he could see that it was expensive, without knowing much about the store it came from; all he knew was that it was the most expensive shop for jewelry in Beverly Hills. Looking at Bane with newfound respect, Devon wondered what exactly Bane did for a living that left him that kind of money to "burn" for a birthday present for his best friend. He couldn't conceive of what Bane bought Carrie for her special occasions like anniversaries, Christmas, and birthdays. Though he wasn't a greedy man, Devon decided that he was going to start exchanging gifts with the Bloodworths for Christmas and birthdays.

"I don't know, Bane. This is awfully expensive. I don't see how I can accept it."

"If you don't want it, I'll take it. Erika will love me forever if I gave that to her!" Devon teased, knowing there was no way Jessica would give it to him. "It's from one of the most expensive jewelry stores in Beverly Hills!"

"There's a very simple way to accept it. You say, 'thank you, Bane.' You give me a hug and a kiss on the cheek. Then you tell me how much you love it and repeat the process when Carrie comes up here. She should be at the house in a matter of hours."

Still uncertain but knowing she'd never win this battle with Bane, Jessica decided to try to take it up with Carrie later, also realizing she'd probably not get very far with Carrie either. At last, she seemed to relent by trying it on to see if it would fit, secretly hoping that it would give her a perfect excuse not to take such a costly present. Unfortunately, her luck wasn't with her that morning, as the necklace not only fit but also looked fabulous on her.

"Thank you, Bane. It's beautiful. I love it." She gave him a huge hug and a kiss on the cheek. "I can't believe you guys did this! It's—" Suddenly she was overcome with emotion, a rare thing indeed.

"Easy there, TNT. We don't want you blowing a gasket." Bane's phone alert went off with Pamela Phillip's cellular number on the screen. "Yikes, I gotta make a call. Don't burn our food while staring at yourself in the mirror."

Bane walked out the screen door out onto the deck. He stared across the lake for a moment before digging out his cell phone. He allowed the lapping of the churning waters to ease his tension. Speedboats pulling skiers were causing plenty of large, fast-moving waves. Again he marveled at the leaves changing so out of season but enjoyed the vibrant colors that replaced the subtle green foliage surrounding the lake.

"This is Bane. What's up?"

"He struck again, as though forty kids weren't enough for one night." An angry tone tinted her words. "Four children, staying in one room to help them keep watch for the killer. One would remain awake for a period while the others slept and rotated duties through the night. Their parents said they had been doing this for several days. That's not the worst of it either, which isn't to say it isn't bad . . . "

"The killer turned the family pet inside out?" Bane injected.

"How the hell did you know that? " her tone slightly irritated.

"Well, you don't think I got into law enforcement because of my stunning good looks, did you?" Bane evaded the question like a master linguist.

"I guess no—." Pamela started to say. "Still, that's a pretty detailed guess."

"I've got a few things to work on here; then I'll call you later." He quickly cut her off realizing his stupidity.

"Alright, I'll get the reports on what we discovered at the scenes sent out to you right away. Bane, watch your back on this one. From what you've told me, this guy may have it in for you. That makes me very nervous."

"No sweat, and we'll compare notes later. Bye." Bane hit the end button before she could remember that she never got a straight answer to her question.

The screen door behind him slid open skeptically, with great hesitation. Jessica appeared in the doorway. "Bane, is everything alright?"

"Yeah, I guess so."

"Uh, breakfast is ready."

"I'll be right in. Just let me finish this cigarette," Bane informed without turning around, his white-knuckle grip on the railing tightening for a moment, causing the strong wood to groan softly. Jessica closed the door and went back to the kitchen to get the food set on the table. Bane lit a smoke and inhaled deeply, allowing the billowing smoke to fill his lungs. The sun was so bright in the sky that he was forced to squint as he stared out at the lake.

Inside, Thunder managed to crawl out of bed and make it into his morning ritual. Once he used the washroom and cleaned himself up, he walked out into the living room. Nodding to Devon as he sat down, Thunder couldn't help but watch Bane out on the deck. He'd heard many dark tales of Bane but knew little about him firsthand, other than that he had the reflexes of a black panther. Thunder never thought of himself as a timid or particularly nervous person; however, Bane's presence set him on edge.

Jessica rounded the corner. "Well, since I've already gotten roped into making Bane breakfast, do either of you want something to eat?"

With his eyes the size of saucers, Thunder exclaimed, "Holy shit! That's one hell of a necklace. Do you often wear expensive jewelry when cooking?"

"No, actually I just got it as a gift. I guess I forgot to take it off." Jessica's hand reflexively went to her neck, stroking the diamond choker.

"Forgot to take it off, my ass!" Devon hooted. "I bet you'll sleep with it on!"

"If you don't mind my asking, are those real diamonds?"

"No doubt about it— this baby came from Rodeo Drive," Devon answered for Jessica. "Bane has extravagant taste, it would seem."

"Bane gave that to her? What does he do for a living?" Thunder inquired, still in awe of the magnitude of the gift.

"He's never answered that directly. Last time I asked him what he did for a living, he said 'I earn money.' When I followed that answer by asking him how he earned money, he gave me a strange grin, telling me he did it by earning a living," Devon answered.

"Okay, don't anyone talk directly to me, even though I'm standing in the room."

"Sorry, Jess. Why would he give you such an elaborate and expensive gift?"

"First of all, Devon, it wasn't just him; Carrie picked it out. Bane was the one who bought it. I don't think I like the connotation you give when you imply it was from him," Jessica argued. "As for the reason he'd give me such a great necklace is because—"

"She's a good friend of mine, one that I've counted on many times and who has rarely failed me. Carrie and I have always put our faith in Jessica, and she comes through almost every time. We had some extra money and decided to buy her a nice present for her birthday." The irritation, which marred his face, caused everyone in the room to whiten.

88

Without saying another word, Bane strode into the dining room for his morning meal. He dined with skills that would make Emily Post proud, but remained silent, brooding while he ate. Bane didn't even look up when Jessica announced she was going to consult some books to research the doll heads. Devon entered the room and sat down quietly next to Bane, his hands fidgeting in his lap.

"Look, man, we didn't mean any offense. It's just . . . you've got to admit that it's kind of an expensive gift for a friend."

"Devon, let me explain something to you. Someday perhaps we'll hang out a lot more, and we'll become closer. At that time, you'll come to realize that money, inconvenience, sweat, tears, or blood are of little consequence to me when it comes to my close friends. Carrie and I had the means to buy her a nice gift that she could make good use of in her career. The cost means nothing to Carrie or I. The sky is the limit for our friends and family," Bane tried to explain.

"Are you staying around for a while? I was thinking that we all could do some drinking games tonight. Erika is looking forward to seeing Carrie again. Besides, I could use some help drinking Thunder under the table. What do you think?"

"Sounds good." Bane finished his meal and began cleaning up. "I'm going to grab a shower and get dressed. Lots of things to do today before the fun can begin."

"Is there an ashtray out on the deck?" Thunder called out.

"Yeah, on the picnic table."

"I'm off for a smoke then . . . "

"I think Thunder has a thing for Jess," Devon mentioned casually.

"In that case, I guess Carrie and I had better begin studying him. He's gotta pass our test, to see if he's worthy of Jess."

Devon laughed, despite the fact that he knew that Bane was serious. He found it amusing that Jessica had held up her end of a bargain with Carrie from so long ago. Carrie thought Jess found the wrong men to get involved with, so if they passed her test, they'd be worth a try. Jessica agreed that it was a good idea to help her break her unfortunate habit of choosing idiots and creeps for lovers. Few men ever passed Bane's high standards; however, more passed Carrie's, and that was good enough for Jess. Devon thought he'd have a stroke if Bane ever approved of one of Jess's prospective dates.

In the other room, Thunder shifted on the couch uncomfortably, hearing he was being discussed. Normally, he'd take part in the conversation or ignore it completely; the problem he had was the fact that if Bane was talking about him, it could mean trouble. The last person he wanted trouble with was Bane Bloodworth; he knew it could be fatal. Thunder was no wimp, but he also knew his limitations. From what he knew, Bane was a far superior warrior, not to mention his extensive contacts that were rumored to be very effusive. At long last, he got up to have that long awaited cigarette.

Bane was gone for a good portion of the day, leaving Jessica to her research. She had always been fascinated by the occult and had collected many books on the subject over the years. To her way of thinking, anything that could be done by the occult could be reproduced as an illusion in the magic act. Her boss thought her preoccupation with the thought of real magic childish and immature. Jessica caught a great deal of ridicule from her colleagues and friends over her minor obsession.

Bane spent the day running between office supply stores and messenger services that would deliver the package full of information he managed to pull together for Pamela. He drove slowly, pondering the implications of the doll heads and the taunting the killer did. Bane couldn't help thinking that he was caught up in a cop movie where the suspect played with the police, laying the blame and blood on their heads if more people were slaughtered. Now that he was involved, every child killed was partly his fault for not stopping the killer in time.

Carrie had reached the lake house twenty minutes after two o'clock and was warmly greeted by Devon and Erika. Thunder had taken his motorcycle out for a drive, to familiarize himself with the area. He hated not knowing where he was and how to get to the places he wanted to go. They had all decided to meet at the Badger's Paw for some drinking later in the evening. Jessica was so engrossed in her reading that she wasn't aware that Carrie had finally arrived. Devon and his lovely bride entertained Carrie while they caught up on what each of them had been doing with their lives.

Before too long, the sun dropped behind the shroud of the planet, only shedding its light in the form of a reflection off the moon. Devon decided he would have to go disturb Jessica if they wanted to get to the bar on time. Knocking on the door firmly, Devon was met with a groan from within the room.

"What? " Jessica called out.

"We've got to get moving if we're going to meet Bane and Thunder at Badgers. Carrie is already on her way to the bar now. She's going to meet us there while you get ready."

"Give me ten more minutes; I just want to get through this section."

Sighing in exasperation, Devon walked away. He knew that her ten minutes would turn into an hour if he allowed it. "Erika, if she isn't done in ten minutes, we'll meet her at the bar. She's got her own car here anyway."

"I've never seen you so impatient," Erika commented.

"I just don't want Thunder thinking we're blowing him off."

"Alright, but let's give her the ten minutes before we go. Did you tell her Carrie was in town, and already headed to the 'best bar in Wisconsin'?"

"Yep, but she's deep into her books. I doubt if anything I said registered fully," Devon answered.

Thunder arrived at the Badger's Paw shortly after Carrie. Ordering a pitcher of beer, he sat down at the bar near the pool table. He took notice of a pretty woman and figured, since he'd have a hard time getting Jessica into bed, he might as well find himself a companion for the night. After taking a long drink from his glass, Thunder pulled himself upright and walked right over to the lovely lady.

"How's it going," were the words Thunder chose to start up the conversation.

"Fine, and you?"

"Not too bad now that you're here. Can I get you a drink?"

"I don't think that's a good idea," she answered.

"Why not?"

"My husband might not look too kindly on that. He's a rather jealous man, not very understanding of men hitting on his wife."

"I'm not worried about him. If you're attracted to me, I'll take that risk," Thunder continued.

"Do you believe in reincarnation?"

"No, why?" Thunder asked in confusion.

"Because it's not going to happen in this lifetime."

"Ouch! You're killin' me. Come on. One drink isn't that much to ask. It's not like I'm asking you to sleep with me," Thunder stated as he put his hand over his heart. "Besides, where is this wonderful man that could keep a woman like you? Shouldn't he be here at your side?"

"If he were here, you'd be in a very bad situation. Look, I don't want to be rude, but he's really jealous, and I don't want to have to try to keep him from tearing you to pieces."

"Why would you wear a sleek, form-fitting black dress like that if you didn't want to attract attention? Seriously, can't we have one drink together?"

"What I wear is for him. As for the drink, he'd kill you."

"I'm pretty tough. What makes you think I can't take care of myself?"

Carrie's eyes grew wide with fear as she saw Bane approach. He walked up behind Thunder. "Mainly because you are hitting on my wife, and that is extremely dangerous. If you continue to hit on my wife, I'll let you experience what your pancreas tastes like."

Thunder turned around to face the voice and went ashen when he saw Bane. "Aw, man! Shit, I didn't know she was your wife. I keep fucking up with you. I'm sorry, man. I'd never mess with your marriage, man. That ain't my style in the least."

"Good, so long as we all know the ground rules. Devon told me you were interested in Jessica. Why is it you're out trying to get another woman?" Bane asked, his eyes narrowing dangerously.

"Well, I don't think I have a chance with Jess, so I figured I'd see what else I could get. Devon said she's hard to impress, thanks in great part to you and the way you treat women. He said she holds you up as a template of what a potential boyfriend should be. Really, I didn't mean any offense. Are we cool?"

"Yeah, no sweat, man. In this case, and only this one, ignorance is an acceptable excuse. It's good you met my wife, Carrie. She's going to judge whether or not you're worthy of our friend. Jessica can be a real catch, and lately, only losers have won her heart. We intend to change that. Jess deserves much better than that," Bane explained. "I've done some checking on you, and from what I've been told, you can hold your own in a fight. That is something that's important in my book. Jessica doesn't need some wussy trying to protect her. In addition, I learned that you consider honor to be a life-leading style, which is another trait that is admirable in a prospect."

"I'd never hurt her."

"You'll never hurt her more than once if you take my meaning," Bane added a bit of steel to his voice when he spoke.

"Crystal clear." Thunder turned to Carrie. "Now that we're friends, can I get you that drink? I guess we should chat if I'm to be under the microscope."

Carrie smiled. "Just get me a glass. I'll have some beer from your pitcher."

From behind the bar, Bane heard a sigh of relief; Nancy was concerned that since Bane had been through a very rough few days, he might simply destroy the guy hitting on his wife. Nancy allowed her natural smile and charm to return to the surface as she drew a frosty pitcher from the refrigerator. She always grabbed a pitcher and filled it when she saw Bane; he always ordered a pitcher when he came in for a night of drinking, another reason Bane believed the adage "best bar in Wisconsin." Despite his love and loyalty to his hometown bar in Illinois, this was the only substitute he would find here in Wisconsin. Often Bane had asked Dave to open a Gators around the lake, but as of yet, he hadn't managed to convince him.

Bane paid for his pitcher with three hundred dollar bills, asking Nancy to deduct the rest of their party's drinks from that until it ran dry. Under normal circumstances, she'd have told him to piss off. However, Jessica, Bane, and Carrie were not only regulars but also friends. It didn't hurt that whatever was left over he would insist on paying the tip, and with their prices being so cheap, there was no way they'd rack up three hundred dollars' worth of drinks. He couldn't see Rick anywhere in sight. He assumed that Rick was in the back making food or feeding Mr. Fuzz.

"What do you say we sit out back in the courtyard? The weather is nice, and there'll be more room for us when Jess, Devon, and Erika arrive."

"Sounds like a great idea to me, Carrie," Thunder admitted.

Devon and Erika arrived twenty minutes later, minus Jessica. Devon explained that he tried to get her out of her room, but she was working on something. Bane felt his cheeks flush, knowing that she was working very hard for his sake; he hated that she was missing out on the fun because of a favor he asked her to undertake. Bane whipped out his phone, rapidly tapping the name in the contact list. The line rang four times before her voicemail answered. Without leaving a message, Bane hung up and dialed again.

He repeated this process seven times before Jessica answered, and she didn't sound happy.

"What? Who is this? "

"Jess, it's Bane. I appreciate your vigilance, but you're missing a good time. You know there will be plenty of time to read that book after we get back from the bar. We're all here drinking and having a blast. Join us."

"You have no idea what I stumbled onto here. It's very strange. I think I have some answers to our questions, but I need more time to be certain."

"That's great, Jess! Remember what the Shining said, 'All work and no play makes Jack a dull boy.' Take a break and come and hang out with us. Nancy already asked about you, wondering where you were hiding out at."

"You win. I'll be there shortly. You're a real pain in the ass. You know that, don't you?"

"If I ever forget, I can always count on you to remind me. See you soon."

Chapter Seven

C rimson walls surrounded her as Pamela crept through the room, diligently trying not to disturb anything. Thick blood coated the walls and as it began to drip, giving off the appearance that the walls were melting. The only footprints in the dense blood shrouding the floor were hers. She couldn't understand how the killer escaped the room without leaving any tracks in the blood that seemed to have exploded throughout the room. Every time she entered a new crime scene she left with more questions rather than answers.

She had to fly out to Dallas to investigate the latest in the series of brutal murders. The worst of it was the home being a halfway house for youths pending adoption. Twenty children, varying in ages from two through thirteen, had huddled in one room for protection. That ploy had failed miserably. It simply gave the killer one place to slaughter his prey. Pamela couldn't get over the amount of blood that laminated the entire room.

Though she was a veteran member of the FBI, her stomach felt as though several fish had taken up residence inside and were swimming around vigorously. Aside from the spinning of the room and the vertigo it was causing her, she persevered with her duties. Again, the killer left his handkerchief as a signal to them it was indeed him, not that there was any doubt who had murdered the children. It was his way of sharing responsibility with the police, making them just as accountable for the deaths as he was.

Despite the plastic slipcovers that Agent Phillips had worn, the ocean of blood that covered the floor slopped across her shoes. It seeped inside her footwear, soaking into her socks, making a squishing feeling between her toes as she walked. She closed her eyes tight against the horror, fighting her urge to run from the room and scrub herself with a bristle brush in an hour-long shower. Mustering all of her courage, willpower, and professionalism, Pamela continued to survey the room for clues. For a brief moment, she thought she saw a flash of movement behind her in the closet.

Pamela whirled around with her Smith & Wesson drawn held out in front of her, elbows locked tight. Blinking rapidly, she discovered she was still alone in the room, save for the chill left in her bones. As she drew closer to the window, a shudder wracked her body; the blinds were closed and dripping with scarlet fluid. With a gloved hand, she pulled the cord, raising the blinds. With a startled gasp, she jumped backward.

The window had a message on it painted in what could only be human blood. It read, *Pamela, get Bane Bloodworth off this case immediately, or face my wrath.*

The killer knew her name and once again was warning Bane off his trail. She didn't know how to tell him that the murderer had fixated on him. Another thought had sprung to her mind, like Tigger in his cartoons. *Bane must be getting too close, or the killer fears Bane. Why else would he be so determined to get him away from the case? This Bane Bloodworth warrants some investigation. I think I'll see what I can find out about him. It's a damn shame he's married. I could really fall for a guy like him.*

The last thought she had stunned her. She hadn't ever really thought about why she was so open with Bane. Normally she was very suspicious of CIA personnel. He had a confidence about him in the way he walked, talked, and moved, as though he knew the secrets to life itself, and they gave him a peace that everyone strove to achieve. Pamela wished that Bane were at this crime scene to help her wade through the atrocity in order to collect clues.

The vibrant colors of the sun setting were smothered by charcoal clouds that rolled in at an alarming speed. The rain was on its way and with a fury that would make the earth tremble in utter fear. Pamela thought it was a foreboding sight to behold combined with the eerie message left on the window.

"Agent Phillips?" a voice called from behind her.

"What? " she implored without turning around.

"We found something in the basement that we thought you'd want to see. Personally, I don't mind telling you— it scares the shit out of me."

"Alright. Get me some new shoe covers; these are worthless now," Pamela ordered acidly, with the edge that she often used to put people off.

When she had gotten cleaned up enough to walk through the rest of the house without tracking the blood across the place, she followed the detective to the basement steps. He stood at the top with no indication of intending to descend the stairs with her. Rolling her eyes at his cowardice, she walked down two steps at a time. At the bottom, she turned to see a man who was eviscerated, suspended in midair. He was face down three feet from the gray cement floor, with his intestines lightly scraping the ground.

Two homicide detectives were circling the body, trying to figure out if there were any wires holding the body in place. One picked up a hula-hoop from the corner and, like a magician on stage, brought it around the body. It went over the body with no resistance, save for the man's innards, which snagged the hoop briefly. When he finished, he stepped backward three feet in outward awe. He'd never encountered anything like it in his thirteen years on the job. His normally tanned face was growing pale, which made his slim build look skeletal.

"What the fuck? That's not possible!" he stammered.

"Photograph the body. Get some video of it while doing that hoop trick again, and get forensics to do a full run on the man while he's still suspended in midair," Pamela ordered, attempting to keep her tone professional. It was a hard struggle for her, for she too was terrified of the sight she was beholding. "When that's done, make certain all copies of this go to my office. No one, especially the press, is to hear about this. Do I make myself clear?"

"Yes, ma'am."

***

After Jessica left the lake house, stepping into the cool evening air, her basement became a source of activity. Two doll heads rolled around on the Ping-Pong table under their own power. Creaking and cracking could be heard, like a baby bird breaking free of its sheltered egg. A dark oozing solution began leaking out of the cracks in the doll heads. The crack itself was along the mouth of the head. If anyone saw the abomination in progress, one would think that the doll was regurgitating something nasty it had eaten earlier.

Jessica had brought the book she had been reading with her as she drove toward the Badger's Paw. It was a study of demons and the powers they possessed. The sources in the book seemed more than credible, which made it a valuable book to those who studied the occult. Bound in a red leather cover with chipped silver lettering across the front, the pages were tattered and brittle from its age, having lasted so long. If Jessica ever considered selling that book to a dealer, it would be worth a great deal of money; the book was by far an antique and written in by some of the great occult minds of the past.

As she drove, her hand continually strayed to the novel on the passenger seat like she was trying to ensure it didn't disappear while she traveled. Red and orange leaves rained down on the windshield of her Explorer, however, when she looked in her rearview mirror, no leaves had fallen from the trees. All of her trips to the bar included an open road with no traffic. This ride was no exception; once more, she envisioned that the world had come to an end and she was the last person left on the planet. The only thing she could hear with her radio off was the beating of her own heart, loud and rhythmic in her ears.

Jess didn't know why she brought the book with her; it wasn't like she planned on reading it while she was at the bar. Something compelled her to bring it, thinking that if she were to leave it unattended, the book might be stolen. Most people would have passed the book by, the yellow brittle pages making it look beaten and battered. She had a terrible feeling that the killer would magically appear from the darkness in order to swipe the book from her before she gathered too much information on him. Subconsciously, she wanted to keep it within her line of sight, ensuring it would remain in her possession.

When she pulled into the parking lot, there were no available spots for her to park in. She swung around back out onto the road and parked along the street. Jessica was reluctant to leave the book in the truck, but bringing it into the bar with her could get it ruined, a fate she couldn't allow for her precious belonging. A spilled drink, a stray cigarette amber, any number of things could happen to damage her book. Without it, much of her research would be futile.

As she approached the front door, a drunk stumbled out and fell down the two steps onto the pavement. The door was starting to swing shut when Jessica caught it in her left hand. While she pitied the man on the ground, she made no attempt to help him up. Instead, she stepped over him, proceeding inside without giving him a second glance. Stepping through the second door, she was assailed by both fresh and stale smoke that wafted through the bar. Music pummeled her ears. The jukebox pounded out Stevie Nicks, the goddess of music, with enthusiasm.

Scanning the room, Jessica didn't see any of the people she had gone there to meet. Rick waved, smiling his greeting as he poured a drink for a customer. Nancy tapped her on the shoulder, which caused Jess to jump slightly.

"They're out back on the deck, sweetie. Where have you been all night?"

"I was busy reading— didn't realize the time. I guess I'll get a pitcher and meet them out there. A pitcher of Miller Lite? I assume they already have glasses."

Nancy nodded and quickly strode to the opposite side of the bar to retrieve Jessica's order. She managed to move through the crowd to the end of the bar nearest the pool table, to wait for the pitcher of beer. When Nancy returned, she had two pitchers of beer, offering them both to Jessica and refusing her money when Jess tried to pay.

"Bane already picked up the tab tonight, sweetie." Nancy reported.

"Figures. How's he holding up tonight?"

"Outward appearances? He seems to be doing all right, but Bane always looks like he's doing well, no matter what happens. It's just his way," Nancy informed.

"I'll talk to you later. I should bring these out to the group," Jessica said as she strolled to the back door. She put one of the pitchers down on a table, just long enough to slide the screen open. After retrieving the second pitcher of beer, Jess went to sit with her friends.

Bane had his feet kicked up on the wooden table and was leaning back in his chair. Thunder was sitting next to Carrie, and they seemed to be involved in an in-depth conversation. Meanwhile me, Erika and Devon were being thoroughly entertained by Bane, listening to amusing stories of things that happened to him over the years. Jessica's timing couldn't have been better, as their pitchers were running low.

"TNT!" Bane shouted with enthusiasm. "About time you got here! Ah, and you brought beer with you; I knew there was a reason I liked having you around."

"That's the only reason?" Jessica baited.

"No, but it's a very important one." Bane grinned back at her; he dropped one foot off the table and kicked out a chair for her to sit in before returning his foot to its original place.

The weather was cool with the breeze blowing; however, it wasn't cold yet. A light jacket or flannel worked well to fend off the panting winds, although Bane was filled with an inner chill that no piece of clothing could dispel. On the outside, he looked happy and jovial, but inside, he knew that while he celebrated with his friends, his gut told him more children were arranged to be slaughtered by the maniacal serial killer. However, until he learned more, there was little he could do to stop the vicious murders.

Two men walked out through the screen door and sat down at the second table outside. The first man was so overweight that his clothes seemed ready to burst at any moment, whereas the second guy had hawkish features masking his face; his long beaked nose and beady eyes made his appearance sharp and wicked. They scanned the group of people already occupying one of the tables, not really sure what to make of them, especially since two of the group were obviously heavy-duty bikers and the others were dressed more business casual.

An eardrum-piercing scream rang out through the bar and floated out through the screen door. It bought the attention of everyone outside, promising an adventure or at the very least something interesting to talk about. Bane leaped to his feet, quickly followed by Thunder. They slid the screen open and jogged inside to see what happened. A woman was standing in front of the ladies' bathroom with the door open wide. Blood was splashed across the floor and written in that same blood. On the wall were the words, "*Get Bane off the case, and give me the book, or you'll be destroyed!*"

Thunder's eyes shot back and forth between the wall of the bathroom and Bane with great apprehension. The woman stood there trembling and inhaling deeply, preparing for another blood-curdling shriek. Nancy and Rick raced to where the crowd began to coalesce. When they saw the condition of the bathroom, they stared in horror. Neither knew what to say to Bane since he was mentioned in the message; however, they began moving people away from the doorway.

Nobody could be seen from where the crowd was standing, but everyone knew that it had to have been mutilated beyond recognition to accrue such a massive amount of blood. Bane stepped forward, pushing his way through the small group of people. With tentative steps, he entered the bathroom, his gun drawn; he chambered a round and pulled the hammer back. Bystanders gasped in shock when they saw the weapon and moved away in the direction that Rick and Nancy were herding them. He cautiously checked the closest stall, looking underneath the door before kicking it open.

Empty, save for the blood, he moved to the next stall. Again he hit the door with a fierce snap kick opening the door violently. Over the toilet was a child no older than two years old; its body was shredded as though it had been through a wood-chipper. A magician's silk handkerchief was jammed inside the toilet paper dispenser. How long the body had been in there wasn't known to Bane, but he had to assume that it was there for at least thirty

100

minutes; he could see the bathroom doors from his position outside, and no one had used the ladies' room in that time.

"Rick, close the front doors; no one leaves until their statement has been taken," Bane called out from the bathroom; Rick was quick to comply.

Bane unlocked his iPhone and dialed Pamela Phillips. "Pamela, we got another crime and message." Their conversation continued for twenty minutes as Bane relayed everything he saw and gave her directions to the bar. She was already in the air aboard the jet she had been allotted by the bureau. Local police arrived on the scene more than twenty minutes later. Before they could get in his face, Bane flashed his ID at them and explained what he required of them.

He sent Thunder outside to keep Jessica, Carrie, Erika, and Devon occupied so that they wouldn't see the carnage with their own eyes. Bane knew that they would each be haunted for many months, if not years, to come upon seeing the horrific scene in the bathroom. Normally, Bane would've had Thunder escort them all back to the lake house, but he felt uneasy about letting them out of his vicinity. If the killer was going to attack them at any time, he'd do it while Bane was far away from his friends. Only one thing about the crime in the Badger's Paw was considered a positive aspect by Bane; the murderer was afraid of him. It was the only conclusion that Bane could draw from the constant demands that he stay off the case.

Pamela had stated that she would not only fly directly to Wisconsin but would have a helicopter ferry her over to the bar to save time. Meanwhile, the local authorities began taking statements from the people inside the bar. Their biggest problem came in collecting coherent accounts of the night from the undeniably inebriated patrons of the establishment. Both Rick and Nancy gave clear accounts of what they saw and heard. However, they were tending to their customers for the majority of the night and, thus, weren't paying close attention to the comings and goings of the clientele.

For his part, Bane was able to reassure the police that no one had exited the bar through the courtyard since he had arrived. Though the killer could've entered and left through the small window in the women's bathroom, no fingerprints were found on the sill. Additionally, no one matching the description of the serial killer described in Jessica's dreams had been in the bar. In fact, Badger's was filled primarily with regulars for most of the night. What had baffled Bane was how the killer could get in and out of an entire bar congested with people without being seen by anyone at all.

As the SID scoured the bathroom for evidence, Bane watched the police take the statements from the regulars of Badgers. Almost all of them were shaken by the tragic death in their midst. It was such a small town environment that murder was a farfetched notion for them, something that happened in large cities, but they felt they were far removed from such crimes. Of course, there was a college campus in the main town, and petty crimes were committed by some of the students. However, nothing like this had ever happened in Lake Edge.

On rare occasions, someone drowned or was run over by a speeding boat, but in general, the mortality rate was low. Scientific Investigation Department had brought in lights and taped off the bathroom while they worked the crime scene. The additional lights did little to dispel the gloom of the situation; the macabre of the bar seemed to deepen even further. The bright bulbs illuminating the ladies washroom heightened shadows in the rest of the building. The darkness washed over the crowd, casting their features into sharp-edged masks of fear.

Bane could feel his heart pounding against his chest and almost heard the thundering beats of the people standing near him. Slowly, the building began emptying out after the police took down everyone's name and address, along with any information they provided. Each person was sent on his or her way, a card for a counselor distributed to each person before he or she left. It was a standard operating procedure for anyone witnessing such a graphic crime. Though the act itself went unseen, the aftermath was beyond comprehension to most people.

The unanswered question loomed in Bane's mind, tickling the back of his brain adamantly. He ran theory after theory over in his head, trying to determine what the killer was truly after. Most serial killers had a distinct purpose. Despite their insanity, they often had a driving goal behind their destruction. His question was very simple, yet evaded his every effort to answer: what book did the magician want? How close was he to catching him, if he was so intractable in his desire to rid Bane from the pursuit?

Glancing out the front window, Bane stood mesmerized by the elaborate dance of the flashing lights. It was an authoritative tango, blue and red hugging close as they flickered against the exterior of the Badger's Paw. Nancy wept silently as she switched off the glowing signs in the windows; the impact of the situation finally set in. At first, the shock had glazed over the pain, fear, and anger over what happened within the walls of what she considered her second home. Rick stood stoically beside one of the touch screen games, hiding his emotions valiantly.

An hour after the initial discovery, Pamela Phillips burst through the front door. Two local police tried to stop her before she got fully inside. For some reason, she didn't have her badge attached to the outside of her jacket like she usually did.

"Let her through; she's with the FBI," Bane stated plainly as Agent Phillips reached into her breast pocket and withdrew her identification.

"Bane, what have we got here?" she asked, not even sparing a glance at the cops that had attempted to restrain her.

"Mutilated infant in the ladies' bathroom." Bane's frown sharpened. "It's not like the rest of the killings. The baby was shredded, its flesh torn to pieces, the blood splashed thoroughly throughout the bathroom. I think the killer was not only sending a message with the words on the wall, but with the amount of destruction to the body itself. Strange thing is, no one reported seeing any children of any age in the bar at any time tonight."

Pamela's eyes shrank as she examined Bane's face, as though she was trying to read his mind. However, it was clear that she wasn't having much luck. His face was a portrait of anger, but it didn't give away anything, other than his unadulterated rage. With a sigh that started from the tips of her toes running up to her head, she pronounced, "I had better take a look at the bathroom. Did you already give the locals their instructions?"

Bane nodded grimly. He didn't much care for the police in the area, mainly because of the hassles they had given him less than a week prior, not to mention the fact that they were not used to handling that type of crime. Several times he was forced to correct them before they made serious errors. While he wasn't really in law enforcement, he had done many things in his lifetime and knew how evidence had to be preserved, especially from the angle of trying to obscure the potential clues that would lead to an arrest.

Agent Phillips approached the bathroom with a strange caution, as though she believed the killer might still be inside. She glanced over the message with a pain-filled expression adorning her face. Pamela hadn't told Bane of the note the magician had left on the window in Dallas. Nevertheless, she wasn't startled to see the bloody letters scrawled across the bathroom wall. Turning to look at Bane, she noticed he was walking toward the screen door with purpose.

"You're leaving?" Her brow crinkled.

"Not at all. I came here with some friends, and I need to check on them. We came to enjoy a night of friendship and comradery. That fucker destroyed that plan pretty quickly."

Pamela nodded as he stepped through the door, out onto the deck.

"Bane? Are you all right? Thunder told us what happened . . . " Carrie asked.

"Yeah, I'll be fine," Bane answered, glancing at Thunder.

"I think I know what book the killer was referring to, Bane."

"All right, Jess, exactly what does it mean?" he demanded skeptically, the stress of the situation starting to make him irritable.

"I told you that I thought I was on to something, and that was what kept me from coming here sooner. An occult book I was reading seemed to indicate that the magician is a demon of some sort. If that's true, then he wouldn't want you to have possession of it, true?" Jess answered calmly, ignoring Bane's obvious frustration with her. "I didn't want to mention it in front of everyone, but seeing as the killer has made his declaration in such a public fashion, I see no reason not to tell you now."

"A demon? Are you serious?"

Jess nodded emphatically. "Yeah, I know it's hard to believe, but some magic is real. Back in medieval times, there were people called mages or sorcerers because they had an ability to harness the energies of reality. They could bend the possibilities of reality to their will. As time progressed, much of those skills were lost. After the witch-hunts, almost all of the real power was lost to the world. Even now, I believe that those who call themselves psychics are actually tapping into the powers hidden deep within them.

"So many things in this world go unexplained; is it really so hard to believe that demons exist? Think about it for a minute; even the Bible tells us that angels were cast down from heaven. Those beings didn't just disappear. They became what the world would call demons," she concluded.

"Uh . . . " Bane stammered, not sure what to think. His entire reality shifted around him, warping in his vision. "You've got to be fucking with me— It's not possible!"

"How do you think that the killer gets from place to place so fast? What's not possible is for a mortal man to traverse the distance between those killings in the time that the murders took place. Can you explain how a normal killer could do that?" Jessica rebutted.

Bane shook his head sardonically. "I guess not. It's just—"

"It's fucked up, is what it is!" Thunder exclaimed.

104

Devon and Erika remained silent through the entire conversation. In fact, they hadn't said a single thing since Thunder went out to babysit the group. Carrie, Jessica, and Thunder spoke in hushed tones while they waited for Bane. No one really noticed that Erika and Devon were quiet. They were too wrapped up in their own conversations. Both were scared, and they believed that Bane's presence had brought indescribable danger into their lives. They resented him immensely the moment Thunder explained the situation inside.

"So you're trying to tell me that some fallen angel is responsible for all these killings and that the book you're reading is the one that it wants? I don't suppose it mentions how to destroy the demon?" Bane asked, obviously scything along the edge between sarcasm and fear.

"I didn't get that far; I was about to cross-reference those doll heads with the demon that I was researching when you called," Jessica responded with exasperation. "You'd better start taking this seriously—it might be your only chance to stop this guy."

"I've never taken anything more seriously than catching this killer, but you're talking witchcraft, spooks, and spirits! How am I supposed to respond to that? " Bane argued.

"With the open mind you claim to have, ya asshole!" Carrie snapped before Jessica could even open her mouth to answer.

"And I'm supposed to go inside and tell that Fed that I'm trying to capture and kill a demon? This is beyond insane! She'd laugh her ass off and probably stop sharing information on the case with me."

"So don't tell her. Just do what you were going to do, but don't just write this off!" Carrie argued again.

"Carrie's right. You can't blow this off. At least read what I've found thus far and make up your mind. You were the one who asked me to check into the occult books for answers, ya know," Jessica added.

"I'm sorry, but I'm with Bane on this one. This sounds really bizarre! Do you guys really think some ancient demon from biblical times has decided to munch a few kids to alleviate its boredom? It sounds a bit farfetched," Thunder joined in the conversation.

Suddenly the porch door skidded open. "Bane, I think we have something inherently strange in here."

"I'll be right in, Agent Phillips . . . " Bane gave the group a meaningful stare before entering the bar once more. "What's up?"

105

"You'll notice that there are two stalls in this bathroom." Pamela paused, awaiting Bane's nod. "Well, there aren't supposed to be any stalls. From what the owners say, it's just one big private bathroom. Or didn't you know that?"

"No, I use the men's room. In case you haven't noticed, I'm male. In the men's bathroom, there is a urinal and a stall, so it seemed logical to me that there would be two stalls in this bathroom." Bane stared in disbelief at the stalls in the ladies' room. "Why would the killer put in a stall? For that matter, how would the killer put up stalls and add toilets? "

"I don't know. I can't understand any of this unless the owners are lying," she theorized.

"No," he responded, shaking his head.

"No? You dismiss it that easily?" Pamela asked, tilting her head to one side.

"No. They wouldn't lie. I know them, not just as a customer, but they are friends. What purpose would it serve for them to lie about it anyway? Besides, it would be too easy to disprove if they were lying. All I'd have to do is ask my wife or my other female friends, and bingo— the truth is revealed. So, no, they aren't lying."

Bane walked into the bathroom once more, flushing both toilets, seeing the water swirl around the bowls clockwise, and disappear. Drawing a knife from its sheath, he tapped against the metallic stall walls, hearing a satisfying pinging click answer him. They were complete with graffiti etched into the bluish paint, the impressions filled in with browning dried blood that was spattered across the entire room. A deep chill rang throughout his body, Jessica's words stinging his ears even after the conversation ended; in his mind, the words shouted louder than any voice ever could . . . *a demon!*

A demon!

Things were starting to crystallize in his mind. After all, how could a normal man sneak into a pub filled with people, with a child that no one saw, install two toilets, complete with stalls to encase them, all within a half-hour time span?

A demon!

He left the bathroom and looked at Agent Phillips, wanting desperately to let her in on the information he had. However, he knew that wouldn't be possible. Not only was he missing all of the facts, but it sounded so farfetched, he hardly believed it himself. Somehow, he had to get through this crime scene and gather his friends around him while they sorted out what they had recently discovered. Moreover, Bane needed to learn how to track and kill this creature before it mutilated more helpless children.

A demon!

"Bane? What is it?"

"What?" He looked up as if coming out of a deep haze.

"You look absolutely pale, almost worse than when you were at your . . . " She let her voice trail off, not wanting to reopen such fresh wounds. Pamela was about to mention his sister's house and their tragic deaths, which would've hit Bane like a slap in the face.

"You just look very upset. What's wrong?"

"I . . . I just can't figure out how the magician could pull this off. If these stalls were illusions, that would be one thing, but they aren't. It's not possible that this guy snuck in here with two stalls, an extra toilet, and a child, living or dead." Bane sighed in frustration. "How are we supposed to catch this guy if he can sneak by an entire room full of people like that?"

A demon!

"What if the illusion wasn't the new stalls?"

"Huh?"

"Think about it. If this killer is a magician, maybe he created the illusion that the bathroom was as it was prior to tonight. But in actuality, he altered the room last night, merely sneaking a child through the bar unseen. Let's face it. If people are drinking and having a good time, how often do they notice every single person in the place?" Pamela mused.

"Even so, someone, even just one person, seeing a man and a child would've come up. Plus, a man walking into the ladies' bathroom would definitely catch some attention."

"Not if he were using his illusions to mask the child and himself."

"Okay, so let's say for argument's sake that is what he did. What is the point of hitting so close to where I'm at? If he's truly afraid of me catching or killing him, why run the risk I might detect him?" Bane questioned, playing devil's advocate.

A demon!

"I don't know, maybe perhaps to take the game to a higher level. Maybe he thought he could scare you off the case if you thought he could get this close to you and you were unaware. The truth is, I have no idea what motivates this creep," Pamela concluded. "Look, you've been here keeping things under control since the body was discovered. Why don't you take your friends home and call me in the morning? I'll have all of the reports in by then."

Bane nodded grimly. "I think I'll do that. They're pretty upset about this, and I hate keeping them here any longer than necessary. The problem was, I didn't feel right letting them leave without my protection."

"You can't take the whole world on as your personal responsibility, Bane. You'll go insane trying to protect everyone," Pamela stated with a full measure of empathy. "I know; I have the same problem. Comes with the job. Call me later because you and I need to get together to compare notes."

"No problem. Get some rest. You look exhausted, Pamela."

"I will if you will," she answered.

"Deal. We'll talk tomorrow," Bane called over his shoulder.

Bane strode over to Rick and Nancy, not quite knowing what to say to them. Their bar had just gotten pulled into his personal battle against the serial killer. It was clear from the expressions on their faces that they didn't hold him responsible. In fact, they appeared to feel sorry for him. He was dealing with some very serious issues, and they could almost feel the weight of his pain, stress, and guilt.

"I'm going to take the group home. Are you guys going to be okay?"

Nancy smiled but said nothing. Rick shook his head. "We'll be fine. You just take care of yourself and the rest of them."

"If you have any problems, call me immediately," Bane said, handing Rick one of his new business cards. "I know what the card says, and I'll explain all that later, but you can get a hold of me through those numbers."

Bane left through the back door, and when he arrived on the deck, everyone stood. "Time to go, people. This is how we're going to do this . . . " Bane announced. "First, I will walk each of you to your vehicles; you'll start the car and follow me to the next person's vehicle until I'm the last. We stay in a close line convoy on the way home. Any problems, flash your lights and honk your horns. Thunder and I are riding motorcycles, so we'll keep pace on each side of the train of cars. Any questions or comments?"

"What would you do if I left the train of cars and ditched you?" Jessica joked.

"Now isn't the time to be a smart-ass; that's my job. Now we do it as I planned, and everyone gets home safe," Bane claimed.

After that, no one had anything relevant to say, at least nothing that would change the plan to get home. Everyone felt comforted by the idea of their convoy; it kept them all together. It was a much safer alternative than each person scrambling home as quickly as he or she could. If the killer could slip into a bar filled with customers and pull off a crime as he had, it wasn't out of the realm of possibilities that he could sneak into the backseat of someone's vehicle.

"Jess, why don't you let me hold on to that book until we get home. If that's a potential reason to target someone, I'd rather be the one the demon sets his sights on. I'll keep it in my saddlebag. The book will be plenty safe there, I promise," Bane requested.

A demon!

Reluctantly, Jessica agreed. They followed Bane's plan to the letter, and before long, they were all headed home. Bane and Thunder raced up and slowed down periodically, keeping all three vehicles covered, within their view. Everyone seemed to drive rapidly toward the lake house, exceeding the speed limit by leaps and bounds. Tires squealed in protest as the vehicles took the corners way too rapidly; the motorcycles were able to speed around the bends in the road far easier than the cars, but their riders worried they might lose control at the vast speeds at which they traveled.

If the convoy of vehicles had known what awaited them when they returned to the lake house, they might not have been so eager in their desire to return home. The vile goo that spilled from the mouths of the dolls had begun to coalesce into mini-monstrous bodies that would serve for the heads. None of the other doll heads had been kept by a family member of the slain children, except for Bane's, which were oozing fluids from within. Tar and black ink mixed would appear similar to the fluid that was creating the hideous bodies for the dolls. A mottled black, green and grey formed as its skin layer.

Instead of hands, the liquid formed into talons that were reminiscent of vampire claws. The fingernails weren't very long, but they were thin and serrated. Though the arms and chest of the creatures were small, they were incredibly muscular, well defined in shape and cut. Sharp black needles burst through the creature's back, running the length of its spine. The area between the toes was webbed, and the same talon-like nails protruded outward from the toenails. A small spike emerged just above each heel and atop both kneecaps.

With the split along the mouth-line, multiple rows of barbed teeth were now visible. The eyes that once appeared to follow a person no matter what direction they moved turned serpentine, the irises rapidly changing into a milky yellow. Where once the features of the face resembled the slain child, it now transformed into something far worse. Deep, dark circles surrounded the eye sockets; profound creases surfaced along the eyebrows, casting a permanent scowl across the doll head's face.

Its legs were like that of animals with large, solid haunches. Both the hands and feet appeared to have three joints in them, as though the feet could be used as an extra set of hands if the need arose. Its mouth formed into that of a small crocodile mixed with a German Shepard. The little creature was carved into very convex and concave angles, the severity of which made it even more terrifying to behold. And a nasty black and green forked tongue slithered out of the mouth every so often.

The exterior coating of the creature resembled tight, expensive, black, leather over muscle and bone. With horrifying precision, the beast formed itself as though it were always meant to exist. The depths of the abomination were unfathomable since evil can't create properly, as it is best suited for destruction. After a few moments, the creatures began to stir, attempting to stand up and move around under their own power. Those first timid steps were off balanced, like the shaky legs of a newborn calf. However, the creatures seemed to adapt quickly to their environment and began moving gracefully, almost unnaturally fluid.

In the center of the basement, they stood, waiting for the return of Bane Bloodworth. It was there that they would ambush him and do what they were created and commanded to do.

Chapter Eight

og drifted across the road like the smoke pulled in from a smoker's first drag. With the haze rising up to embrace the night, the travelers moved swiftly, but more cautiously. An inferno could be seen blazing in the distance; one of the houses off the lake was on fire. Though the smoke was dark, it appeared grey and silver against the iridescent glow of the flames. The night reached out its taloned claw toward Bane, as he rode ahead of the convoy of vehicles to get a better look at the burning building.

Before racing forward, Bane gestured to Thunder to stay with the group, guarding them against whatever may happen into their path. The group of cars returned to their lake house; before piling into one truck, they too wanted to see which home was burning. Bane looked at the water, and it seemed as though black oil glistened against the fiery embers of the flaming house. Flames licked the sky above the line of tall trees, as though they could burn the clouds themselves.

The two-story dwelling had wisps of flames and smoke pouring from windows on both floors. Such structural damage was done to the building that the roof was beginning to sag. Screaming wails of the emergency vehicles responding to the fire sliced through the fog-encased wind. Bane watched in sheer awe of nature's true power; he was always mystified by flames. The way they leaped, danced and consumed never ceased to amaze him. To him, there was something inherently intoxicating about any flame, but more especially large ones.

As the Ford Explorer slowly approached where Bane was watching the house burning to the ground, he spun on his heel and drew two Ruger semi-automatic handguns from under his coat. If the occupants of the truck had hostile intentions, they would have been blown into Swiss cheese in an instant. However, recognizing the truck like the one belonging to his old friend Jess, Bane returned his weapons to their proper place. Through the windshield, he could see the wide-eyed fear of staring down the barrel of two guns on the faces of Jessica and Carrie.

Carrie was the first one out of the truck, pulling the seat forward to allow the people in the backseat to exit behind her. Jessica quickly followed, walking toward Bane with her eyes bound tightly to the flame-covered home. On either side of the burning house, owners were hosing down the side of their homes, trying desperately to ensure that the fire didn't spread. The fire trucks were getting closer, which was obvious by the approaching noise they generated.

"I wonder if anyone is still inside?" Jessica asked.

"By the time I got here, there would've been no way anyone still inside could have survived. Forgetting the smoke inhalation factor for a moment, those flames have completely filled that house. I doubt any part of that place has been left untouched by the flames," Bane answered her, shrugging his shoulders slightly. "When you factor back in the full measure of smoke inhalation, no one could be alive inside those walls."

Thunder made the sign of the cross over his body, in a small prayer for the owners of the blazing home. Erika clung to Devon tightly, burying her face in his broad chest; his arms circled around her, giving her a comforting reassurance. Jessica came to a halt next to Bane's Harley, watching the destruction with a morbid fascination. Bane pulled out a cigarette, placing the filter between his lips; with a flamboyant, fluid motion he whipped out his Zippo lighter and lit the cigarette; in that same movement, Bane closed the lighter and slid it back into his pocket.

"Hey, you got one for me?" Jessica asked.

"I didn't know you smoked," Thunder mentioned.

"I don't really smoke. I mostly mooch." She stated.

Thunder had his cigarettes out before Bane could respond to her request. Jessica took one from his pack and waited patiently while Thunder lit it for her. His chivalrous gesture didn't go unnoticed; Jess was very impressed with him. It was commonplace for Bane to light her smokes, but she already knew that beneath Bane's rough exterior laid the heart of a gentleman. She found it odd that it never occurred to her that Thunder might be like-minded.

The wail of the fire engine's sirens sang a sad song of destruction. At last, they had arrived and ordered that the motorcycle and Ford Explorer be moved back immediately. Bane and Jessica were quick to respond to their demands and moved their vehicles out of the way. When they returned, several firefighters were trying to keep them at a distance. Bane flashed his badge at one and shoved another aside as he walked to where Carrie, Thunder, Erika, and Devon were standing. They too were being instructed to move along, that there was nothing more to see there. Of course, no one believed that line of garbage for a second—as if the firemen telling them that the action was over, would deceive their eyes like a Jedi mind trick or something.

One of the firemen grabbed Carrie by the arm and began pulling her back. Bane's anger flared to life; he drew his handgun, aiming it at firefighter's head, "Take your hands off the lady, now," he ordered in a firm voice.

When he got no response, he moved forward to show the fireman that he was in grave danger. "I said take your fucking hands off that lady, or I'll blow your fucking head off!" Bane shouted through clenched teeth.

Without hesitation, the firefighter released Carrie and raised his hands above his head, showing he was no longer a threat. Bane said nothing, simply returning the gun to its holster. The group moved back a little to give the first responders room to work, but remained to watch the fight between water and flame. Six fire trucks and two ambulances arrived to attempt to quash the rising flames. Deep inside, everyone there knew that the battle would be a losing one and the house would be reduced to charred rubble. Only the concrete foundations would survive the inferno, and then only because it melted at a much higher temperature.

Crackling subsided to the sound of hissing, as tons of water was being sprayed at the burning home. The constant rush of fluid did little to diminish the soaring flames rushing outward from within the toasted building. Squad cars began wheeling around the corner, to help control the crowd that began to gather to gawk at the tragedy. Bane turned to his friends, nodding his head slowly. His face turned into a grim scowl. They all knew what the end result would be the moment they arrived; so staying would do them no good.

"I'm heading back to the house. This thing is gonna burn all night. We'll get just as good of a view from the balcony if we want to watch this thing later," Bane announced. "Besides, there isn't any beer around here, and I'm feeling rather parched."

"I'd rather stay and watch for a while," Jessica stared blankly.

"Me too," Erika added.

"I've gotta take a piss, so I'm going back to the house." Thunder informed.

"I'll stay with the girls if you two want to head back to the lake house." Devon offered Thunder his key chain. "Take my keys so you can get in."

113

"Like Bane or Thunder would actually need keys to get inside!" Carrie laughed.

"While my wife does have a good point, keys do make the effort much easier." Turning to Thunder, Bane said, "Hop aboard. We'll be there in a few seconds."

Bane started up his bike and revved the engine several times before dropping it into gear. Like a shot from a gun, the two bikers were barreling down the road toward the lake house. After a few brief moments, they arrived in the driveway and climbed off the Harley. Walking shoulder to shoulder, they approached the front door; each feeling that something wasn't quite right. Bane pulled a .44 Desert Eagle Automag from its holster and held it out to Thunder.

"I assume you know how to use one of these?"

Thunder accepted the weapon from Bane, and with a whimsical smile, he answered him. "We both know you checked into my past, and so you know I can handle just about any gun placed in my hand. My only question is, do you have a round already chambered?"

"Always. Just flip off the safety, and you're good to go."

"I guess you feel it too, huh?" Thunder asked as Bane drew two additional weapons from under his trench coat.

"Yeah. Something, or someone, is waiting inside for us." Bane flipped off the safeties and drew the hammers back on each firearm. "You open the door. I'll lead in. Cover my back, and we'll do a full room-to-room search. If you can't wait to piss, I'd recommend using that tree over there, because once we're inside, we may need to focus our attention elsewhere."

"Good idea," Thunder agreed, moving quickly toward the tree to alleviate the pressure on his bladder. As soon as he had zipped his pants back up, he nodded to Bane that he was ready. They approached the door warily, stepping through the outer screen door. Thunder used the keys Devon gave him to unlock the front door, and Bane threw himself inside, eyes seeking out a target. Thunder was quick to follow him, his weapon held pointing at the ceiling.

Bane backed into the bathroom once the front door closed; he spun and checked inside the shower stall. With an abrupt shake of his head, Bane told Thunder that the shower was empty. He put off checking the basement until after they had checked the entire upper level. Nodding in the direction he wanted Thunder to take, Bane circled around into the family room. Thunder moved through the kitchen, into the dining room, and back into the family

114

room where Bane stood motionless, as though listening for something. They then proceed to check the solarium, which was a simple task since it was open to the family room.

The hall that was normally a narrow avenue seemed even smaller as they moved through it. The first door they encountered led to another bathroom; this time Thunder checked the room, only to find it void of anything threatening. Even though they had encountered nothing dangerous thus far, their hearts clamored rapidly, their pulse increasing by the moment. On the left, they moved into a bedroom, where they checked the two closets and under the three twin beds. Again there was nothing to be found in that room, yet it did nothing to make them feel the least bit safer.

They ignored the small linen closet, due to the fact that no man could hide within the tiny confines of that indent. Bane moved to the last door in the restricted hallway; it was another bedroom with two twin beds and two closets; the room held no monstrous villains waiting to slice them into fish sticks. Only the basement had gone unchecked thus far.

In hushed tones, Bane explained how he wanted to approach the basement. "Look, you go out through the front door, circle around to the outside door that leads into the basement. I'll take the stairs down; if there's trouble, kick the door open and get in there fast. Otherwise, I'll unlock the door for you, and we'll finish the search. That way we have all the bases covered."

"If there is someone down there, you'll be in the more dangerous position. You've got a wife and a grieving family to worry about. I should be the one to slip down the steps into the basement. I've got no family to miss me if something goes wrong," Thunder suggested.

"No. We do it the way I planned. You've already shown you can't sneak down those steps with the stealth we want. Besides, with all due respect, I'm better prepared to handle myself if the shit goes bad than you are. We both know my reputation, and while some of it is bullshit, as most legends are, a good portion of it was earned with my blood. I'm the one that has the skills for this part of the search. Now I'll give you a slow count to ten to get to that door down there; then I'm going to be on the move. You hear a whistle or a gunshot, you bash through that door, gun blazing. I'm putting my faith in you, Thunder."

"Start the count once I'm outside the front door, and don't worry, Bane. I won't let you down," Thunder vowed solemnly.

"Get moving. I want this over before everyone decides to come home."

They exchanged determined looks, and Thunder raced out the front door. Bane eased the door to the basement open a crack, listening for any type of movement, and began his count. When he reached nine, he pulled the door open all the way and slipped onto the first step. Keeping his feet placed along the outside of the stairs, he avoided the steps he knew to squeak. Proceeding down the stairway, until he was at the last step, Bane took a moment to prepare. He leaped off the bottom step, rolled forward into the room, coming up into a standing position.

Swinging his guns in wide arcs, covering the entire room, Bane was irritated to see no one standing within his line of sight. Four doors connected to the basement room, one to the outside, another to a master bedroom, a closet, and the fourth to the laundry room. His eyes strayed to the Ping-Pong table several times, but couldn't determine what he was missing. Dropping to one knee, Bane checked under the bunk and the twin bed. When he saw nothing to shoot at, he moved quickly yet silently to the outer door.

Bane opened the door, wincing at the grinding noise it made as it opened. Thunder shot him a questioning glance and was rewarded with a grim shake of Bane's head. Keeping his voice to a whisper, Bane decided on the best way to search the basement. "Alright, you stay here. Keep your weapon aimed between those two doors. I'll check the master bedroom first; it's got an attached bathroom. Once that's done, I'll sweep through the laundry room, with you here making certain nothing slips out behind me, and we'll have the entire house covered."

"What about that closet?" Thunder asked.

Bane cursed himself for forgetting such an important detail; it wasn't like him. "Check it; I'll cover you. Then I'll head into the bedroom."

Thunder pulled the door open with great trepidation, but no creature from the abyss waited within. With a shrug, Bane flung the door to the bedroom wide open. Reckless abandon not being the tactic for the evening, he entered slowly. Outside the cicadas had gone silent, as though anticipating a great misfortune about to befall humanity. Gooseflesh rose across Bane's skin, with a painful chill sliding down his vertebrae. His instincts were well honed, and if his body was telling him something was wrong, it was usually right. At that moment, his mind rewound to earlier in the night when Jess told him what she had found . . . *a demon!*

With a peculiar feeling welling up inside him, Bane knelt down to lift one side of the bedspread, so he could see under the bed. He recognized the feeling, but hadn't felt it in such a long time; Bane almost forgot what it felt like. That emotion was fear. Rising to his feet, he walked over the bed toward the bathroom. Using the extra spring from the mattress, Bane leaped in front of the bathroom doorway. His weapons held out at arm's length, he entered and found nothing. Quickly, he returned to Thunder, knowing that only one room remained unchecked.

"For this last room, I'm going in fast and furious. You follow me in, slow and cautiously. Anything other than me moves in there, blow it the fuck away. I've got a sinking feeling that something is in this house, and this is the only room left."

"Be careful. I'll be right behind you," Thunder whispered.

Bane lashed out at the door with a powerful sidekick, knocking it open violently. In the same forward motion, he plunged into the room sideways, a gun pointed out to each side. He spun in a circle, covering the entire room. Dark shadows loomed in every corner, yet nothing stirred. Thunder followed more cautiously, and fear shown clearly in his eyes. Upstairs, voices could be heard entering the house. Bane's face contorted into a snarl and motioned for Thunder to go keep an eye on them. At first, Thunder didn't understand the gesture, until Bane repeated it a second time, and that time he also caught the irritation marked on Bane's face.

Thunder backed out of the laundry room and ascended the stairs two at a time. He caught the first glimpse of Jessica walking through the door when he was only halfway up the staircase. She looked down at him, confusion an integral part of her expression. Thunder reached the top step and blocked her from going further into the house.

"What the hell's going on? " she demanded.

Then several gunshots reverberated throughout the house, causing everyone to jump. Thunder grabbed Jessica by the waist and hustled her out the front door, along with everyone else. At first, Jess, Devon, and Erika stood in shocked silence, not really knowing how to react. Carrie, on the other hand, was jolted into action.

Carrie immediately ran to the back of the Hummer, pulling down the back hatch. Her hand moved along the side panels of the truck, seeking out the telltale indents. She began opening a hidden cache of weapons within the wall of the vehicle. Several types of weapons were stashed throughout the Hummer; fortunately, she chose the panel she was looking for. Drawing out two Mossberg pistol gripped shotguns, a long oriental katana, and a small caliber handgun, she threw one of the shotguns to Thunder and kept the other for herself.

Carrie chambered a round into the shotgun and looked around shrewdly. As she tossed the katana to Thunder, she shouted, "Get that to Bane as soon as possible! It's one of his favorite weapons. I'll keep things cool out here until you guys get back."

Thunder had second thoughts about leaving the group unattended, but he also figured that a woman couldn't stay married to Bane Bloodworth without learning a thing or two about the art of combat. He turned quickly and ran back into the house, hoping that whatever was going down wouldn't be over before he got there. It never hurt to be able to tell people you helped the legendary Bloodworth out of a tight spot. Something like that would be an enormous boost to his own reputation.

Shots continued to be fired, but what Bane was firing at Thunder couldn't imagine. How many shots from a 9 mm could a person stand before being put down, permanently? Though Thunder hadn't been keeping count, he knew that Bane fired off at least seven shots or more. He knew that Bane possessed a deadly accuracy, especially at close range. Thunder was reminded of the conversation held out on the deck of the Badger's Paw; Jessica was talking about demons, which to his way of thinking, would be hard to kill. Beads of sweat sprang up across his forehead and along the back of his neck.

Thunder wasn't more than halfway down the steps when he saw Bane backing his way toward the staircase. "Bane!"

"Get back up the stairs! Go get everyone into my Hummer. Have the engine running!" Bane ordered.

"I've got your katana here. You want it?"

Bane nodded, and Thunder tossed the sword down to him, which Bane caught without even looking up. He slid the katana over his head and under a shoulder, securing the sword to his body. As soon as his sword was in place, Bane pulled out another gun. Thunder realized that Bane holstered one of the guns he had been using, most likely because it was empty and Bane didn't have time to reload it yet. He couldn't help marveling over the arsenal that Bane seemed to be toting around with him. Not to mention that Bane had added his favorite katana to his carried weapon list.

"What are you waiting for? Get moving! They're just absorbing my bullets!" Bane growled as Thunder stood hoping to catch a glimpse of what had Bane Bloodworth so visibly terrified. Thunder had heard many things about Bane, from the streets and conversations with Devon and Erika, and he thought it was impossible to pierce Bane's "got it under control" surface,

118

not that he believed that Bane was never afraid, just that nothing could make Bane show that fear openly to anyone.

"I've got a shotgun, man— I can help! Carrie's guarding everyone with another one. You need me more than they do!" Thunder countered.

"No! We're getting the fuck out of here! I need that Hummer loaded, running, and ready to go! Throw me the shotgun and grab the book out of my saddlebag. Then get everyone into the damn truck! Now!" Bane shouted.

A vile, beastly, wicked hissing sound filled the air for a moment at the mention of the book. Bane was firing rapidly with the gun in his left hand, while he holstered the empty one in his right hand. Risking a quick glance up at Thunder, Bane was able to catch the shotgun with his free hand. Adjusting his grip on the shotgun swiftly, Bane fired at an area just out of sight of Thunder as he began ascending the stairs. After Bane replaced his handgun, he ejected the spent shell, chambered another round into the shotgun, and fired again.

"Everyone into the Hummer! Carrie, start it up, then move over. We're getting out of here!" Thunder yelled as he came bursting through the doorway.

Thunder raced to Bane's Harley, rummaged through the saddlebags trying to locate the book that Bane took from Jess. Resonating blasts were coming from the house, while Thunder pulled the book out and ran to the Hummer's driver seat. He pulled the truck out of the driveway and backed it over the lawn, leaving the back hatch open and aimed at the front door, making it easier for Bane to leap into the truck. Though he was being bombarded with questions from everyone in the truck, Thunder remained silent. His full concentration was in the rearview mirror, waiting to see Bane appear in the doorway.

A silhouette appeared at the front door, lit briefly by the muzzle of the shotgun. A distinct click jarred everyone in the Hummer; the gun was empty. Bane sprinted toward the truck; leaping forward, he landed inside it and shouted, "Go! Go! Go!" Carrie was about to hand her shotgun to him when he opened another panel in the back of the truck. Jessica threw a few things out of her bag, and smoke suddenly engulfed the foyer of the lake house. Grass and mud were being kicked up by the powerful wheels of the Hummer, giving the impression of a tornado swirling behind them.

Bane whipped out a Heckler and Koch MP-5 heavy machine gun, hoping the 10 mm rounds it fired would do more damage, or at least kick his foe backward. The fact that it was fully automatic meant he didn't even have to aim all that well. If his unseen adversaries came into his line of sight, he'd simply hose the entire area down with a wide-arced spray of bullets. Bane pulled the bottom part of the hatch up to keep himself from sliding out of the truck. Propping himself up on the back window, Bane prepared to open fire. The Hummer jostled and bumped as it emerged back on the asphalt.

"Where the fuck are we going? " Thunder shouted, not knowing the direction he was supposed to be taking.

"Anywhere but here, and fast!"

Thunder rammed the gas pedal to the floor, shifting gears as quickly as possible. Racing up the street, everyone was looking out the back to see what had Bane so panicked. If anything was, in fact, in the doorway of the house, it was well hidden from their view by Jess's smoke trick. Questions were being shouted in fear at Bane, but his concentration on the front door remained unassailable.

"What is it? "

"What did you see? "

"Was it a demon? "

"What did it look like? "

"Are you okay? "

All of the questions were ignored; Bane seemed locked rigidly guarding the back of the truck. Jessica reached out a timid hand, tapping Bane's foot lightly. He whirled an arm around, catching her wrist painfully in his muscular grip. She winced from the pressure he exerted on her arm, but simply waited for him to release her. He stared at her without recognition; his eyes were wild and out of focus. Jess had never seen such terror in his eyes before; the very thought of it froze her heart solid as an iceberg. Bane released her wrist as he returned his full attention to the fading image of the lake house's smoke-filled front door.

Bane opened fire on the doorway as they rounded a corner in the road, taking them out of the line of sight of the house. Only when he was hitting nothing but trees did he cease his hysterical firing. Devon and Erika were stiff in their seats, fear overwhelming each of their five senses. Devon thought that the evening in jail would be the worst thing he could ever fathom happening to him, but at that particular moment, he vowed never to make that assessment again. Fate seemed to have a way of making liars out of people when they made assumptions.

"Now that we're out of danger, would someone like to tell me what the fuck happened back there? " Jessica pleaded.

"I don't know, man. We were searching the house. Both of us had bad feelings about going inside. We didn't find anything upstairs, but we started going through the basement when you guys came home," Thunder explained, his voice still shaking from the ordeal. "Then we all heard the gunshots and scrambled outside. You now know as much as I do at this point. Should I stay on this road or turn off somewhere?"

"Take a right at the next street; follow it down for three miles—" Jessica started to say.

"No fucking way that just happened!" Bane shook his head and began chanting, "It's just not possible."

"What's not possible? Bane . . . Bane!" Carrie tried to elicit a response from him, without much success; he simply repeated the same phrase over and over. His reaction did little to quell the rising flood of fear, threatening to wash away their senses.

In the back, Bane became a flurry of movements as he reloaded each of his guns. Pulling open small compartments all over the truck, he began loading up on heavy-duty weaponry. A grenade belt, with six fragmentary grenades attached, was removed from a small cavity. While he shrugged off his trench coat, Bane was still pulling out items from their secret locations. His bandoleer not only had shotgun rounds down the front but underneath, sixteen shurikens were concealed.

Bane replaced one of the knives he had attached to his forearm with a small Derringer, which only had two shots, but it could be popped into his hand in seconds, provided the right movements were used to eject the tiny weapon into his hand. He pulled the bandoleer on before strapping the grenade belt around his waist. Several times Bane checked the guns in their holster to ensure they would deploy quickly and easily if they were needed. Bane also thoroughly checked his "bag of tricks" and ninja sword to ensure all of the equipment was inside. With a small blade, Bane cut a hole through the top of his trench coat, leaving an opening for his sword to fit through.

After he shrugged into his trench coat, Bane replaced the sword in its sheath, from the outside of his coat; it gave him faster access to it. Inside a locked compartment, Bane removed three Beretta .22 caliber semiautomatic. He passed the first one to Jessica, who promptly gave it to Carrie. Again Bane gave Jess another gun. When she tried to hand it to Erika, Erika strained away from the gun; she wanted nothing to do with the weapon. Bane shrugged and gave Jessica the third firearm.

121

Though driving, Thunder checked his .44, making certain it was ready for action. He didn't realize that in the very center, in the back of the truck, Bane was pulling out an oversized gun and setting into a preset location. With a battery-powered drill, Bane secured a chain-gun into the center of the Hummer, aiming out the back window. Carrie had never seen Bane pull out that weapon, though she knew he had bought it through a military contact in another state. Despite his rapid and vigorous arming procedure, Bane hadn't stopped chanting to himself, "It's just not possible."

Devon shifted restlessly in his seat; his mind was in a flurry of its own activity. In his mind, a war was being waged, debating whether or not to request a weapon from Bane. He held no doubt that he would get one if he asked, but he wasn't sure he really wanted a gun. Of course, he wanted to help protect his wife, sister, and friends; he just wasn't used to handling firearms, not to mention that the idea of shooting at someone made him more than a little queasy. Devon held a reverence for life, and taking a life would've violated all of his values.

Long ago, Devon learned to take Bane very seriously. In a casual conversation, he mentioned that he was being hassled at work by an annoying manager who "rode his ass" every chance he got. Bane looked him squarely in the eyes and asked if that person were to disappear forever if Devon would mourn his loss. At the time, being very inebriated, Devon said he wouldn't care one single bit. Two weeks later, when that manager turned up missing, his mind relived that conversation, and he was wracked with guilt. He felt if he had kept his mouth shut, the manager would still be around.

Bane never really took responsibility for what happened, evading even the simplest questions on the subject. However, it was clear to Devon that Bane had a hand in what happened to the annoying manager. The lesson he learned was an old cliché, "Be careful what you wish for because you just might get it." At the time, he didn't think less of Bane, because if anything, Bane had done it out of a sense that he was helping a friend, even if Devon didn't really know that he was signing the man's death sentence in such a casual conversation. He also learned that his sister's friend from high school had some very scary contacts.

Finally, the debate was ended when Bane thrust a revolver into Devon's lap. Carrie explained how to remove the safeties while preparing to fire. Bane continued to chant his same tune over and over.

"It's just not possible."

"Bane!" Carrie shouted as loud as her voice would allow. "Snap out of it! What the fuck happened in there? "

"So little . . . so very fast—just absorbed my bullets. Barely slowed down, just kept advancing. It's just not possible. So fast. Hideous to look at. Didn't stop them—couldn't stop them. They kept coming," he rambled as his mind grappled with what he had seen. Nothing in his life filled with dangerous experiences had ever prepared him for what had just happened. "They were so damn fast!"

"What was so fast? What did you see? Damn it, Bane. We need to know!" Jess screamed, her fear having stepped off the precipice of rationality into the gaping chasm of terror.

"The doll heads— they weren't just heads! They had bodies, and they moved—fast! Faster than I've ever seen anything move! Holy shit, they were fast."

"They were fast—we got that already. What else?" Jess shouted in frustration.

"Terrible, they were so disfigured, like the gates of hell belched up the two little—" Bane couldn't even come up with a word that accurately described them, but it didn't stop him from trying. "Creatures, beasts, freaks, no! Abominations! That's it!"

"From the gates of hell? As in miniature demons?" Carrie pried.

"Okay, so the guy is a fucking demon! So he created those nasty . . . things! I believe now, all right! Is that what you wanted to hear? I was wrong; you and Jess were right! Does that make you feel any better?" Bane ranted.

"No, but at least it's a start. Now that you know, you'll be better prepared to combat whatever the demon throws your way," Carrie admitted.

"Where's that fuckin' book? I want to read up on what I'm fighting against," Bane stated frantically. "Tell me we got the book! Please tell me we didn't lose that too!"

"I grabbed the book, just like you asked." Thunder reached down, snatched the book from the floorboard, and held it up so Bane could see it. "I told you I wouldn't let you down. Now maybe you'll trust me?"

Jessica took the book from Thunder and mentioned the turn they wanted to make was coming up shortly. Flipping through the brittle pages as quickly as she dared, Jess stopped at a page and scanned the text. "I knew it!"

"Knew what?"

"I was thinking that those doll heads would show us which demon we were dealing with, and it appears that it does." Jessica paused then began reading aloud from the book.

"'Xanithsabar, a mean spirited demon, was the third archangel to be cast down from the heavens. During his exile from the kingdom of heaven, he has been using powers that appear to common folk as magic. With every action in which he uses his skills, he is slowly drained. The only way for him to regenerate the energy expended is for him to feed on the innocent. Virtuosity is the key, for the less innocent his prey, the less abundant the energy he receives.

"'He makes ample use of creatures known as avatars, miniature versions of himself. They're able to camouflage themselves, using illusion and misdirection. However, a kinsman of the slain can only release these avatars unto the world. In their possession, the avatars have life spring forth inside them, drawing on the dark energies of grief to power their animation.' Is that what you saw? The avatars of the demon?" Jessica asked when she paused in her reading.

"I'd have to guess that's what I saw." Grinding his teeth, Bane decided he would have to split the group up for their own safety. What bothered him the most was he'd be forced to take Jessica with him. She alone had a full grasp of what the book described, and without that knowledge, he'd never be able to stop the demon.

How can I ask her to put her life at risk? On the other hand, her life is already in danger, so I'd only be asking her to help me put an end to that beast. But if she gets hurt, it'll be my fault. How could I live with myself if I was responsible for harming her in any way?

Bane debated in his mind.

Drawing a deep breath, Bane made his announcement. "Okay, here's how I see this. All of us are not involved in this mess. If we all stick together, we're just dragging the innocent into a world of pain that they can easily avoid." He paused, briefly collecting his thoughts before continuing. "So we're going to split up as soon as possible—"

"I'm in. I said I'd back you up, and I meant it," Thunder declared.

"I'm in too. I vowed to stand by you for better or worse," Carrie announced.

"You're going to need me as well; I'm your only hope for figuring out how to stop Xanithsabar," Jessica added.

124

"Jess, you're right. I'll need your help desperately. However, no one else is going with. Thunder, you're going to guard Carrie, Devon, and Erika. If any harm comes to them, your dead body is the only excuse I'll accept."

"Which means to guard them with my life, right? No problem. I would do that without being told. Are you sure you don't want me there for backup?" Thunder asked.

"I'm positive. I don't want to have to worry about their safety while trying to stalk and kill a demon. Lord, be merciful; we're going after one of his fallen angels," Bane stated. "Devon and Erika will stick with you and Carrie; Jess and I are going after that demon."

"Where are we going for shelter tonight? I don't think driving around will help ease my nerves much."

"Thunder, my man, you're right. We'll go to my house up here. Though the construction isn't complete, there is a room in the basement that I call the 'safe room.' It's got reinforced walls, an independent power generator, and plenty of room to stretch out. I know they finished the work on that already; I checked on their progress a week ago. We'll go there to figure out our next move." Bane closed his eyes picturing the room in his mind's eye. "I think we'll be safe there for the night. Come morning, the hunt begins. We take the battle to the demon, and like the angels from heaven, we'll defeat this fucker, but this time we'll beat him once and for all!"

Thunder couldn't help thinking how inspirational Bane sounded. Despite the fear of the supernatural, Thunder thought that they all might just get through the situation alive. A thought occurred to him as they drove toward Carrie and Bane's house.

"Does that room have a bathroom?"

"Thunder, when I said a safe room, I didn't mean it literally. It's more like a disaster shelter with several rooms, including a bathroom, kitchen, and a fairly nice sized library to boot. I figured that if a disaster struck, it would be good to have some form of entertainment locked inside with us. Who knows how long a disaster could go on, so I prepared for the worst. Even if the house caught on fire, that room would remain at whatever temperature the thermostat is set at. Plus the air is filtered, purified, and recycled, so no smoke would get inside." Bane had started to pull himself out of his panicked state and was reverting to his instincts once more. "If for some strange reason, something goes wrong in there, Carrie has full access to the weapons room, though I find it hard to believe you'll actually need it."

When they arrived at the house, Bane was quick to get out and inspect the area. Unlike at Jessica's lake house, he had no ill premonitions about going inside. Thunder escorted everyone inside, while Bane began preparing the shelter for his guests. He had built the shelter with the thought that one or more of his friends or family might be caught in the disaster with them and had several small bedrooms installed for just such an instance. Bane prided himself on being prepared for any situation, no matter what the personal cost.

Once everyone was safely within the walls of the shelter, Bane sealed the door. "Make yourselves at home. We've got alcohol in the kitchen if anyone needs a drink. I'm going to get some shut-eye; I'll need to be well rested for tomorrow. I suggest you get some sleep too, Jess. It's gonna be a long day, filled with fraught and danger."

"I doubt I'll get any sleep tonight, after all, that's happened," Jessica complained.

Bane and Carrie disappeared into one of the rooms and closed the door, leaving Devon and Erika standing in the middle of the room, still in a state of shock. Jess walked into the kitchen, pulled out a bottle of single malt whiskey, poured a generous amount into a glass, and sat down at the table. Thunder was torn between trying to get Devon and Erika to snap out of their horror-bound minds and his desire to sit with Jessica. In the end, Devon solved his dilemma by taking Erika by the arm and leading her into one of the bedrooms. Only two bedrooms remained for guests of the Bloodworths.

"How are you holding up?" Thunder asked gently.

"I'm scared half to death. How are you?" Jessica revealed.

"Pretty much the same as you. Will you do me a favor?"

"Sure, what's the favor?"

"Be careful out there. I'd really like the opportunity to get to know you better. I know Bane will watch out for you, but I'm going to be worrying about you anyway," Thunder admitted, staring at the table as a method of avoiding her eyes.

Jessica gulped down the three fingers worth of fiery liquid; it burned her throat all the way down, but it warmed the chill that hid deep inside her. Going completely out of character for her, she stood up, moved behind Thunder, and began massaging his neck. While he wasn't sure how to respond, due to the threat looming over his head of Bane not approving, Thunder stayed where he was, enjoying the contact. Carrie seemed okay with the idea of Thunder courting Jessica, but he didn't know where Bane stood on the issue. That worried him greatly.

She brushed her warm lips against his neck, whispering, "Come on. Let's move into the bedroom."

"Are you sure that's a good idea? I . . . err, I mean, you're gonna need your rest and all."

"I'm far too wired to sleep right now, but I think you might be able to help me get rid of some of this nervous energy." Jessica entertained her invitation once more. "This isn't like me. I'm not usually this forward, nor do I sleep with men indiscriminately. But I'm attracted to you, and I think you feel the same toward me. So if I'm going out there tomorrow and risking my life, I want to feel alive— really alive, before I do. What do you say?"

Seconds felt like minutes to Jessica; she had gone out on a limb saying all that she had. She could feel her face burning with embarrassment, almost as hot as the whiskey she just gulped down. Jessica had made herself very vulnerable, another trait that she rarely displayed, and she was hoping like crazy that she wouldn't regret being so bold. Though only five seconds passed before Thunder spoke, Jessica was certain she was standing there for thirty minutes.

"Lead the way, beautiful." Thunder smiled.

Jessica picked up Bane's katana from one of his many sword racks and put it in Thunder's right hand. She gave him a seductive smile and playfully pulled him toward an empty bedroom. Though the violence that had entered her life over the past several weeks disgusted her, something about Thunder attracted her like a moth to a flame. After she closed the door to the bedchamber, she smiled slyly at him. He drew the katana from its sheath, twirling it around skillfully, and her smile grew proportionately. She had desired what he had in mind, having brought it to his mind. With a simple yet elegant swing, he split her top open; not a scratch was left on her body, but both her blouse and her bra fell off her heaving breasts. She was impressed by his exceptional skill with a bladed weapon. It was his heart that scared her, rather than the katana itself. With another expert slice, her shorts fell by the wayside, exposing her red Victoria's Secret panties. A quick twirl and the sword was returned to its case. Seconds later, he used a tanto blade to allow himself access to her blooming flower of love. She didn't mind that he had laid waste to her clothing; it was something she had fantasized about since she met him. Now that she had no more apparel, she looked at him expectantly.

Running the cool metallic surface along the length of her body, the eroticism of the moment expanded to mythic proportions. She cooed softly in response to his motions, knowing he was in complete control of the blade. Placing the weapon in her left hand, he freed his hands to frolic across her savory physique. Additionally, he showed his faith in her by giving her control in the situation. Passion ruled that instant like a king with a golden scepter. As his fingers danced along her love button, she slid the blade along his arms.

Goosebumps flared up across his appendages; a sweet minute of elation filled the air. She pulled the oriental knife away from his skin as she began to quiver from the gratification he gave her. With a subtle smirk, she demanded, at the point of his blade, that he lick her with his inimitable talent for giving orgasms. With a nimble thrust from his pelvis and he was deep within her. Because there was no warning, she accidentally sliced into his arm with the knife. It wasn't a deep cut, nor was it a particularly painful, so he paid it no mind. Before she could apologize for her transgression, he kissed her with his entire being.

He opened his eyes to see she was staring up at him with undisguised affection. Using his left hand, he gripped her bottom and rolled her on top of him. Blood stained the sheets, but neither paid any attention; they were both too wrapped up in their moments of ecstasy to care. Murmuring and sighing with pleasure, he proceeded to make love to her as she had never been before. The difference between him and other men was his passion. It filled the room like a flash flood racing through the streets. In and out, the pleasure simply grew with every gentle yet forceful thrust. Their passionate lovemaking proceeded well into the night, closing in on the dawn.

Chapter Nine

"Jess! Open the door!" Devon shouted as he pounded on the metallic door. His face was bright red, not as much out of anger but through embarrassment. "Mom's on the phone; she said she heard you last night on the radio—"

Jessica's voice could be heard from inside the room. "Oh my God! No way! Please, no!" she cried out.

"When you didn't answer your cellular, she called mine. You were doing a sex show last night! What the fuck's going on? "

"I'll be right out, and keep your voice down. I don't think the entire world heard you yet," Jessica snapped.

"Not me, but apparently they heard you."

She was mortified to know that anyone in the country could've listened to her most private thoughts during an intimate act. Jessica quickly pulled on a silk robe that was left in the room for guests, muttering curses the entire time. Thunder slept through the entire conversation between Devon and Jessica. Slipping out of the room, closing the door behind her, Jessica was startled to see that her brother was still standing in the hallway. She felt the heat flood her cheeks causing her to blush. Jess had a difficult time looking him in the eye; she watched the floor and walked into the kitchen.

"What the hell is Mom talking about? It was all she could do to keep Dad from going completely ballistic," Devon demanded as he followed her into the kitchen.

"Look, it's a long story, with no explanation at the end— so cut me some slack, alright?"

"Good morning! I'm afraid our radio system was messed up last night; we couldn't get any channels in. Thanks for the entertainment though, Jess," Bane chuckled as he entered the room. "I didn't know you were into that kind of stuff; it came as a big surprise to me."

"Fuck you, Bane."

"You know for someone who had a lot of sex last night, you certainly are grumpy this morning. I'm usually in a pretty good mood after a ride in the sack." Bane laughed, relentlessly teasing Jessica. "Maybe it wasn't as good as you made it sound. Or perhaps Thunder didn't find it as exciting as you did."

"Look!" Jessica shouted as her temper lost control. She stood up, glaring at Bane as though looks could kill. "You need my help, so you had better get off my back! This is no one's business but mine! So just back off!"

"Easy, Jess. It was just a joke. Geez," Bane answered, looking somewhat taken aback. "You need to learn to relax and allow jokes to pass sometimes. I was just fuckin' around with ya; it's not like I was trying to piss you off."

"Well, sometimes your jokes aren't funny," she answered acidly.

"Guess not," mumbled Bane turning to go get dressed in his fighting gear. He wanted to be absolutely sure that he was prepared if they were going to hunt the hunter.

"I don't know what his problem is; he wasn't humiliated like I was last night," Jessica complained bitterly.

"I think he was trying to break the tension, Jess. What's with you lately anyway? It's like sometimes Bane's your best friend, and other times he's your greatest enemy," Devon responded.

"He really pisses me off sometimes— that's all."

"Yeah, well, I can remember a time when you would laugh at his jokes and make some in response. Now it seems no matter what he says, you take an adversarial position. So I guess I'll ask you again. What's going on?"

"Dev, you can't possibly know what it's like to have your most inner thoughts broadcast across the nation. Do you really think I went on the radio last night to let the world know what a good time I was having? For some fucked up reason that I can't figure out, my thoughts are sent out all over the radio wherever there's static. It's a total invasion of privacy, and there isn't anyone I can blame for it because I don't know what's causing it," Jessica ranted.

"So instead you're blaming Bane for it? Look, I don't pretend to understand the whole dynamic behind your friendship with him. It seems to me that you two would have very little in common if you didn't attend the same high school at one point." Devon locked eyes with Jessica, making certain he had her full attention. "But because you did, you two have grown to be pretty good friends. I guess what I'm getting at is that I've noticed on more than one occasion that he does everything in his power to look out for you, which makes me wonder why you're so hard on him lately?"

"What do you mean? " she pouted.

"Well, for example, instead of staying with his family and grieving over the loss of his nephews, he came up here to make sure you were alright. Christ, Jess! The man just lost several family members and is coping the best he can; I'd think, considering how much you like him, you might be a little more sensitive to how he feels. I'm sure that he's tough as nails, just like he shows the world, but even so, he's gotta be hurting inside."

"What's the point you're trying to make?" Jessica asked, looking around in an effort to make sure no one else was in earshot. Guilt over her last outburst hit her hard; her brother had a very succinct way of cutting through all the exterior garbage, striking straight into the heart of the matter.

"I'm just saying it wouldn't be so terrible for you to ease up on him a little. He's going through a lot, and your snapping at him isn't going to help anyone."

"Since when did you become part of the Bane Bloodworth fan club?"

"For all intents and purposes, he pretty much saved our lives last night. Sure, none of us saw what it was he protected us from, but anything that had him that shaken must have been nasty. If it weren't for him, we'd all probably have walked right into whatever had him so rattled. Truth be told, I'm not a big fan of his. I think that a lot of this situation is because of him, not directly, but he brought it into our lives. Regardless of how I feel about that, it's clear he'd kill or die to keep us all safe," Devon stated bluntly. "I'm not going to say that I won't worry about you while you're out trying to kill the serial killer with him. However, if you have to go looking for trouble, I can't think of anyone who would sacrifice more for the sake of your safety than that certified sociopath, Bane."

"He's not a sociopath. Bane simply has a very colorful and, let's say, dubious past. That past is the one thing that makes him so dangerous to his enemies, and so protective of his friends," Jessica admonished her brother.

"See? That's what I'm talking about, Jess! One minute you're biting his head off; the next you're defending him! I've never seen you run so hot then cold on any subject before. So he's not a sociopath, but he's damn menacing. What are the odds that if he didn't come back up here that the killer would have gone to Badger's last night? Jess, just think for a second. Even though he brought most of this down around our ears, he's also the only one likely to get us out of this mess. Erika and I talked the whole thing over in depth last night." Devon paused, adding dramatic effect. "She's scared to death but feels ten times safer in this shelter than anywhere else right now. And even though I'm pissed off at him for all of this shit, I can see that he's doing all that he can to fix the situation."

"What do you want me to do?" Jessica asked, knowing that the preamble was leading to something.

"Try not to push his buttons; the man is living through a personal hell that none of us can fully understand. On the surface, he looks like he's handling it well, but it's gotta be taking a toll on him. When he snaps from the strain, he's going to take anyone nearby with him; I don't want to lose my older sister due to her habit of playing games with the emotions of someone as unstable as Bane."

"That's really sweet, Dev, but he'd never hurt me. His aversion to hitting any woman is such an integral part of his character that even to defend me from another girl, he'd feel the guilt of the damned if he had to strike her. Besides, he's not nearly as unstable as he leads the world to believe; Bane does have a white-hot temper, but deep inside he's simply a teddy bear."

Catching only the last sentence as he entered the room, Bane remarked, "That's grizzly bear. I think you've got your bears mixed up."

"Yeah, you're just a mean, nasty, wicked man with no redeeming qualities, Bane," Jessica said, her words oozing with sarcasm.

"Something like that. Hey, Jess, I didn't mean to offend earlier. If you want to know the truth, when Carrie and I heard what the radio was putting out, we turned it off. We're not perverts or anything, ya know." Bane sauntered over to a steel cabinet and removed several breakfast bars. "We hit the road in an hour, so if I were you, I'd go get ready."

"I've got a good place for us to start looking. After I fell asleep, I dreamed of several killings. I also got a strange feeling that one or more of them haven't happened yet. I can't explain how I know that; I just do."

"That'll make things a bit easier on us, Jess, although I have to ask you once more if you're sure you want to come along. This could be very dangerous, and I don't want you to get hurt," Bane stated in between bites of his breakfast bar.

"You'll never find the demon without me, not to mention you won't be able to stop it without my help. While you drive, I'll keep researching, and learn all I can that will help us kill the damned thing once and for all," Jessica stated adamantly.

"Can a mortal man," Devon paused and nodded his head toward Jessica, "or woman kill a demon? According to you, demons are fallen angels, from heaven and all. If the archangels Michael and Gabriel could only cast them out of heaven, but not vanquish them, how do you guys intend on doing it?"

"I've never believed in an undefeatable enemy. Everything on this planet has a weakness; it's simply a matter of seeking out that weakness and exploiting it," Bane stated boldly.

"How can you be so confident when you don't really even know what you're up against?"

"That's really simple. If you walk into a battle thinking you'll lose, chances are you'll find a way to make that happen. However, confidence can be a weapon unto itself. As Jess said, she's going to continue to learn about this creature, and the enemy you know is far less scary than the one you don't. Once we discover exactly what this thing is capable of, we can develop some defenses against it. Plus, she'll discover the creature's Achilles Heel, and then I'll use that flaw to destroy the fucking thing." Bane turned and looked at Jessica. "Hey, I've got some extra web belts and other battle gear. You'll have to adjust them for your size, but you may want to be well armed. I'll give you your choice of firearms and a few knives, not that I think you'll have much need of them since I'll be there kickin' ass for you."

"I'm not sure I like the idea of walking around like a mobile arsenal. While I'm sure that having every weapon known to man on your person is a good style choice for you, I don't think it's the best idea for me. I'll carry a small gun, and my usual party tricks, which should make up for my lack of weaponry," Jessica informed, shaking her head slowly. "Besides, I'll have several books that will need tending to anyway. Do you think we can go back to the lake house to get a couple of books I need?"

Bane's jaw locked into place; it took him a long moment before he relaxed and was able to speak. "I don't know. We'll park down the street. You can tell me what you need from there, and I'll grab them if I can. It could go one of two ways if I have trouble in there; first, I may come hauling ass out of the house and sprint to the truck. Or, I may leap on my bike and fire it up. If you hear my Harley come to life, start moving because I'll be close behind."

"You're going into the house alone? " Devon exclaimed in shock.

"Yeah, why?"

"After whatever you went through last night, you're telling me you'd willingly return for more of the same? Damn, Bane, you've more balls than I ever gave you credit for!"

"This time I'll be better prepared, and the element of surprise will no longer be working against me. Plus, if the books TNT wants will help me catch and kill this fucking creature, then I'd be willing to risk it all for them. I once heard a phrase that is called 'the way of the warrior,' which goes something like this: When you live, live without regret; fear is just the flame in which courage is forged," Bane recited, picking up one of his tanto knives. Suddenly he grew much more agitated and tossed the blade onto the counter. For some reason, it didn't feel right in his hand, as though it was out of tune. His mind flashing to the murders once again, the faster and more menacing his voice became. "That motherfucker killed members of my family, he made this thing personal, and for that, I'm going to lay him out across the altar of pain. I'll show him how we all must sacrifice to the jaws of misery at one time or another! He's going to know the wrath of God, divine destruction handed down through the avatars that are my fists!"

"If anyone can, it's you, man," Devon admitted, hoping to mollify Bane, while he shot his sister a look that clearly said, "And you don't think he's unstable?"

Bane rubbed his temples with his eyes closed. "I'm sorry. I didn't mean to yell. I guess I'm a little more pissed off than I thought."

Quick to respond, Devon was waved away the apology as irrelevant. "No problem. We totally understand. I'd be a mess if I had to go through what you have these past few days. We're very impressed at how well you're handling everything."

Bane nodded in agreement, even though he knew the conversation he walked in on had much to do with some flawed aspects of his character. Whether those flaws were real or in the eye of the beholder wasn't of issue. Jessica had a defensive tone and was conceding that Bane had a bad temper, which to Bane meant that Devon was worried about her being out on the road with him hunting a demon. He didn't blame Devon for his concern; in fact, it made him like her brother more.

"I'm going to go say good-bye to Carrie and call Agent Phillips to figure out where we'll have to meet her. In the meantime, we're gonna need to concoct a story as to why I'm bringing along a magician's assistant with me where ever I go," Bane announced, tossing Jessica an old flannel that he wore often. "We'll grab you a change of clothes from your lake house. That'll have to suffice for now, plus whatever we can dig up for pants."

Singing birds swooped from the sky, attacking Agent Phillips at every opportunity. Clowns were pelting her with blood from their seltzer spray bottles, while the sounds of several children's shows played loudly in the background. Kids were playing ball in the street, but none of them wore their heads to the game. Children on bicycles, tricycles, and big wheels were cruising along quite well, considering their bodies were decapitated. Strange white rabbits were flooding the alleys, appearing from out of nowhere.

She ran, but the road turned into four-foot-deep raw sewage; immediately she began to sink deeper within the obscene smelling fluid. Kicking her feet wildly, Pamela started to wade through the urine, feces, regurgitation, and other unidentifiable things in the hope of making it to the sidewalk. However, the going was much more difficult than simply swimming through water; the sewage had the consistency of clam chowder mixed with maple syrup. When she finally reached the edge of the sewage, a foot from a headless child pushed her head under the repugnant liquids.

Suddenly Pamela Phillips awoke, chilled to the bone, but covered in a thick sweat. Her breathing was rapid and discordant. She glanced around the room and pulled her pistol out from under her pillow. Pamela felt reassured by the weight of her weapon, and she held it like a talisman to ward off her nightmares. Her eyes coming to rest on the newspaper photocopies sent by her office, she knew that through reading them she'd learn the truth about Bane Bloodworth.

Scooping up the papers, Pamela walked into the bathroom and started the water for a hot bath. After testing the water with her toe, she slid inside the bathtub, while keeping the paper in her hands far above the water. As the soothing waters eased her tense muscles, she began reading the sheets. The first in the series was a photocopy from the Chicago Sun-Times.

Child Gone Wild or Wild Child Hero? -By Natalie Wolfson

In a startling exclusive interview, we had the chance to interview the teen who saved his entire family. This chilling tale begins two years ago in a small northwest suburb of Chicago. The teen's sister began dating whom she thought to be a nice boy, but who turned out to be a family's worst nightmare. A three-month relationship developed and endured their two clashing worlds; it ended in tragedy. When the Bloodworths forbade their daughter to see this troublesome young boy, he set out for revenge.

With a gang of thugs, he rapidly began to kidnap members of the Bloodworth family, starting with the girl's parents, aunts, uncles, and then cousins. One by one, family members disappeared, and the local police had no leads, suspects or clues. Through sources he refused to disclose, the girl's teenage brother located where his family members were being held.

Some critics say that the teen should have gone to the police with his findings, but he was able to persuade a grand jury that doing so could have cost the lives of the people he meant to save. Instead, he took justice into his own hands. Using unregistered firearms and a sword he had won from his martial arts teacher, the teen attacked the warehouse.

Police believe that he entered under the cloak of night, slipping in through a broken window on the second floor. He admits to using lethal force in the extraction of his family members from that building. However, he is quick to point out that, to him, it was a matter of self-defense.

Prosecutors maintain that his preparation before the incident demonstrated that he had premeditated murder on his mind. Lawyers for Bane Bloodworth countered this by reminding the court that had he entered the building unarmed, he would have been in far more danger, and thus, still constituted self-defense.

Twenty bodies, both male and female, were found in the warehouse the following day as the rescued family members went to authorities, informing them of their safe return. It was at that time that Bane Bloodworth was arrested on twenty counts of first-degree murder.

As of this morning, Bane Bloodworth was released from a Cook County Courthouse, without any charges being brought against him. No one can say for certain if Bane Bloodworth belongs behind bars, but it is a question to ponder. Is this wild child a hero or villain?

Pamela's eyes were as big as saucers, and her jaw was slack; it was beyond her comprehension how a teenager could enter a building and kill twenty people without any help, then somehow down the road still manage to join a federal agency. All members of the intelligence agencies were required to take a polygraph test before being given employment. Surely, Bane wouldn't have met the criteria for a member of the CIA with his background. Yet, somehow he slipped into the agency without setting off any red flags.

She couldn't get access to his record, or any information on his training. For every instance she tried to gather some shred of information on Bane

Bloodworth, she was called by her superior officer telling her to back off. Though she had a high level of clearance, it wasn't high enough for her to get inside his personnel file. His entire life had been classified, and obviously, those precautions were set into place recently.

Pamela felt guilty for checking up on Bane; she really did like him. She admired his courage, determination, convictions, and she thought he was very bright. However, in the back of her mind, she sensed that he was a covert operation specialist; which were usually deployed when dealing with something the government had unwittingly unleashed on the world. Stacks of articles were left untouched as she decided to learn nothing more that might taint her view of her ally Bane Bloodworth.

Suddenly her phone rang, causing her to jump from fright. "Hello? Shit! I'll be there as soon as possible. Anything else? Fine, have the jet fueled and ready to go. I'm on my way."

Pamela grabbed a quick shower and swiftly dressed in fresh clothing before rushing out the door. She knew her assistant would have someone collect her belongings and have them sent to the next hotel where she would stay. It was just another way for them to save time when she was needed. Pressing the button on the elevator several times with great impatience, the telltale ping of the elevator arriving sounded. She got into the metallic box and pressed the button for the garage, where her car was kept.

The only advice that her father had ever given her was that the truth would attend to itself. She had seen innocent suspects get railroaded by abusive polygraph examiners, while the guilty went uncaptured by passing the controversial test. One thing always remained the same; the truth always surfaced; however, most of the time it happened after it was too late. So her faith in her father's advice left her skeptical, to say the least.

Pamela reached the car she was driving, slid the key into the lock, but couldn't get it to turn. After several attempts, she was at last able to get the door open. The sound of footsteps echoed off the concrete walls, giving the impression that they were coming from all directions.

Wasting no time, Pamela climbed behind the wheel, locked the door, and started the engine. With a slight squeal from her tires, she pulled out of the garage and out onto the main road. She considered calling Bane but didn't want to wake him at such an early hour.

If he was anything like her, Bane wasn't getting much sleep, and every minute of slumber was deeply treasured. Over and over, her mind replayed the newspaper article she had read about him, and her concern about him increased.

Chapter Ten

He approached the house, slowly and with great caution. Bane's sword was in his left hand, while a Ruger semi-automatic handgun occupied the other. Once he was inside, he raced through the house to pick up the books and clothes Jessica would need. He grabbed his bag on his way out, but saw no trace of the little creatures he fought with the night before. He left the house and went directly to his motorcycle, the one that was meant for a James Bond film.

When Bane pulled around the corner and met up with Jessica, she was sitting impatiently in the driver's seat. He drove up the ramp attached to the trailer, locking his bike in place. He hopped down and lifted the ramp before moving to the driver's side of the Hummer.

"Slide over. I'm driving."

"What? Why should I slide over? I can drive this thing just as well as you can."

"Such typical arrogance. I should've expected as much. Look, we agreed that though I need your help to catch the magician, I still call the shots. If you don't want to help me, then just leave me the books, and I'll drop you off at my house."

"Come on! I'm all ready to go; the mirrors are perfect!" Jessica crowed.

"Just move over, will ya? "

"Fine!" came the petulant response.

By the time Bane got inside, Jessica was already pouting in the passenger's seat. She refused to even look at him, pretending she was alone in the vehicle. Bane hit a button, and his seat, side and rearview mirrors all adjusted to their preset locations. Even the compact disc player began to play Stevie Nicks, the most amazing singer he had ever heard. He closed his eyes for a moment, gathering his thoughts before he shifted into gear, pulling away from the side of the road.

"You just love throwing your weight around, don't you? " Jessica complained.

"Damn it, Jess. It's not like that! If we run into something that would force us into using evasive maneuvers, are you so damned confident your skills are higher than mine? I've been trained for this shit all my life. A few

139

years ago, you were still living in your ivory tower, playing daddy's little princess. We can't afford to be innocent, so leave the naïveté at the door!"

"Oh, the big bad Bane Bloodworth's off to save the world, is that it?"

"No, I'm not in this for the world." A dark look concealed his face when he paused, to look out his side window. "This all came to me because the killer mutilated my nephews! How many children are in your entire family? How many of them have been butchered by this bastard? This fucker knows you're in the game now, so who knows what could happen now?"

"Thanks for putting my mind at ease," Jessica snapped sarcastically.

"Jess, this isn't an outing in the park. If it were, I'd have packed some beer and food. I'm not trying to scare you, however; I am trying to get you ready for what you're about to witness," Bane said sympathetically. "I know that we've got to get to him before he gets to us."

"I guess I had better get reading then," Jess admitted, putting on her wounded puppy face.

"You might want to put your own clothes on," he said handing Jessica, her bag.

"In front of you? You wish!"

"Jess, you've got a great body. And let's not forget when we all went skinny dipping in the lake. I've seen it before," he stated calmly before switching to sarcasm. "Seeing you naked is my heart's desire."

It was clear she had nothing more to say, as she retreated into her usual sulking silence. Bane didn't really blame her for it; after all, she had lived a rather sheltered life, which he referred to as the "Ivory Tower Complex." In her mind, the things Bane had done in his life, past and present, weren't truly real. Now she had no way to deny all that he confided in her was true. The walls of her illusions cracked and crumbled; however, to her credit, she didn't show her terror on the outside. Bane could see it clearly, but then again, he had known Jess for many years.

Bane was actually getting used to her chilly silent treatments; she always expected him to apologize for things that were beyond his control. This time, though, Bane realized the stakes were far too high to even bother with. She'd have to get used to it in her own way, in her own time. Perhaps then she'd find some sort of growth that eluded her for many years. Jessica began flipping through the pages of the book she had treated so carefully before, indicating her frustration that Bane had yet to apologize.

Not this time, princess. I'd spill my last drop of blood for you, and I love you dearly; but I'm not about to say I'm sorry for your rude awakening. Sometimes you're the most caring and generous person I know; other times you become an iceberg. I guess I'll never truly figure you out. I suppose in some way you're probably thinking the same about me. I wish I could comfort you, take you into my arms and tell you it will all be all right, but I can't. *You need to see and feel how serious a situation we've got ourselves wrapped up in*, thought Bane sadly.

They drove in silence for almost an hour; the only time that shield of stillness was smashed was when Pamela called to get a situation update. Immediately Jessica disliked the FBI agent working the case, for whatever reason, she couldn't tell. By that point, they made it into Lake Zurich, down Route 12. As misfortune would have it, they had a killing off a street called Long Grove Rd. Pamela Phillips was already there waiting for Bane to arrive. He turned on the flashing beacon and slammed the pedal to the floor.

Driving like a madman, Bane whipped down Cuba Road, sliding almost out of control before he got the truck righted, fish-tailing around the corner onto a small unpaved road, Deer path, slowing down a bit so not to lose control over all the potholes in the road. He almost wished that it was winter because at least then the potholes would be compacted in by all the snow. Jessica held on as best as she could, with the unpaved road jostling things to and fro.

"Whatever she said to you doesn't mean you have to drive like a nutcase! You're gonna get us killed before we reach whatever our destination might be," Jessica exclaimed.

"Relax. I've been over this road a thousand times. I know it like the back of my own hand. Besides, this is exactly why I wanted to drive in the first place. We're headed to a crime scene; you can come in if you'd like; however, I don't think it would be wise."

"Why not?"

"Because they are children mutilated; it's not a pretty sight. I can't get most of what I've seen out of my head. I close my eyes, and I see nothing but carnage."

"Oh," Jessica stated, gnawing on her lower lip. "Maybe I could lend some insight into the scene though. I mean, you didn't bring me here for my looks."

"Really? Who says I didn't have you tag along for your looks? Beauty can help erase some of the horrors I've seen in these places."

"Because then you would've brought your wife."

"Alright, so you have additional qualities I need on this hunt. Just don't rule your looks out of hand," chuckled Bane, trying desperately to add some lighter notes over the tension that was building within them both.

"Sometimes you can be really sweet; other times you're a real jack-ass. I still can't figure you out after all these years."

"Yeah, well, from what I've heard, you ladies like a little mystery in your lives. Besides, after all the time you've spent with me, I still can't figure myself out. So it's no surprise that you're having trouble with it."

They came to an abrupt end to the unpaved road and turned left onto Long Grove Road. Still pressing the pedal to the floorboards, Bane raced by cars that were pulling over for him. Two minutes later, they arrived at the house Agent Phillips had called from. Ten Killdeer police cars were surrounding the entire block. Bane drove over the sidewalk to pass their cars and pulled into the driveway of the house. Several of the police approached the Hummer, hands on their side arms.

"Let me handle these morons. I've had dealings with them before, and they're not only incompetent but complete assholes," Bane stated, getting out of the Hummer.

"Who the hell are you? "

"Bane Bloodworth, Central Intelligence Agency. I'm working with Agent Phillips on this case, so go back to doing your jobs of guarding those streets. It's all you're really good for anyway." Bane held up his hand before they could object. "I'm in no mood to fuck around with you, so do as you're told, or I'll call your superiors."

Bane heard the passenger side of the truck close with a thump. Jessica decided to go inside with him, for better or worse. He nodded grimly to her, and she followed him up to the front door. They ducked under the yellow crime scene tape, noticing blood spattered across the marble tile floor. Bane escorted her around the blood evidence and toward the stairs. He knew that if Pamela was anywhere, it was in the children's room.

His phone vibrated against his chest; he looked at the caller ID screen. Bane suppressed a chortle; it was Pamela wondering where he was. Holding his index finger over the fingerprint reader, he answered the call.

"Hello?"

"Bane, how long until you get here? This one is really bad, a sleepover gone way out of control. At least ten children, the parents, and a baby kitten— all slaughtered. So how long will it take you to get to where I'm at?"

Standing in the doorway behind her, he said, "Shouldn't be too long." Turning his phone off, he had Jessica avert her eyes and tapped Pamela on the shoulder. Her cat-like reflexes showed clearly, as a muzzle of her weapon was pointed right at Bane's face. When she finally got over the shock, she lowered her gun.

"Don't ever do that!" Pamela shouted.

"Sorry. Anything new?"

"No, just more slaughters, butchers, and mutilations. Same magician's handkerchief. All of it is simply too much," Pamela answered.

"Let me have a look at his call sign; I'd like my associate to look it over. She worked in magic before I made her my assistant. She might be able to tell us more about it."

"She looks as though she might get sick coming in here, so I'll bring it out." Pamela offered caustically.

Upon her return, she handed the bagged item to Bane instead of Jessica. "Here. Let's see the wondrous insights she has that the other magicians I've consulted haven't come up with."

"Pamela, this is Jessica; Jess, this is Agent Pamela Phillips. You two crossed paths in Richmond, Wisconsin, at the Badger's Paw."

"These are used with a black light shining on them. If directed the right way, it conceals what the magician is doing. However, when used the opposite way, it'll wipe a number, name, and picture off one object and put it on another. It's all part of the illusion," Jessica stated. "That's the most I can do with this while it's in the plastic bag."

"Sorry, miss, but we might have wasted your time. We already knew that much."

"My name is Jessica," she said with more edge in her voice than Bane had ever heard her use before. "If you keep these things sealed up, how the hell do you expect me to learn anything about the handkerchief? "

Bane took the plastic bag back and stuffed it into his pocket. When Pamela saw that, she nearly started to scream. Bane forestalled her tirade with a handheld in the air. "Look, we've got a ton of these things; I'd like to keep one to examine."

"By the way, we were sent a package that had your name on it this morning. It's in my rental car, so on the way out, just grab it from the trunk," Pamela said coolly.

"Jess, in the back of the Hummer is a metal briefcase. Would you go out and grab it for me? This is important, so please no grief over it." He winked at her, and she calmed down.

The moment that Jessica went down the stairs, Bane turned to look at Pamela. "What was the reason behind that hostility? "

"What hostility?" Pamela asked in an innocent tone.

"Never have I seen you so . . . pissy. You might want to take a few days off or something. Clear your head, and look at it from a fresh point of view," Bane suggested, knowing that her arduous and haunting work of late wasn't behind the bad mood.

"It has nothing to do with that," she stated with an air of indignation.

"Then what does it have to do with? You were pretty rude to my assistant, and I'd like to know why."

Repressing her real reason, she responded, "Because you're a married man traipsing about with a pretty brunette, all while claiming to try to help me catch this killer. You men are all the same, shacking up with beautiful women when they should be focusing elsewhere."

"Look! She's a friend of mine, and now my personal assistant. That's where it ends, period. I'd expect you to act like a professional and treat her with some respect," Bane chided.

Pamela found Bane very attractive and secretly wanted to date him. She knew it would never happen while he was married; he was far too honorable to do otherwise. Pamela knew that she was merely transferring her desires onto Jessica, and it wasn't really fair. However, her pride wouldn't allow her to back down on Jess. She decided instead to apologize to Bane and try to keep herself in his good graces. He was very motivated in the case and very intuitive. Bane picked things up quickly, which made his catching up on everything he had missed before taking on the case easier.

"I'm sorry, Bane. I was letting my personal feelings get in the way of our work. I misjudged you, and it was wrong. Please accept my apologies."

"No big deal. Please try to remember she's a close friend of mine. I take hostility toward her very personally. Our relationship goes back all the way to high school. She knows me almost as well as my wife, not to mention that she is also taken." Bane glanced over his shoulder, noticing Jessica returning. "I realized something of a pattern going on in this whole mess. The magician is leaving a specific area in the country alone. Every state has been hit at least once, save for Indiana. From what I understand, the hotels in Indiana are booked for months. Parents are trying to keep their children safe. Apparently, they caught the pattern before we did."

"Interesting," Pamela mumbled as she scratched the information into her notebook. Glancing over at Jessica, then looking into Bane's eyes, she asked, "Do you want to take a look at the room now, or perhaps just skip it this time?"

Bane looked over his shoulder at Jessica; she had her jaw set and a determined look on her face. She obviously had chosen to go in on her trip to the truck. Jessica had steeled herself against the horror she might see. Her heart roared with each beat, and her palms were sweating. Bane knew that if he went in there, Jess would follow him in. Heaving a sigh, he entered the room and looked around, taking in as much as he could and as quickly as he could. He didn't want to keep Jess in that room if he didn't have to.

As Jessica looked around the room, her mind blazed in terror. In a flash, she was sweating profusely. The room swam around her—red, flesh, power ranger pajamas, toy ray guns, walls smeared with blood, a closet door slightly ajar. Suddenly she saw nothing but stars, and then darkness. Bane caught her in his arms before she hit the floor; he had noticed her swaying back and forth just a few seconds prior.

"I think I better get her out of here; I'll keep you up to date."

"I understand."

Pamela watched Bane carry Jessica out of the house in his arms, still feeling some jealousy toward Jess for getting to spend so much time with Bane. The dark storm clouds were rolling in as Bane got Jessica settled in the passenger seat, effectively eclipsing the pre-autumn sun from the sky. Carrying the airtight steel briefcase, Bane strode to Pamela's car and withdrew the package with a fear-filled knot in his stomach. He opened it, and within were the two doll heads of his nephews.

A gasp of horror and shock escaped his lips, despite his best efforts to contain it. He already suspected what the package had inside, but it still surprised him, which was the reason he brought the steel briefcase. With hands that looked like he was handling hot potatoes, Bane snatched each head and put it in his briefcase. Locking both sides, Bane returned to the Hummer to check on Jessica. She was still out cold; he pulled out his bandana and dabbed away the perspiration on her sweat-covered face.

Being a bit over paranoid was a trait that Bane had always been guilty of; this was no exception. He checked her pulse and spoke softly, trying to bring her back to a conscious state. She groaned softly, and immediately he

145

turned on the air conditioning, letting the cool air soothe her. When at last she came to, Jessica basically leaped into Bane's arms, sobbing uncontrollably. He rocked her back and forth consoling her.

"Shh. It's alright, sweetheart. Let it all out. That's it; take a long deep breath. It's gonna be alright."

Jessica was embarrassed that she crumbled as she had, but it all became too chaotic for her senses to handle. The swirling flashes she took in from the massacre not only horrified her but also made her feel physically ill. With the tragic combination, she was lost in darkness in a matter of moments. Now that she was back, she remembered each sight as though she had stared at it for hours. Jessica was happy she could share her tears with Bane, which she rarely showed to anyone.

Bane felt closer to Jessica than he had in such a long time. She seemed to build more walls every time he scaled, rammed through, or dug underneath one of those emotional blockades. With her crying uncontrollably on his shoulder, she shared with him a portion of herself that she showed no one else. He couldn't tell how long they sat there rocking back and forth. Strangely, Bane found that while he was giving his strength to Jessica, she was comforting him just as much as he was for her.

After Jessica managed to get herself under control, she glanced up at Bane and saw that his eyes were misty. In each eye, a tear threatened to spill over his lower eyelids.

"Bane? Are you okay?" Jess asked with a cracked voice.

"Yeah, why?" he answered stoically.

"You look like you might cry— that's why."

"I hate to see you cry; it upsets me, I guess."

She hugged him tightly around his neck. "You always act like the typical tough guy; every now and then, you show your kind, sensitive side. I've got to admit I like that person better than the usual hardened Bane."

"And I like it when you share your emotions with me. You show me a great deal of faith to allow me to see you when you're unguarded."

"Bane, I made such an ass out of myself in there. Those people will never take me seriously now."

Bane pulled back and looked her in her bloodshot eyes. "Hey, everyone has had a bad moment like that. Well, at least most law enforcement have, so they will understand. They'll just think you're a rookie, getting her feet wet. Don't you give that a second thought, alright?"

"I think we can beat the demon to his next target if we hurry. It's going to happen in Elmhurst, where I used to live. The child there will be devoured tonight. I can feel it in my blood. Maybe it's information I got while I was out cold. I'm not sure—" Jessica changed the subject before Bane cut her off.

"But what do we have to lose?"

"We've got to get there before sundown, or we'll miss him again," she explained.

Bane shifted into gear and drove across the lawn to leave the area, heading directly for Elmhurst. Jessica seemed a little surprised that it took so little convincing for him to follow her lead. However, he did bring her along for several reasons, and despite his attempts at humor, none of those reasons had to do with her looks. Lighting a cigarette for the first time since the night before, Bane switched on the twenty CD, disc changer under the backseats allowed for a wide variety of music. He kept at least five to ten tracks dedicated to Stevie Nicks and Fleetwood Mac.

Bane didn't have the eclectic tastes in music that Jess did, but there was a wide variation in the music he chose to put into his disk changer. From eighties music to heavy metal, a good portion of musical variety had still shown through. As they drove down the road, gloomy dark storm clouds began rolling in from the south. The storm turned the day from vibrant colors to a dull institutional gray, while the rain fell in large shards of silver splashes across the windshield.

Bane had flipped on the whirling red light that would force vehicles to yield and clear the way for his Hummer. It would be a few hours before sunset, and he knew that the traffic from the Lake Zurich area to Elmhurst would take at a maximum of an hour drive. That was including moronic drivers that crept across the expressways at a snail's pace. It was as if people forgot how to drive in the rain, even though they had done so many times before. With the density in each drop, floods emerged in the gutters, spilling slowly into clogged sewer drains.

Houses looked menacing, as did the bright red lights that flashed when the people in front of the Hummer hit their brakes. The roads began to look like dark asphalt as it was saturated by water and released oil. Neither thunder nor lightning accompanied the storm; it was just a heavy downpour. Growing tense, and increasingly irritated by the drivers in front of him, Bane finally flicked on the red revolving globe a top of his truck. After a few screeches of his siren, people seemed to put more stock that his vehicle had the right of way.

Though he wasn't racing down the road recklessly, Bane was driving faster than he should, considering the visibility and road conditions. In his right hand, he held Jessica's shaky left, while maintaining control of the vehicle with his left hand. The radio played the inspirational works of Mozart, soothing both their nerves. Bane was worried about Jess; she was still shaken up after what she had seen. The most noticeable sign was that she was clutching Bane's hand so tightly as if letting go would be the end of the world.

As the ramp on to York Road appeared, Bane switched off his flashing dome light, sliding into traffic as though he had been among the line of cars all along. "How long until you think this is going to go down?"

"Two hours, twenty-two minutes." Jessica shrugged when Bane cast her a sidelong look. "Don't ask me how I know it. I just do."

"Okay, let's say I see this guy. His little buddies seemed unaffected by my attacks; what's the best method of combating this fucker?" Bane asked.

"Well, your guns will do little good against the demon, too modern a weapon to affect him. You'll do your best work with your katana; the older it is, the better."

"I brought a bunch of swords, but I do have the two-hundred-year-old katana that my sensei gave me after my last tournament."

"Speaking of which, I noticed you specifically left one katana behind, one that you usually take with you."

"I think it had enough of an adventure last night, and the next time Thunder touches one of my weapons without my permission, that weapon will be the one that he uses to defend his life against me," Bane stated with great irritation, sliding his right hand free and placing it on the steering wheel.

"Hey! I thought you didn't listen?"

"Well, I heard enough. How do you think I had the sense to throw you my flannel shirt and pick up more clothes for you at the lake house? Interesting fantasy, but you were taking a great risk without knowing how good he was with a sword. My god! He could have killed you; my weapons are inhumanly sharp!"

"I still can't believe you were listening."

"After he put the sword away, I stopped. It just had me worried. How do you think I'd feel if one of my own weapons was the cause of your death?

" he countered. "What kind of a pervert do you take me for anyway? For crying out loud, I was looking for a radio station, and then I heard your secret little thoughts about him as he began twirling *my* sword!"

"Lighten up. It was no big deal. No one got hurt, and it was fun, all right? It's not like he hurt your precious sword or contaminated it in some way. I don't know why I have to justify myself to you. If you weren't eavesdropping, you'd never had known!"

"My swords and I are attuned to the same Chi rhythms; that's the big deal."

"Plus, you must have been listening longer than that. You grabbed your tanto knife from the rack and tossed it onto the counter!" Jessica rebutted.

"That's why it didn't feel right. You were using it for your sex games!" Bane lapsed into a very angry silence, trying not to say something he'd regret later. He hit a button on his steering wheel, changing to the music to match his mood. That was when Metallica doused the truck with pounding bass, heart thumping drums, and wailing guitar riffs. Bane turned the volume up to its maximum and slammed the gas pedal to the floor.

When they got to the building where the murder would occur, they had some time to kill. So Bane pulled out one of the occult books and began searching for the name, Xanithsabar. Jessica was about to complain and caution him, but with the music so loud, and Bane ignoring her, she knew the effort would be futile. Besides, the more he knew, the safer Jessica would feel. Fortunately he didn't start a cigarette as he'd normally do while sitting down to read; instead, he pulled out a thermos from the back seat, took several deep gulps, and passed it to Jessica without looking up once.

Two hours passed by through the doors of music and reading, and when Bane's watch started to beep, he knew it was time to get inside. He cut the music and turned to Jessica. "Alright, I'm going in."

"*We're* going in," Jessica corrected.

"Any idea if the parents are home?"

"Not a clue."

"Well, I better get the rest of my gear on," Bane reported as he got out of the Hummer and opened the back door. Jessica followed him out of the truck and waited for him to hand her items they'd need while inside. Instead, he placed a sword under his coat and another over one shoulder, making certain neither caused an obstruction with his other weapons. Just as he was about to close the door, Jessica stopped him.

"What about me? I'm going in too, ya know."

"I don't think that's a good idea."

"Deal with it— I'm going. So give me a sword or something."

"Jess, you don't know how to use a sword. You're just as likely to hurt yourself as the killer. Here are a couple of guns that you can shoot; that should suffice for now." He started loading her web belt with spare clips of ammunition for the two guns she carried. "Follow my lead in there, and do exactly what I say. No arguments, clear?"

Jessica nodded her head, despite the fear that surged through her veins like a bolt of lightning. In the street lamps, her face looked like a mannequin—rigid and unmoving. Bane pulled out his identification, so when he arrived at the door, he'd have no trouble with the parents. The building was red brick with white shudders and aqua doors. Two-car garages separated each door from the other in the group of townhouses. He took one step up onto a slab of concrete that rose to the doorway; he rang the bell, awaiting a response.

Bane noticed the peephole's slight glow was diminished; then someone called out, "Who's there?"

Holding his badge in front of the eyepiece, Bane responded, "Special agent Bane Bloodworth. I'm on the child mutilation case; I need a moment of your time."

The door opened cautiously, and a woman's pudgy face took a closer look at his identification, and then opened the door wider. "This is my assistant Jessica. We're afraid that your child may be the next victim. May we come in?"

"Oh my god!" she shouted, retreating from the doorway. The woman was about to charge up the steps from the door before Bane caught her.

"Ma'am, let me go. If he is in there, you'd be in great danger!" He passed by her. Gun drawn, Bane took the steps two at a time.

Her husband looked astounded to see Bane running through his home with a gun in his left hand. When Bane reached the second set of stairs, he could hear snaps and scrapes. Bane's legs pumped harder to get up to the bedrooms. Jessica could be heard running behind him, but Bane had a great lead on her. Bursting through the only door that was closed, Bane caught his first sight of the mysterious killer. The evil creature looked exactly as he expected him to from the descriptions in Jessica's dreams.

In the magician's hands was a small child, whose head was totally mutilated. Bane fired off several shots before he remembered that guns would do little against such an ancient enemy. By the time he drew his katana, Bane heard Jessica gasp in terror behind him. The magician half-hissed, half growled at them, with the whites of his eyes turning red.

"Xanithsabar! You die tonight!" Bane shouted, attacking the demon with a forward thrust from his katana.

"Oh my poor little Robert!" came a cry from the hallway.

Xanithsabar dove into the closet, closing it behind him. Bane grabbed the door handle, flinging the door open, only to be blinded by a retina-burning blue burst of light. When he looked again, the demon was gone, and so was the small child!

"Damn it! Shit! Damn it. Damn it! Shit!" Bane shouted out in his fury.

"Where's my baby? Where is my baby? " the mother cried out from the hallway.

Jessica stood numb, staring at the spot where the magician had been devouring the child. Behind her, the child's mother and father stood weeping in fear and loss. Bane sheathed his sword and examined the room. Finally, the child's father entered the room. "Where the hell is our baby? I don't think that's an unreasonable question for a parent to want to know."

"Sir, to be honest . . . I just don't know. I'm looking for clues right now that might give me an idea where that creature took your child. So please step back; I need to be sure you're not contaminating evidence. I know this is frustrating, but this is the best we can do right now," Bane answered using his most sympathetic, yet commanding voice.

Snatching out his phone, he called Pamela, "We've had another one. This time he left witnesses." Bane gave the address of the crime scene so she could have her people go over the place for evidence. Plus then she would be stuck answering questions Bane didn't want to, such as how he knew ahead of time it was going down, or how the guy escaped into a closet and was gone in a flash.

He examined the wall where his bullets impacted; they seemed to go straight through the magician. It was the reminder he needed to use his sword, but that too didn't hit him. The fear he had in his heart just wanted him to get out of the door. Bane escorted Jessica out of the room, with the parents following him closely, asking a thousand questions at once. Finding it hard to keep his mind straight enough to get out of the house, he could give them no answers. Jessica was so shaken that she was acting as though she were an automaton; her body was just going through the motions.

Bane led Jessica out of the house and into the Hummer, pulling away from the scene as quickly as possible. He needed to find a place to crash out and absorb what he recently witnessed. His mind was speeding him toward the abyss of insanity. Nearby he located a Holiday Inn and swung into the parking lot. Leaving Jessica in the car, he got them checked into a room, and then drove the car around to the nearest entrance to the room.

Without being in his right mind, Bane completely forgot to grab any bags from the Hummer. He cautiously led Jessica to the outer door, down the hallway until they reached the room. Sliding the key card into the lock, Bane waited for the light to blink green before entering their suite. Bane placed Jessica on the bed and checked the room thoroughly before flopping down on the other side of the bed. Nothing in his experience had ever prepared him for hunting demons. He'd hunted men that acted like demons, but never the real thing.

His mind was reeling with no hope of recovery, teetering on the precipice of the horizon. Jessica had basically shut down; her body still moved when guided, but for all intents and purposes, her mind had left the building. Bane's phone rang, over and over, going unanswered; the caller ID on the phone showed it was Pamela Phillips. He didn't have a clue how to explain everything he saw, but it was a good bet that she had learned of how they arrived during the commission of the crime— she would demand to know how.

Jessica rolled over and grabbed Bane's left arm, holding it like a teddy bear to ward off the bogeyman. Bane didn't even move, his eyes staring straight at the ceiling, his brain replaying what he'd seen in a heart-stopping loop. He couldn't get a grip on what was happening, and since it was beyond his experience, Bane felt incredibly vulnerable, whereas he used to be so confident in any situation that he even carried that confidence in the way he walked, talked, even slept, as though the world would be all right so long as he was in it.

Bane wasn't megalomaniac as to believe that nonsense; rather, he rarely felt threatened. He had table manners that Emily Post would be envious of, a natural talent for combat that even Bruce Lee would covet, and the charisma to make even the most pessimistic think positively in him. While Bane never found himself to be very attractive, most women tended to disagree, an anomaly he had never solved, a puzzle that was missing several pieces, just like his case.

Bane withdrew a cigarette from the pack in his coat pocket; with his right hand, he lit the tip. Inhaling the billowy cloud of smoke, allowing it to fill his lungs, Bane started to relax enough to meditate so when he was done with what he called cancer tube, he would be ready to try to grasp everything that happened in the past two weeks. "Not another one," Jessica groaned. You're gonna stink up the room." She then lapsed into silence, still clinging to Bane for support. He continued to pull in fulfilling carcinogens into his lungs and expelling them without regard to Jessica's protests.

After crushing his cigarette out in the ashtray, Bane concentrated on his breathing, slowing his heartbeat and lapsing into his own mind. Twenty minutes after he began meditating, and things started to clear up for him a little, all he saw was darkness.

When he awoke at nine-thirty in the morning, he noticed that Jessica was draped across him. Bane nearly leaped from the bed in shock when she moved and felt their skin shift. *We're naked! Holy shit! How the fuck did that happen? I gotta admit she looks damn good naked, but what the hell happened last night?* Bane thought in confusion. He'd never admit it to himself, but it felt good to have such intimate contact with someone after what they'd been through. Bane had no idea how far things had gotten, or if anything happened between himself and Jessica.

He seriously hoped that nothing happened. Bane would never willingly violate his wedding vows. Carrie was already going to be very pissed off about them being naked in bed together, but if she discovered that he cheated, she'd never forgive him, not that he could've forgiven himself. It was completely against his belief system and code of honor.

"Jessica, wake up. We need to talk—."

153

Chapter Eleven

Pamela Phillips found it hard to concentrate on the pages in front of her. Bane wasn't answering his phone. He obviously struck a good lead and didn't have time to call her, but where did that lead come from? According to her reports, he fired several shots without hitting the killer, before drawing a sword and attacking in melee form. Bane had him cornered in the closet, when the magician hit Bane with a pyrotechnical trick to escape. However, neither of the parents of the missing child saw anyone use that hallway. The blinds over the window hadn't been disturbed, nor had the quarter-inch layer of dust that covered them.

She couldn't believe that Bane was that bad a shot, especially after reading the newspaper articles about his proficiency, not to mention his method of changing tactics inside the room, using a sword when his shots missed. Pamela found Bane's methods completely unconventional but figured that was why he made such a good agent. When she phoned his immediate superior, he had nothing but rave reviews for the man. He had stated that there was no agent better than Bane Bloodworth. She thanked Tom for his time and ended the call.

Pamela feared that this was the most dangerous serial killer ever encountered. The closest in ferocity and sheer numbers was Pedro Alonso Lopez, known as the Monster of the Andes, though Lopez had covered far more ground, three countries, whereas the magician was localized to the United States. Lopez had managed to kill over three hundred children before he was apprehended in 1980. The magician had tallied up four hundred, fifty-six child murders, and was still on the loose.

Restless and worried, Pamela began field stripping her sidearm; most people employ different methods of relaxing, but she enjoyed the way everything had its place in the firearm. Once the weapon was clean, she could reassemble the gun, bringing order out of chaos. For her, that meant a lot, since it was her job as an agent of the bureau to bring order from the cases she was assigned. Federal homicide cases tended to be very messy; she cut through all the crap and got the job done.

Looking at the table before her, she picked up the Smith & Wesson and deftly dismantled the gun. Cursing softly, Pamela rose from her seat, walked across the room, and retrieved her cleaning kit. Each piece of her weapon was cleaned thoroughly; the parts that required oiling were swabbed with the gun oil. After a quick wipe down, she put all the pieces back together. She slammed the magazine into the gun and chambered a round.

The view from her room wasn't a great one; she had taken up residence in a room at the Holiday Inn down the road from the crime scene. The couple in the room next to her seemed to enjoy a very avarice sexual relationship. They had the walls shaking; even the paintings were being shaken loose from their mountings. Screams and squeals of delight penetrated the room like a sword through silk. They seemed to be at it all night long; for hours on end, they writhed in passion.

The couple kept her up all night, not that she could've slept much anyway. Pamela had a very rough time sleeping when she was involved in murder cases. Until they were solved, she would view the crime scenes, the aftermath, along the back of her eyelids. However, the couple's loud lovemaking disrupted Pamela's attempts to sleep. Finally, Pamela decided to take a long soak, followed by a quick shower to start her day. She'd try to call Bane after lunch. If he still didn't answer, then she'd begin to worry about him.

He was a very tough guy and could handle himself in the most dangerous situations. However, he did have to babysit that Jessica woman. Pamela still believed that something was going on between Bane and Jess, but knew her feelings might lead her in the wrong direction when it came to him. She was fascinated by him; something about the way he moved made her has sparked a fire deep within her.

Looking out her window she wondered aloud, "Where are you, Bane Bloodworth?"

***

"Wha . . . what?" Jess murmured sleepily.

"Wake up!" Bane stated in a state of panic. "TNT! We're naked!"

Her eyes blinked up at him lazily; then suddenly she understood what Bane was saying. At that point, Jessica was totally awake, like being hit with a bucket of cold water. She started to move over away from Bane, taking the covers with her.

"Whoa, easy there. I said *we* are naked. Unless you want a good view of what I got; I'd leave me with one of the sheets."

"Did we —?"

155

"Screw? I don't know," Bane interrupted quickly. "I can't seem to remember much about last night. At all!"

"Neither can I," she admitted, clutching the comforter all the way over to her clothes that were folded neatly on the dresser.

"Wait!" Bane shouted as he leaped from the bed, naked as the day he was born. However, this time, he was holding a gun. That hadn't happened when he was born, despite some rumors to the contrary.

"What?" Jessica cried out.

"How likely is it, that if we did have sex, we'd take the time to fold our clothes? You? Okay I could see that, but I'm not that anal-retentive. I'd simply toss my shirt and pants to the floor for later pickup," he explained, keeping his gun aimed at their clothing. "It seems too easy a trap to spring— back away."

Bane kicked at his shirt, pants, and socks. Nothing stirred, so he ventured closer; he went so far as to pick up the shirt and give it a good shake. No tar monsters were hiding in the folded clothing. He tossed Jessica her clothes, not thinking that in order for her to catch them, she'd have to drop her blanket. Bane simply slid into his pants, pulled his shirt on, and then thoroughly checked the room for signs of intrusion.

By the time Jessica squirmed into her bra and panties, Bane completed his security check on the hotel room. No indications that anyone had been in their room, besides them. Wired beyond frustration, Bane grabbed his cigarette pack from the pine-paneled bedside table. He lit a cigarette while he paced the room in his bare feet. Once Jessica had her clothes on, she noticed that Bane seemed to be talking to himself silently because he was gesturing like he was carrying on a normal conversation.

"Hey, Bane?"

"Yeah?"

"Will you bring my bag in from the truck? I need clean clothes and a hot shower."

"No problem. Just bolt the door and wait for me to come back. Don't let anyone else in."

"I'm not a fucking idiot, ya know, and I'm not ten years old," Jessica snapped.

Bane left the room shaking his head, going to retrieve a clean shirt for himself and the bag Jess had requested. He realized she was under stress as well, so he didn't want to pick a fight. Complying with her wishes quickly usually avoided an argument pretty well, most of the time. Stepping into the

156

midmorning air, the sounds of traffic on the road filled his ears. Bane walked casually toward the Hummer, as though he wasn't holding a Ruger in his right hand.

Bane fished his keys from his left pocket and opened the truck's rear door. Sounds of baseballs rolling around echoed from the steel briefcase. He grabbed a black silk shirt, Jess's bag, and the briefcase hauling them back to the hotel. Once inside, silence rushed Bane's ears, except for the occasional burst of energy from within the briefcase. Since his hands were full, Bane had to kick on the door in order to knock.

"I've got a big fucking gun in my hands, and I'll shoot! Go away!" Jessica shouted from inside the room. "My friend's coming back here soon, and he'll kick your ass!"

"Your friend doesn't want to get shot with one of his own guns, and I've got too much in my hands to properly whoop my own ass. So open the door." Bane answered with a slight smile.

Jessica peaked out the curtains; in her left hand was indeed a big gun. Seeing it was Bane, she opened the door, bolting the moment he was inside. With one hand, she snatched her bag and disappeared into the bathroom. What amazed Bane was that she took the gun with her into the bathroom. He figured her for a smaller weapon, but she had been trained on revolvers for her boss' magic act, which got Bane thinking about the fact that he hadn't considered her boss for a suspect.

He was a magician, so the evidence would fit. She never really talked about him, saying as little about him as possible. Her boss would know about Bane, since every time he met one of Jessica's friends, he or she seemed to already know him. Obviously, she talked about him frequently, probably telling one of the amusing anecdotes he was involved in. Jessica was unaware of the killings until she went on vacation, far away from him.

Bane began pacing again; his thoughts turned away from the case. He was trying desperately to recall the events after he started meditating. Just as he was starting to catch on to what was going on, darkness fell over his mind. So he either fell asleep before he understood everything or his memory had an extensive gap. Jessica said she too was having trouble remembering the previous night. Perhaps they were drugged at some point?

His hand ran across the rough surface of his stubble-covered face, casting a dark shadow over his cheeks. Instead of doing his hair, Bane tied it under a bandana to keep it out of his way. With a few sprays of cologne, he donned his silk shirt, tucking it loosely into his pants. After he shimmied into his extensive web belt of weapons, Bane approached the briefcase. In the background was the sound of running water from the shower.

He didn't open the steel briefcase because if they had to get out of the building fast, Jess was far too naked and wet to be sprinting for the truck. However, Bane did want to hold the case in his hands. By the feel of the movement, he hoped to ascertain if the doll heads he put inside had changed shapes. When in doll head form, they didn't seem to pose a threat; in their tar monster shape, they were terrifying and dangerous. From the way the briefcase rocked, Bane figured that the doll heads were still dormant.

Dropping the briefcase on the linen-stripped bed, Bane finished getting dressed for the remainder of the day. Though the weather didn't call for it, Bane wore a sleeveless leather trench coat that covered most of his weapons. It brought down more heat, but not much more. The black coat was meant for spring and fall weather. He checked his weapons, before securing them into place. Bane rolled up his sleeves as the shower stopped, returning to his pacing mode. He caught his reflection in the mirror, which revealed a typical biker—the look he was going for. Most people underestimated bikers.

Not liking the sleeves on his silk shirt with his coat, Bane tugged at the seams until the entire arm was showing. He repeated the process for the other side and then smiled at himself in the mirror. "I'm stylin' now," Bane muttered to himself. A few minutes later Jessica returned from the bathroom fully dressed. She had taken one of his holsters and diminished it to fit her by pulling on the straps; the gun seated securely in place.

"Ready to go?" Jessica asked, combing her wet hair before packing her bag.

"Yeah, we should be ready. I want you to be in the driver's seat of the truck."

"Oh? I get to drive for a change?" Jessica asked playfully.

"Yes, you get to drive the truck. I want you to unhitch my bike from the trailer. I've got a headset for my iPhone; the Bluetooth rocks! We'll keep in touch that way for this afternoon."

"Wait. You're not ditching me, are you?"

"No, Jess. I'd never do that—."

"We still don't know if anything happened last night, so there isn't any reason to feel uncomfortable around me or to you. I'm going to lay a trap, and maybe snag a lead. I want you a safe distance from the trap," Bane continued as though he hadn't been interrupted.

He gave Jessica a gentle hug. "Jess, even if we did actually have sex, I wouldn't feel uncomfortable around you. Yes, I'd be hurt because I betrayed my wedding vows, but it wouldn't be your fault. It would be one more precious memory that only you and I would share— that is if we do remember it at all."

"Hey, if you had sex with me, you'd remember it, buster!" Jessica smacked him on the arm.

"Doesn't speak well of me either, Jess. Anyway, I want you in Palatine until at least noon. We'll meet at the Gators bar off of Rand Road, and as I said, I've got the headset for my iPhone. If this works out, I might have a real chance of catching this fucker once and for all! I will have the perfect bait."

"Alright, you go play hero but remember you'll need me when you face the demon. You've got to promise me that I'll be there when you take on that fight. Promise me— on your honor."

Bane walked her to the door silently; he moved like a ghost, not making a single noise as he took each step. His mind was reviewing all he had to do for the day: First, he had to get some information on Jessica's boss, and then he would mess around with the doll heads. After he gathered his strength, Bane would contact Jessica for the final showdown between the demon and them. He was working his mind overtime on this case, and finally, he seemed to think he had a viable way to destroy this sucker.

"Okay, fine, Jess. I'll pledge on my honor. I promise you will be there— I promise," he said as he closed the door behind her. Something about the way he said that, and the look in his eyes, sent a prickly chill cascading down from her skull to her buttocks.

Chapter Twelve

arm winds blew softly through the curtains of the hotel room. Outside the sun melted across the electric blue sky. Bane, using every ounce of caution he had deep within himself, opened the steel briefcase. Tightness constricted his chest, with anticipation pounding against his lungs like a sledgehammer; only to be released when the case had been opened. He found that the doll heads were still in their proper form, so he pulled out one before resealing the briefcase. Bane placed the head on the desk, and while he waited for it to do something, he began using his iPhone to surf the Internet.

Most of his searches on Jessica's boss came up with show dates and fan sites. Bane grew frustrated, wishing he had gotten his computer from the truck before Jess left. His suspicions didn't dissipate with the lack of information he wanted; in fact, it increased exponentially. Bane nearly jumped out of his seat when his phone's alert went off, scaring him half out of his mind. Looking over at the doll head, making certain it was stationary, he checked his alert.

Without taking his eyes off the doll head, he called Pamela. "It's Bane."

"Where the hell have you been? I've been trying to call you all last night, and most of this morning!" Pamela interrogated, surprised to hear from Bane.

"I had a rough night; that magician is one scary mother-fucker! I needed time to collect my thoughts. How did my background check go?"

"Your what?"

Bane chuckled. "The background check you ran on me. How did it turn out? Was it everything you hoped it would be?"

"How did you—?"

"Did you really think I wouldn't hear about it?" Bane grinned for all he was worth. "I mean, you even called my people, like they wouldn't let me know you contacted them."

"I was just —"

"You were just trying to see if I'm as good as I seem to be, and weren't worried in the least about my involvement in the case, right?"

"Err . . . uh, yeah."

"Well, I've got a few quick leads to follow up on before I'll have anything to report. Do me a favor. Do some research on the Resplendent Roberts— where he is, what he's been up to for the last few months, and everything from down to what his cat eats for supper."

"I want to know what the hell happened last night."

"And I'll tell you, once it all falls into place. You wouldn't buy my explanation right now anyway, so let's save it until I have my ducks in a row."

"Fuck your ducks! What if some kid gets killed because you didn't share your information with me? The blood will be on your hands then!" Pamela snarled.

"Then I'll have to bear the weight of that guilt— but I've got no proof. Until I do, I can't use that information," Bane stated calmly. "My nephews were killed; don't you think I want to stop this guy? I've got to get him, but only if I get the right one. It's meaningless if we don't catch the correct serial killer. I don't want to mangle an innocent man!"

"I've kept you up to date on every crime scene, each clue, and everything I knew. Don't you think it would be fair for you to do the same for me? If you get a tip to where this guy is going to hit next, share it with me! Damn it, I've been on this case from the beginning. Besides, you're the one that lost him last night— not me."

"Excuse me? If you were there, he'd have torn you to pieces with his bare hands. At least I got out of there with my life!" Bane countered, an angry tone piercing his voice. "When I know something for sure, I'll let you know. So, please, just do that research. I've got work to do right now, so I'm hanging up. Good-bye."

He closed his hand around his iPhone hard, staring at the doll head shaking under its own power. Bane noticed the room growing warmer by the second, and his heart was exploding beneath his chest. Sweat ran from his left temple, straight down his cheek. He knew that his body was dumping gallons of adrenaline into his bloodstream. Energy surged through his muscles, pounding behind his eyes.

Bane watched a crack appear along the mouth of the doll head, resembling a vicious sneer. The crack began spilling out black oozing tar along the dresser. With sword in hand, Bane approached the head for closer examination. While he was trying to walk over to the dresser, his feet didn't move. They were trapped inside a serious pool of fear quicksand. Closing his eyes, Bane yanked his feet into motion through sheer will power. Though he didn't fear death, he wasn't in any hurry to die.

More rapidly than before, the unidentified ooze began to form into a body for the doll head. Suddenly, rows of sharp barbed teeth appeared within the open mouth of the creature. The liquid formed into talons, reminiscent of vampire claws. The fingernails weren't very long, but they were narrow and jagged. From its back, sharp black needles burst through the thick black skin running the length of its spine. A small spike emerged just above each heel, and atop both kneecaps.

All of a sudden, the eyes blinked. When they opened again, the doll's irises were serpentine, and the rest changed to a murky yellow color. It rose rapidly; having already learned to control its body from the last time Bane encountered the creature. Strangely, the shoulder blades on the creature's back were throbbing visibly. At last, two leathery looking wings appeared from its back.

Preoccupied with its new body parts, the demon's avatar fell prey to Bane's rapid attack. His blade streaked through the air, slicing the creature's legs off. The legs reverted to a liquid form; causing the creature to shriek in pain with rage. Bane nearly dropped his sword to cover his ears in order to shield them from the painfully high-pitched screech. Wincing, he twirled his sword into position for another strike.

The creature pointed at the goo that once were his legs and snarled at Bane menacingly. Flapping its wings it lifted off the dresser, hovering just off the surface. In midair, the creature did a somersault, while launching its dark needles from its spine. Bane threw up one arm to shield his face while twirling the sword defensively in an attempt to knock the needles from the air. Several of the needles pierced the skin on his left forearm sending a shocking pain up his shoulder.

Having distracted Bane, the creature landed on a set of reformed legs from the ooze that had been severed from its body. Hissing wildly, the creature catapulted itself at Bane, claws flailing chaotically. Bane backed away, still whirling his sword in a defensive spin; he didn't like the new development. His left arm had gone totally numb, paralyzed in some way. He had to admit his fear was reaching the point it was when he ran from the creatures before.

Then it struck him that was exactly what he needed to do. After he escaped from them at the lake house, they must've reverted to their natural state. So, with a quick slash of his sword, a wing dropped to the floor, and Bane made a hasty retreat.

***

The demon growled and frothed at the mouth over the failure of the avatar. With a voice rumbling like a storm in the depths of hell, the demon cursed venomously, "That damn Bane Bloodworth! How dare he try to thwart me! I should've had him broken by now! The rat fucking asshole! I've done most of my best tricks, and yet he lives, not to mention his emotional wellbeing is just as stable as it ever was!

"I should have eliminated him myself last night. If that moron Bane manages to decipher half of the information in the books he's read so far, I might have to up the ante! I must strike at him in a most personal way. His wife and friends will do for now!"

When the demon concentrated, speaking in jarring tongues, it couldn't seem to enter the bunker in which he knew they were hiding. All the closet doors were shut tight, and for some reason, they all had locks on them. And the beds were all supported by concrete lifts and box springs, giving it no room to appear under. It snarled a malevolent curse on Bane for being such a paranoid, yet well-prepared mortal. The demon decided that a new plan was in order; Bane was starting to catch on.

It didn't have to take the direct approach; there were plenty of closets and beds in the rest of the house. The demon would just have to get them to open the door to the bunker in order to kill them. That effort would definitely break Bane because he took great care to seal them away from harm. It could go after other children in Bane's family, but that was old. The demon preferred to be original.

When Bane started meditating the night before, the demon could sense the truth being revealed. It couldn't allow Bane to remember what he had learned when he thought it all through. For the demon, it was easier to perform a memory loss chant than deal with Bane Bloodworth if he knew the truth. He would also then know how to destroy the demon, and it couldn't allow that; its life span had lasted for centuries, and no mortals were about to change it.

The demon stepped into a makeshift closet, before shimmering and disappearing.

***

Pamela watched out her window in amazement as Bane raced out of the hotel she was staying in and hopped on his motorcycle. In a flash, he was racing away before she had a chance to even contemplate how to get his attention. She hadn't noticed the Hummer in the parking lot, because her car was parked in front of the building causing her to walk through the hotel to get to her room. What was remarkable about the way he took off was that he never glanced back—even once.

Pamela knew she had pissed him off on the call earlier, so she decided to do the research he had requested before calling him back. That would lend her the perfect reason to get in touch with him again. Something about him captivated her; she wasn't sure if it was his open and honest approach to the world or if she was simply lonely. However, she couldn't help noticing how good he looked as he rode away.

Agent Phillips called her assistant to order several agents onto the task of crawling up "The Resplendent Roberts's" ass and learning everything about the man. If Bane thought he was tied into the killings in some way, she had to at least act on the lead. Even though she was certain Bane was hiding something from her, he seemed ahead of her on this case. She needed his help to catch the killer, and though he didn't seem to trust her enough to tell her everything, Pamela realized that was typical of a member of the CIA, to which the unnamed agency she believed reported.

***

Jessica phoned Bane when she got into Palatine; she could hear his motorcycle racing down the expressway. She pictured his long hair and sleeveless trench coat whipping in the wind, his eyes shielded by mirrored sunglasses that wrapped around his face languidly. The day turned out to be a pleasant one, with a light breeze and the sun shining in the sky. So many different shades of blue colored the sky; one would be hard pressed to attempt to count them all.

"Bane? You sound shaky. Are you alright?"

"Yeah, no sweat. What's up?" Bane brushed aside the concerned voice.

"I've made it into Palatine with no trouble. Did you get what you needed?"

"Not yet, but I'm working on it. Hey, let me ask you a question." Not pausing to hear her answer, he asked, "Where is the Resplendent Roberts right now?"

"He's working on new illusions for the act; that's why I had time off before our next show," Jessica responded skeptically. "Why?"

"Where would he go to practice or create these new illusions?"

"He goes to his cabin in the mountains; that's where he set up a large stage for him to practice on. Doesn't have a phone, television, just a CD playing Jukebox with his favorite titles in it, and tons of room to work. What's going on?"

"Do you have the address of the place? I want to send some people out there to protect him. If he means something to you, he could be in danger now that you're part of this," Bane lied, knowing if Jessica thought he was investigating Roberts, she'd become adversarial defending her mentor.

"Yeah, sure, no problem. He's not going to like the interruption though; he takes his illusions very seriously."

"I suppose he'll take care to remember that they'll be protecting his life."

"Oh my god!" Jessica shouted.

"What? " Bane asked, opening the throttle on his bike even further, topping speeds of ninety miles an hour.

"I just got a flash of your house by the lake, but it was a brief image of the house. What do you suppose that means?" Jessica asked with concern.

"Meet me at the gas station at the corner of Route 12 and Route 22 in Lake Zurich. We're heading back up there."

"Again? Jesus, we're starting to go in circles!" Jessica complained.

"I don't think we have a choice. I'm gonna put on some speed here, so I'll call you when I get close to the gas station."

"Alright, talk to you soon. Drive safely."

A terse laugh was all she heard before Bane disconnected the line.

After hitting the end button on his cell phone located at his hip, Bane opened his throttle up all the way. The motorcycle lurched forward in an explosion of power. He wove in between cars and trucks at incredible speeds, using the shoulder when there was no room to pass any other way. Cars honked at him as he rocketed past them in a reckless, psychotic manner.

Behind him, flashing lights were approaching rapidly. As he glanced in his right mirror, Bane shook his head in irritation. While trying to maintain control of his bike at such a high rate of speed, Bane fumbled with his stupid "smart" phone, trying to dial the emergency dispatch. Normally Bane had no trouble dialing numbers while riding; then again, he didn't often ride that fast.

"Emergency dispatch. What is your emergency?" came the voice.

"This is Special Agent Bane Bloodworth, I'm traveling on Route 53 on a motorcycle. I'm being pursued by a marked squad car. My identification number is . . . " Bane prattled off the information the dispatcher needed to verify him as a law enforcement official.

"How can we assist you, sir?"

"First, you can ask him to stop following me and instead request he clear the way for me. Hell, just not distracting me with the flashers would be fine. I don't like it when anyone tailgates me, and I'm traveling at a very high rate of speed here! I prefer to concentrate on the road," Bane ordered rapidly.

"Yes, sir, we've contacted the unit. She'd be happy to provide an escort. To what location are you going?"

"Routes 12 and 22. From there to Wisconsin, but getting me to the gas station at the intersection will suffice."

"Yes, sir. We're happy to cooperate."

"Thank you." Bane hit the end button returning his hand to his handlebars.

The squad car pulled around Bane, he waved a grateful hand at the car as it swung in front of him. Traffic moved to the right, accommodating the cop car's flashing lights. At that rate of speed, every pebble felt like a boulder threatening to toss him out of control. Fortunately, Bane had full confidence in his motorcycle and his ability to ride it. He paid top dollar to ensure it was fit perfectly for him, and it was a one-of-a-kind beauty. In minutes, they were entering Lake Zurich from Rand Road; the traffic was light, so the sirens were no longer needed, yet the flashing lights continued.

He slowed his bike as he approached the gas station; he saw the Hummer at one of the gas pumps being fueled, but he couldn't see where Jessica was. Pulling into the lot after Bane, the squad car rolled down the passenger side window.

"Are you sure you don't want an escort to the border, sir?"

"No, that's my Hummer; it's equipped with a siren and flashing light. Thank you very much for your assistance, officer. You're an excellent driver. I'll be certain to extend our appreciation of your work to your superiors," Bane answered charmingly.

166

Bane drove his motorcycle onto the trailer and began securing it before Jessica appeared from within the building. She was carrying a carton of Marlboro Lights, two one-liter bottles of Dr. Pepper, and a new pair of sunglasses. Jess was visibly surprised to see Bane strapping his bike into place when she walked out. Restraining her urge to run over and give him a big hug, Jessica settled for a relieved smile.

"Bane!" Jessica shouted. "How did you get here so fast? "

"Wheels of fire, Jess. Wheels of fire."

Rolling her eyes knowingly, she then asked, "I assume you're driving?"

"Yeah. We gotta haul ass. If your flash has anything to do with our family and friends, we've got to get there before something happens!"

The blood drained from Jessica's face but to her credit, didn't say a word. She walked around and removed the nozzle from the gas tank, then carefully topped off the tank of Bane's bike before completing the transaction. Meanwhile Bane got behind the wheel, and had the Hummer running before Jess even got inside. Just as Bane was about to drive off, he pulled to the back of the gas station parking lot and unhitched the trailer. He wanted to make good time, and that would be easier without hauling a trailer carrying motorcycle around with them.

"Jess, call this gas station and let them know we've left the trailer here and will be back for it as soon as possible." He tossed her his identification. "Let them know this is an emergency and that nothing is to happen to that bike."

Tires squealed in joy, as the smell of burnt rubber flooded the air in tufts of smoke. Already traveling at twenty miles an hour, Bane flipped on the beacon and swung into traffic, without sparing a glance to see if anyone was coming. Jessica pulled her seatbelt on. She opened a pack of cigarettes and lit one for Bane. She pressed the filter against his lips as he stared at the road ahead. He accepted the cigarette and pressed the window button to allow the smoke to be pulled out of the truck.

"I got you something to drink too. Just let me know when you're thirsty." She paused. "Bane, do you think they are all okay?"

"I hope so. Your flashes lately seem to come before the crimes. They're in danger, but I don't know if the demon could get inside that shelter I had made."

"That had to cost a small fortune! How do you pay for all of that?" Jessica inquired.

"With money. Most people don't take frog skins for payment, not that I've got any frog skins to give them anyway," Bane answered evasively.

"Holy crap! Slow down!" Jessica yelled, looking at the speedometer.

"No time. Just hang on," Bane said. He had the pedal pressed hard against the floorboard. "We'll find out how fast we can make it to the lake in times of emergency. What gives? You used to love a good adventure."

"Well, I've seen enough adventure for one week. I'd like to survive to see next week, but with your driving, that's not too likely," Jessica bantered, trying hard to keep the conversation light.

"How many people in this truck have rolled a Ford Explorer? Raise your hand now?" He glanced at her. "You'll notice that my hand isn't going up. Talk about my driving, will ya? Anyway, what's the key to killing the demon? How's it accomplished?"

"Silver-bladed weapon in the heart. Anything else will simply piss it off," Jessica stated flatly.

Wasn't there a reference to the eyes in one of those books? Bane wondered, trying to recall what he had read. "Then I guess luck is on our side. I've got a sword set that is bladed in silver. All three pieces have silver blades. I won them in a contest when I took second place. Fortune smiles on idiots, small children, and Bane Bloodworth."

"Bane, can I ask you a personal question—one that you've never answered before?"

"I suppose, but I won't promise to answer it."

"When you had your name changed, why did you pick the last name, Bloodworth. I mean, you kept your first name, but changed the last one."

"Old nickname from my past, not to mention it rolls so well off the tongue." Bane grinned.

"Really? I can't believe you told me that. You've never come close to answering me on that one. Why now?"

"Oh, for crying out loud, you ask more questions than a five-year-old!" Bane grinned widely.

"How long do you think that it'll take us to get to your lake house?"

"With the light traffic, my speed, and the flashing dome to keep people out of our way, I'd say twenty to thirty minutes. Try calling them. See if anything's going on."

"Bane, what if they are fine? And what if we had sex last night? I don't want to talk to any of them if they heard that."

"Jess, I think we'd know if we had sex. You'd have a hard time walking and would have the most satisfied look stuck on your face for days." Bane smirked.

"You couldn't handle me anyway," Jessica said, keeping the tone as light as Bane's

"If there were five of you, I'd still be able to finish you all off and still be waiting for more." He laughed.

"You wish!"

"No way. Just one of you in this world is plenty. More than one would be completely catastrophic."

"Hey!"

"Reach into the back of the truck there and pull out the red case with the blue dragons painted on it. That's the one that has my silver swords inside; we might as well get those ready. Too bad my throwing stars are made of steel; those would've made a good ranged weapon."

His heart was quivering in his chest, with a highly irregular heartbeat. A dark, gloomy depressed feeling settled over him the closer to Wisconsin he got. Jessica seemed oddly serene, considering the danger everyone might be in. Perhaps she had just settled back into her own mind to keep from thinking about it all. Bane couldn't help feeling as though he were driving headlong into doom. However, if that was his fate, he accepted it with no regrets.

All he ever asked for in his life was to die for something he believed in. Nothing could be nobler than a death like that. It was a selfish wish, mainly for extra glory, but he didn't give that a second thought. He was just hoping everyone would survive an attack by the demon. Bane would do whatever it took to ensure their safety— even give his life. Now he prayed that he'd get to the house in time to prevent another personal tragedy.

Twenty-five minutes later, they arrived at Bane's lake house, and his feelings of dread were building rapidly. When he pulled into the driveway, he stepped out of his Hummer and replaced his katana with the silver one, strapping the rest to his body. Each step bringing his pulse to an alarming rate, without realizing it, he had begun to run toward the front door. Jessica followed him at a small distance, allowing him the room to maneuver.

Arriving at the doorway, Bane noticed the door was slightly ajar. He kicked the door, allowing it to slam into the drywall behind it. Entering quickly, checking the rooms as he went, Bane raced down the steps toward his shelter. His breathing became erratic; he felt as though he was having a heart attack. Sweat saturated his skin; he looked like he'd just gotten out of the shower.

Pulling his sword out in an effort to give himself some comfort, he discovered that he was having a panic attack. Bane had read an article on panic attacks but never thought he'd become a victim to one of them. Jessica had reached the top of the steps behind him and was cautiously creeping toward him. He forced himself to continue, despite his swimming vision and lightheadedness. Bane knew he didn't have the strength to continue alone; he called out to the Lord in his mind.

The basement was dark, and the light switches weren't working. It didn't bother Bane much; he saw better in the dark than he did in the height of the day. Jessica, however, was another story. She was having trouble seeing where Bane was and kept whispering his name urgently. He didn't want to give his position away but didn't want Jessica to get lost in the darkness. Instead, he grunted every time she called out so she could follow his voice.

As they skulked through the basement, the only sound was their ragged breathing and Jessica's light footsteps. They rounded the corner, to an open doorway. Bane dove through the entryway and came up in a roll, looking deep into every shadow for signs of trouble. Jess tried the lights in the room, and they flickered to life, causing Bane to wince. When they stood there quietly, only the dull hum of the fluorescent bulbs overhead could be heard.

Bane wanted nothing more than to enter the override code and charge into the shelter. Something inside of him wouldn't let him move; he stared at the keypad on the exterior of the bunker. Jessica watched him with a strange curiosity as if she were trying to read his mind. After only sixty seconds but to Bane felt like hours, he mounted enough courage to approach the keypad. His hands were shaking, palms were sweaty, and he was having trouble focusing on the numbers from each button.

"Bane, we've gotta know."

"I know." Heaving a deep sigh, Bane opened the door to the shelter. The inside door was shut, which meant that someone had locked down the entrances. Another code would have to be input to open the interior door, which only served to make Bane more pessimistic. What kind of attack or fear would make them seal themselves in so completely?

At last, Jessica looked concerned; she'd never seen the inside door sealed, nor knew that it could even be sealed. Bane pushed the buttons slowly, ensuring not to make a mistake when he heard a soft click from the door. Jess looked at him quizzically, as he moved back to the door and began pushing it silently aside, which automatically reset the mechanism, in case the doors needed to be sealed again. Bane had thought it a good redundancy, and he thought of ways that even smoke couldn't get inside his bunker without his permission.

Inside, the shelter was cloaked in shadows, the only light coming through the doorway behind them. "What the fuck is with the lights? " Bane whispered. He reached for the light switch, and nothing happened; however, Bane kept flashlights charged on the side of each doorway in his shelter. Sometimes even he was amazed how paranoid he had become over the years. Before he could will himself to turn the flashlight on, he knelt in prayer.

Chapter Thirteen

Though the darkness brought about an increasingly devastating despair from deep within Bane, he forced himself to switch on his flashlight. He found it odd that his shelter was without power. With a primary generator and two backup generators, it was inconceivable that they had no power. Flaring up, the light beam lanced through the gloom, intensifying the depth of each shadow in the front room. No signs of trouble appeared in the entryway, giving Bane some comfort, but not nearly enough.

He turned to Jessica. "Wait here for a minute. I'll check the shelter and call you when the coast is clear." Before she could object, like she always did, Bane held up a hand to forestall her outburst. "If the demon is in there, you'll be the first person I'll call for."

"Alright. This is your show, but call me if you need me."

"I will. Keep alert. Who knows what's going on around here?"

Bane drew his sword, after shifting the flashlight to his left hand. Carefully, he crept inside the shelter, eyes darting back and forth, seeking out each shadow. The kitchen was undisturbed; no plates or silverware were left sitting on the countertops. In fact, the room was immaculate. Bane lit a few candles and placed them on the dinner table, giving off flickering lights and making the shadows dance along the walls.

He could feel his pulse pounding against his temples, throbbing in his wrists and in his neck. Each vein expanded and retracted rhythmically, yet the pace was far too rapid to be healthy. The complete lack of noise made the situation even more nerve-wracking. That constant hum was conspicuously missing, making him more stressed. There was no power, air conditioning, or oxygen filter, and computer systems were off-line.

Turning toward the hallway, Bane felt his heart drop as he approached the first door on the left. He tucked the flashlight under his left arm and turned the knob. Returning the flashlight to his hand, Bane thrust the door open and entered cautiously. The room belonged to Jessica and Thunder, at least while they were in isolation. Even in the dim light that was given off from the flashlight, the walls clearly showed the thick layer of blood. No corpse was in the room, but the blood was so plentiful that whoever shed it was definitely dead.

Rage boiled Bane's blood, his eyes narrowing into a harsh scowl as his jaw set. Leaving that bedroom, he quickly made his way to the next room. Again the sight was horrific but devoid of bodies; Erika and Devon were nowhere to be found. The sheets from their bed were soaked and twisted into a hundred little knots. Claw marks had shredded the pillows, leaving the goose feathers sticking to the bloody bed.

The last room for him to check, at least for signs of life, was the master bedroom. It brought him more fear than he had ever realized possible. While he had to know what was going on, he wasn't looking forward to seeing what might be contained within. After he checked his bedroom, he'd still have to go through the rest of the shelter to locate the bodies, or to be sure the place was empty.

With a trembling hand, Bane opened the door to where Carrie was staying in the shelter. Bile rose in the back of his throat, seeing the carnage that was left intended for him to find. All the bodies that were missing were located inside the master bedroom. Claws shredded their flesh; huge bites were taken out of the victims, and the magician went so far as to arrange the bodies in lewd positions. Carrie was hanging from the ceiling by her wrists, but not by rope or chains. Bane couldn't see what held her wrists in place, but he couldn't bring himself to investigate further.

Each person was completely naked; even some of his or her skin was missing, adding further insult to injury. Bane staggered backward out of the room, returning to the hallway. Walking like a drunkard, he managed to make it back to where he had Jessica waiting. His pale pallor, sunken eyes, and sweat covered body made him look as though he was strung out on potent narcotics, vision swimming in an ocean of depression, with waves crashing over his head.

"Bane? What the Hell?" Jessica asked in shock over his appearance.

"All dead," he mumbled. "They're all dead."

"What? "

"That fucking bastard killed them all! I don't know how that shithead got inside, but he murdered our friends and family! We've got to put a stop to him; now it's even more personal! He invaded my home, my sanctuary!" Bane shouted angrily.

"Devon and Erika?"

"Dead."

"Carrie?"

"Dead."

"Thunder?"

"Dead! They're all dead! Torn to pieces, shredded by that creep's deadly talons!" Bane shouted as he dropped to his knees. He was emotionally exhausted and overwhelmed by the current situation. Then Jessica saw something she rarely ever witnessed; Bane broke down into a fit of deep sobbing. Tears ran down his cheek unhindered; nothing could ebb the flow of tears that were billowed from his eyes.

Jessica was torn between seeing what happened and comforting Bane. He not only lost friends and nephews but his wife as well. Now it appeared his sanity was about to become another casualty of the demon. She bent down, putting her hand on the back of his neck, gently massaging it. With his snake-like speed, he reached out and held her against him, sobbing on her shoulder. Caught in his tight grasp, Jessica gave up hope of seeing what happened to her brother and everyone else.

"I didn't get a chance to say good-bye. I never had the opportunity to confess to her about what happened between us." He wept.

"We still don't know if anything did happen. I doubt anything happened unless you wore a condom. We women can tell these things, you know," Jessica answered, consoling Bane.

"I had a memory flash on the way to meet up with you at the gas station. If we didn't have sex, then you're the most amazing imaginary lover I've ever met," Bane explained in-between his sniffling. "Even though we weren't in control of our actions, I still had a responsibility to inform my wife of what happened. Now I'll never get that chance."

"Then why I don't I remember anything happening? Something tells me you're not so inept that I'd easily forget all of it. Carrie used to rave about your prowess in sexual matters. Bane, look at it this way; she's in a better place now. I doubt she blames you for what happened because now she has all the answers she could ever possibly want."

"How are we ever going to be the same knowing that we had sex?" Bane asked.

"We're close friends. I don't recall the sex; it was just an intimate situation. We'll go on as we had before, cherishing the memory of our time together. Nothing that I can think of should cause us any guilt. We weren't thinking clearly, and obviously, things got out of hand. So please, try to calm down. You're the only one who can help me destroy the demon."

"I thought you were supposed to help me destroy the demon," Bane said with his body shaking, weeping uncontrollably. "I failed— I failed them all. Each of them trusted me, and I let them down. Jessica, you should run far and run fast. Get as far from me as possible; I'll only fail you too."

For Jess, none of it felt real; she hadn't seen the bodies, nor had she been given a chance to miss her friends and family yet. All Jessica could see at that moment was the apparent breaking point of her best friend Bane Bloodworth. Strangely, Jessica felt closer to him than she ever had before; he had let her see a side of him that he showed to no one. It was a privilege she didn't take lightly; she knew how comfortable he was around her in order for him to break down so badly in front of her.

"Bane, you didn't fail them, and you've never failed me. Don't think like that. You can set things right. I need you. I can't do this without you!"

"No. I'll kill this fucking thing, but you'd be in far too much danger."

"I have to be there."

"I can't risk your life too. Don't you understand? "

"Bane, the safest place on the planet right now is at your side. No matter what trouble we may be walking into, I'll be in far less danger if I'm with you."

"How the hell did I get caught up in all of this mess? I was living my life, and all of a sudden, this demon thing starts fuckin' with me. I'll make it pay, dear God in heaven. I will send this creature straight to hell!" Bane snarled as he began changing his sorrow to rage. A flame ignited inside him, lighting an inferno of fury. Jessica even took a step back when she looked in his eyes. Something about him had suddenly changed; a dangerous edge took over his weeping demeanor.

Like someone flipped a switch in his mind, he shed no more tears. His breath became slow and calm with a silhouette of power untold. Every pore of his being oozed with a violent malevolence that encompassed his entire body. Bane's eyes were alight with an inner glow, a dark and murky luminance. Jessica was afraid; she didn't recognize the man sitting before her and grew more scared as he rose to his feet. Bane stood like a titan among mere men, a perfect example of madness made mortal.

He would look no more dangerous if he held smoldering balls of flame in each hand. Bane didn't need to have bolts of lightning shooting out of his eyes; they were terrifying enough on their own. His muscles bulged, appearing as though they might burst through his skin at any moment. The leather he wore creaked as he moved to gather his belongings from the floor.

Jessica must've looked away for a moment because when she glanced over at Bane again, he already had a lit cigarette hanging out of the side of his mouth.

"Let's go kick some demon ass," Bane said, pulling his hair into a ponytail for better management.

They had no idea how much time had passed while they were in the basement of Bane's lake house. As he ascended the steps, he could see the spiders of dusk were spinning ever-widening webs of shadow across the house. With a coolness that chilled Jessica to the core, Bane reported the deaths he located in his home to Pamela Phillips. His monotone voice held no hint of humanity, just the metal resonance of a robot given the bitter taste of life. He didn't even wait for an answer. Bane reported it and shoved his phone into his pocket.

"Where are we going?" Jessica asked as they got into the Hummer.

"To get my bike."

"Which one? The one at the gas station or the one up here?"

"Both. You can ride a Harley, can't you?" Bane asked in that same frigid tone that tainted his normally jovial voice.

"Yes, but I didn't think you'd allow me to ride either of your precious motorcycles. Aren't you the one who said it would be sacrilege?"

"Things change," he stated simply; then he whispered to himself, "Things change."

"How are we going to work this? I mean, the trailer is in Lake Zurich, and your regular bike is up here," Jessica asked, trying to draw him out of his shell a little.

"I'll ride the Harley to the gas station, and then we'll take the bikes to a new location."

"Where."

"Hell's front door. Where else?"

"I hope that's just a disturbing metaphor." Jessica tested.

Bane ignored her last statement, as though she said nothing at all. His eyes were fixed on the road ahead of him. They never deviated from his driving. It didn't take long to get to Jessica's lake house, but by the time they arrived, the sun was almost completely shielded by the planet's horizon. Placing his headset for his iPhone on his head, Bane clipped the phone to his belt. Turning the gas on, he kick-started the Harley, bringing his hog to life.

He allowed the bike to warm up for several minutes while he grabbed some items from the back of the truck. Jessica tried to see what he was taking, but her view was obstructed by the boxes strapped down in the back. When Bane passed in front of the truck, he was carrying a backpack, the contents of which were indiscernible to the naked eye. Riding his motorcycle was just one more way for Bane to isolate himself from the world.

Jessica wasn't comfortable with the change that had taken over her best friend; he wasn't himself. It was a disturbing transformation that seemed to take place right before her eyes. Though she tried to be supportive and bring him back from the dark place he was hiding within his own mind, nothing seemed to work. She put the Hummer in reverse and pulled out of the driveway, speeding away to Route 12, knowing that Bane could easily catch up to her.

The last thing she wanted was to fall behind and make Bane wait for her at the gas station. In truth, she didn't really know if he would wait for her. What made her the most nervous was that she hardly knew the Bane Bloodworth that had emerged after seeing the aftermath of his wife and friends slaughtered mercilessly. In her rearview mirror, she saw Bane approaching at a viper's speed. Swerving around the Hummer, he took the lead, heading toward Lake Zurich.

Though he was traveling at a rapid pace, Bane allowed Jessica to keep up, always keeping her in his side mirrors. She had the flashing beacon turned on to clear traffic from their path, not that there were many cars on the rural roads. However, when they reached the main streets, the beacon would come in handy for her staying close to Bane, who would simply weave in and out of traffic. A single pickup truck drove slowly down the center of the road, refusing to yield the right of way to Jessica.

Bane swung back and fell in next to the truck; without batting an eyelash, he pulled out his Ruger and fired two rounds. Each shot took out the driver's side tires on the pickup truck; Bane was able to drop back out of the way before the truck lurched across the road into a ditch. Jessica stared out the windshield in shock. Bane always had a quick temper, but he was usually able to contain himself. The change he had undergone snapped the boundaries between his urges and his self-restraint.

As Jessica passed the wreckage and Bane, he nodded at her with a blank look on his face—no satisfaction from following his instincts, no regret marking his visage, not the slightest indication that he felt any emotion whatsoever. What worried her the most was the fact that he would simply shoot someone if they stood in his way and would show no signs of remorse. He had shut himself off emotionally, which made him the most dangerous person she knew.

Bane opened the throttle wide, and his front wheel lifted off the ground like a mighty steed rearing up before charging forward.

Jessica diligently followed the motorcycle and its rider out of Wisconsin. She did notice that Bane took three phone calls while he was riding out in front of her. Who the calls came from, she could only speculate, but something about the way he glanced back at the Hummer after each call made her shift in her seat. The CD player changed discs, and a new song came out of the speakers. "Death Has a Name" by Rantin' and Ravin' held an ominous warning for the future.

By the time they reached the Wisconsin-Illinois state line, sunlight was being obscured by leaden storm clouds. Strong winds buffeted not only the tress, which bent against the force but Bane on his motorcycle as well. Soon needles of rain tattooed the earth with fervent liquid, causing gutters to overflow. Puddles massed in length and depth, causing the water to be sprayed up at the unprotected Bane with a subtle splashing sound. Bane removed the rubber band from his hair, allowing the rain to run freely through his mahogany-colored locks.

Jess watched him closely through her water-soaked windshield and wasn't anxious to drive a motorcycle in the maturing storm. She was a competent rider, but she was in no way confident as to her riding skills in the rain. Lightning crackled and splintered among the coal clouds, illuminating the sky for brief instances; each flash was accompanied by a bone-jarring crash of thunder, sounding like an enormous bomb going off overhead.

***

Pamela arrived in Wisconsin via helicopter fifteen minutes after Bane called her. She entered his house through the front door, which he had left open for her. Though the renovation had yet to be completed, the house itself was very stylish. Once more Pamela felt a pang of desire for Bane; his taste was impeccable. Some of the finest artwork was displayed in the rooms that were completed; from sculptures to paintings, everything was top of the line. She wondered how he had the money to afford such luxuries on the meager pay of a law enforcement worker.

She had brought with her a large complement of federal forensics and scientific investigation personnel. Pamela felt she owed Bane the best people for investigating his home and his personal tragedy. Though she never wished harm on his wife, she did think that it might allow her the opportunity, somewhere down the road, for a possible date with him. She descended the spiraling staircase to his basement where he told her the bodies could be found.

Agent Phillips was in the lead, followed closely by her staff. No matter the crime scene, she always insisted on being the first one to walk through the area. Once she absorbed the entire spectacle, she'd allow her team to get to work. However, the first observations were crucial to her, due to the fact that it wasn't tainted by her team working and collecting the clues. When she saw the bodies, it was clear to her why Bane had sounded so strange. Witnessing that type of grisly view of his wife and friends would cause anyone severe stress.

Her skin was crawling like fire ants with their den kicked over, so when her phone rang, her skeleton nearly leaped from her skin. With a shaky hand, she plucked her cellular from her pocket and answered it. The evidence technician couldn't hear the voice on the other end, but whatever she heard shocked her beyond belief. All he heard was Pamela's reaction, as she paused to listen every so often, then asked more questions.

"He's where? Did you actually see them firsthand?" Pamela stated after listening to the report from the other end. "How's that possible? Well, let them know exactly what's going on. I don't care how, but get them to Illinois as soon as possible. Time is of the essence, in this case, do what you have to in order to get them there fast! I'll call Bane and let him know what's happening. We've got to hurry; he's in grave danger."

Pamela turned to address her team. "You guys wrap this place up; call in a team to clean this mess up after you collect everything you need. I'll foot the bill for it. I'm going to Illinois, and I'll be taking the chopper."

"Yes, ma'am," her team said in unison.

"Annie, you're in charge of this crime scene. Oh, and, Miss Carbonara, make sure there are no slip-ups. I'm counting on you."

"No problem, Agent Phillips. I've got it under control."

Pamela rushed out of the house, barreling through anyone who was unfortunate enough to be in her path. In a one-part whisper, another part prayer, Pamela mumbled under her breath, "Hold on, Bane. I'm coming. Just watch your back and be careful. I'm on my way."

Chapter Fourteen

Sheets of rain-washed over the canopy top of the gas station, shielding the patrons pumping fuel into their tanks. From under the protected top, the rain looked like a waterfall pouring down from above. Many residents of Lake County were considering building arks and herding animals two by two aboard their vessels. Thunder reverberated so intensely that it literally shook the ground when it exploded in the heavens. The cloud cover was such a thick blanket over the sky that it almost appeared to be the middle of the night.

Illinois was under flash flood warnings for the northwest portion of the state, extending far into Indiana. Sump pumps were working overtime in the basements of every house in the area, attempting to keep the homes free of water. Re-enactments of rivers played themselves out in the gutters, where act two consisted of disappearing down the storm drain.

Bane entered the gas station, flashing his identification at the clerk, informing him that he was there to recover his motorcycle. While the clerk looked at him as though he was insane, Bane paid him no attention. He simply grabbed a pack of cigarettes from a display and tossed them onto the counter. After he paid for his purchase, Bane exited the building, returning to where Jessica was waiting for him. Despite the dangers of smoking near the pumps, Bane lit a smoke and enjoyed the first drag immensely.

"What are we going to do now? It's pouring out there. Do you seriously want to ride motorcycles in this mess?" Jessica asked.

"We proceed as planned; we're going to the forest preserve off of Quentin Road by Dundee."

"Deer Grove?"

"Yeah. We'll need the bikes to plunge deep into the woods. My Hummer won't fit."

"Those are street bikes!" Jessica complained.

"I'm aware of what type of motorcycles they are; however, this ends today. For better or worse, by god, this ends once and for all," Bane growled irritably.

"I don't know if I can handle such a powerful motorcycle in the rain, let alone going off-road in a forest!'

"Then I guess you'll be walking into the woods because I'm going with or without you."

"Alright, okay. I'm with you. Just don't blame me for any damage to your bike if I wipe out while off-roading," Jessica conceded.

"Then let's get moving. Time is growing short; I can feel it in my bones. No more blood will be on my hands because of this fucking demon, Xanthsa something."

"Xanithsabar, the demon's name is Xanithsabar," Jessica stated.

"Whatever. The fucker is toast; it's just a puny imitation of Satan anyway."

Jessica looked visibly upset about how callously Bane was dismissing the demon and its supernatural powers. Bane didn't notice her reaction because he had already made a break for his motorcycle under the tarp. With the protective tarp removed, Bane unstrapped the bike from the trailer and moved it onto the pavement. He disengaged several booby-traps so that he could get the motorcycle to start. Climbing onto his custom-made hog, Bane started it up.

Jessica got onto Bane's other bike and followed him out into the downpour. They traveled up Route 12 for a few miles, turning right onto Quentin Road. Their destination was only a ten-minute drive in clear weather, but traffic was moving like a snail on sedatives. Passing the cars would only further endanger Jessica, so Bane fought his urge to race by the slow-moving vehicles blocking his path. Though they were both being drenched by the constant hard-hitting rain, only Bane seemed not to acknowledge it.

After an aggravating twenty-five minutes, they had finally reached the entry into the forest preserve. They drove along the concrete road that wove through the trees, allowing access and parking to patrons of the park. Area five was Bane's destination; he knew those woods like the back of his own eyelids. He could be blindfolded and dropped into the center of the preserve and find his way out in less than five minutes. When they reached the area known as circle five, Bane hopped the curb and started into the woods.

Jessica took the move into the forest a little more carefully, more timid than was in her nature. Her tires spun in the wet grass, tearing up the lawn and kicking mud up against her back. Bane's motorcycle seemed to handle the terrain very well, or he was just that good at riding. He made it all look so easy, while Jessica struggled to maintain control of her bike.

The leaves on the trees wept tears of rain down to the soft earth, further soaking the ground. Tree trunks were dark, yet glistened off the headlight of Bane's motorcycle. Even the areas with sparse tree disbursal lent no light to the forest; the sky was far too overcast to illuminate anything. However, shadows crept out of every crevice among the dense portions of towering vegetation. He came across what was normally a small creek that ran through the preserve; which now was a free-flowing river.

Bane slid to a halt, looking over his surroundings with the eyes of a predator. By forcing the demon to confront him in the forest preserve, Bane placed the battle on his own turf, thereby swinging a Lilliputian-sized advantage to him, and every little bit helped. Since the ground was far too saturated for his kickstand to do him any good, Bane leaned his bike against the trunk of a large maple tree. A short distance away, he could hear Jessica making her way toward his direction. Only when the sky roared like a lion did her motorcycle engine fade from his audible range.

Lightning struck a tree fifty yards away from him, bursting it into scorched shards of timber. Despite the tremendous downpour of rain, flames flared up around the splintered tree. As Bane watched the fires eat away at the tree, Jessica arrived, having trouble stopping her ride. By the time she succeeded in bringing her bike to a stop, Jess was at the very edge of the drop off to the creek. Her face, while she dismounted, was white as a snowflake. Jessica's bottom lip was trembling; her eyes threatening to spill tears down her cheeks.

She didn't have the forethought that Bane had about the kickstand, so when she was no longer holding onto the bike, it fell to one side and then was gone. It slid down the muddy embankment, landing in the water with a loud splash. Jess turned to look fearfully at Bane, knowing he'd be furious over her carelessness. However, Bane had no emotion on his face, simply gazing at her with a blank stare. A chill ran through her body like a bolt of electricity, but it wasn't from the cool wind and rain.

"Bane, I'm sorry. I didn't think that it would do that. I'll pay to get it fished out and repaired, I promise," Jessica apologized.

"Don't worry about it," was all Bane could manage.

"Well, what the hell did you expect? You dragged us out into the middle of a forest on street bikes! You knew damn well I couldn't handle your motorcycle as well as you can," Jessica exclaimed in her defense.

When Jessica felt guilty, she often became defensive, looking for a way to place the blame elsewhere. In all the time Bane had known her, she had never truly been at fault for anything, at least according to her. She had once missed a very important day when Bane needed his friends around him, but instead of being sorry, she made him apologize for putting so much pressure on her. Bane didn't know why, but he never could stand her being angry with him. He always approached her with an apology on his lips.

"I said, don't worry about it."

"What the fuck are we doing out in the middle of nowhere anyway? Do you really think the demon is likely to show up here? I don't see any small children around here as bait."

His face still a mask of emotionlessness, Bane looked her up and down. "I don't need a child to bring the demon here. I've got better bait than that."

With that said, he produced the book the demon wanted from his saddlebag, holding it at shoulder length. It was the only literature that told the demon's strengths, weaknesses, and how to destroy it, something that the demon couldn't abide anyone having in his possession. Bane knew that so long as he contained the means to destroy his nemesis, the demon would come for him. A subtle glint in his eye showed confidence in himself and his plan that left Jessica wondering exactly what he was up to.

"So how long do we have to wait for Xanithsabar to show up? I'm getting soaked straight through to the bone," Jessica asked impatiently. "And what are we going to do once Xanithsabar arrives?"

"Kill it," Bane answered flatly.

"Kill it? That's your big plan? Are you out of your mind? You've got to have a better strategy than that. Xanithsabar is thousands of years old, not to mention a fallen angel from heaven! We can't just leave this to chance."

"I've left nothing to chance; you're going to have to put your faith in me. Speaking of which, let me take a look at your gun. I want to be certain it's ready to rock and roll."

Jessica's brow creased in confusion as she withdrew the weapon from its holster. Bane didn't move toward her, forcing her to come to him. She handed him the gun, and he received it by the barrel. He ejected the clip and the bullet from the chamber. With that done, Bane inspected the weapon. Upon seeing it was in perfect working order, he pulled a fresh clip from his pocket and loaded it into the handgun. Bane chambered a round into the pipe, so all that Jess would have to do is flip off the safety and fire.

"What's with the new magazine of ammunition?" she wondered aloud.

"Different bullets, high impact but low recoil. They'll make the gun kick less when you fire it but will pack the punch I want," Bane explained.

183

"Oh cool! You know something; you're really a dangerous person to go up against. I'm damn glad I don't have to go up against you. Your knowledge of weapons is absolutely mind-boggling!" Jessica exclaimed.

"Jessie, anyone can learn about weapons, it simply takes time. I happened to start learning at a very young age," he said with a subtle shrug of his shoulders, but he kept his eyes locked on Jessica as though he was waiting for something.

"Jessie? You haven't called me that in a long time. I like the way your voice tilts when you call me Jessie." She beamed a smile at him.

Bane nodded his head like a sage dispensing wisdom to loyal subjects. He said nothing; instead he pulled his pocket watch from his jeans. Checking the time, he snapped the cover shut and returned the watch to his pocket. The corners of his mouth twisted into a shrewd smile as if he knew something that the world didn't. Jessica was taken aback by this sudden smile because Bane hadn't shown any emotion since he saw his wife's corpse.

However, since he wore a smile, she felt she was in some way responsible for his newfound elation. Blushing fiercely, Jessica took a long breath and said, "Bane, I never told this to anyone before, and I know this is hardly the time to do so. Yet, I fear that one of us may die today. I don't want that to happen without you knowing my long-guarded secret. I've had a sincere crush on you for years; our friendship has meant the world to me. Even though you recently lost your wife, I want you to know you're not alone. I cherish you as a friend and love you with all my heart. Anything you need from me, you'll have it."

"Jessie, I've known for years of that love. I have always been very complimented by it. My friendship with the woman I've known for so many years is something that I'll cherish until the grave if that is the will of God. I'd gladly hold the hand of death to keep that woman safe and happy. Never doubt that."

Jessica smiled so widely that her face seemed to stretch just to accommodate it. Bane turned away, looking into the forest for an unseen foe. It was at that moment that Jessica pulled out her semiautomatic handgun and aimed it at the back of Bane's head. Her irises flashed an iridescent red glow, and she bared rows of serrated teeth. Jessica's form bubbled and transformed into that of an old magician, clothes and all. Bane held his silver-bladed katana in his right hand, his eyes scanning the shadows diligently.

Four blasts were issued from the demon's gun; the flash from the muzzle wasn't very bright. Just as Bane said, the recoil was almost completely null. Instead of seeing Bane's skull being blown through the back of his face, nothing happened. Xanithsabar couldn't imagine that he had missed so badly with each of the four shots. So he fired until the clip ran empty, and still, no damage was done to Bane. He looked at the gun with confusion and anger.

"I loaded it with blanks, asshole," Bane said, turning to face Xanithsabar.

"Well, well, Bane, aren't you clever?" The demon tossed the useless gun aside. "So what was it that gave me away to a half-wit like you?"

"First of all, was the fact that when I started to meditate, I remember a soft chanting, then I awoke with a large gap in time. Additionally, you took a handgun after telling me that bullets wouldn't affect a demon. The only reason you'd need a gun would be to shoot me. Then, the real Jess hates the name Jessie; she'd have blown up at me for calling her that. Finally, Jessica would never tell me she loves me. Sure, she has a crush on me, but she'd never tell me," Bane concluded. "I don't know how you know so much about Jessica or her feelings, but you were still missing several key points of her personality."

"So many clues. I'll have to correct that in the future. Once I kill you, I'll assume another form and torment someone else," Xanithsabar stated whimsically.

"Why did you choose me? What the fuck was that all about? " Bane snarled.

"I like the challenge while I work. All I need is ten more children, and my power will be at its zenith. Then I'll be able to unlock all of my magic. You've proven to be a worthy adversary. I hadn't expected you to cause me so much trouble. I thought for certain that my illusions would keep you from guessing my true identity."

"That's what you get for thinking, shithead. It just shows what a total fuck-up you really are. Some demon, can't even out-think a mortal man. Humans are the chosen of God for a reason; we're smarter than creatures like you. Today I'm the hand of the Lord, and you're going to be exterminated! And what kind of name is Xanithsabar anyway?"

Eyes glowing with fury, the demon's chest rumbled violently. "I believe it's time for you to die, little man."

"How did you know so much about Jess's character, personality, and some of her quirks?"

"Comes with the change. The problem I ran into was when I'm in a form; I'm stuck with their personality and some of their feelings. I surface now and then; to shape the way things happen. Otherwise, I allow the persona to run the show," Xanithsabar explained. "Plus her damned necklace I replicated seemed to broadcast the thoughts I had in her persona. That was something I hadn't anticipated."

"Well, the change wasn't as good as you'd like to believe. Jessica is far more self-involved and self-absorbed than you portrayed."

"When in this form, I am forced to remain completely tidy, which is due to his personality disorder. He's an obsessive-compulsive clean freak! You know how much energy it takes to keep this outfit clean when devouring children's brains? "

"How'd you get me to sleep with your Jess personality? What did you think you'd accomplish? " Bane asked, stalling for time to come up with a plan of attack.

"A simple spell while you were already sitting in your subconscious. I simply gave you commands to do what I wanted and made you forget the pieces of the puzzle that you had figured out while meditating. I was so fortunate that you put yourself in that state; you made my work much easier than it would've been."

"So I've been raped by a demon? For what purpose? "

"Because I thought it would destroy you. Your honor would never permit that type of transgression against your wife. Then the problem arose; you didn't remember our having sex. So I had to wait for that memory to resurface. However, I grew bored and decided to kill your wife instead." The demon laughed a taunting chuckle at Bane. "They never knew what hit them; I approached the outside door of the shelter. Of course, they'd let me inside in Jessica form. Before the door closed all the way, they were already dead."

"Lucifer himself will torment you when you are sent to hell because you're such a failure!"

Xanithsabar's hands began gurgling as talons tore through the skin; slowly the demon shed his human appearance. When it rose up, the demon was over eight feet tall, with black leathery wings protruding from its back. Its skin was thick like an armadillo's armor plating. Horns protruded from the skull; the canine-like snout was a horrifying aspect. Xanithsabar was enveloped with bulging muscles, yet looked every bit as quick as a rabbit on speed.

With one taloned claw Xanithsabar knocked over a three-foot tree trunk with very little effort. It was meant to intimidate Bane, and that demonstration was quite effective. If the demon hadn't slaughtered his nephews, sister, and wife, Bane might have made a run for it. However, his pain and rage wouldn't allow him to leave the battle without one of the opponents ending up dead. Feeling that his katana was inadequate, Bane drew his wakizashi, an oriental short sword, as well. Florentine, two-sword style, was one of Bane's favorite types of swordsmanship.

Though there was little light by which to see, the silver swords glimmered off the red glow coming off the demon's eyes. Bane dropped into a defensive fighting stance, waiting for Xanithsabar to make the first move. He was relieved to see the demon had shifted form the first time; he'd have a difficult time seeing himself kill his friend, even if it wasn't really her, although the second shift placed him at a distinct disadvantage. Marshaling all of his courage and patience, Bane waited for the first attack from the demon.

Xanithsabar shimmered in a blue flash of light and was suddenly behind Bane. Spinning rapidly, acutely aware of the demon's location, Bane crossed his swords to block the incoming attack. The claw clanked against the swords, sounding like metal hitting metal, driving Bane to his knees. Then he was forced to step back several paces to help recover from the vicious, bone-jarring blow. His courage was beginning to wane, but his hatred was growing with each passing moment.

***

Pamela triangulated Bane's location by running the GPS on his cell phone. With the real Jessica Annie Braun alongside, she rocketed down the road. She was using a local squad car with lights flashing, sirens blaring. Pamela was doing her best to try to explain the circumstances, considering she wasn't entirely sure what was going on. For most of the helicopter ride, Agent Phillips grilled Jessica on family members, relatives, and anything she could about someone who might look so much like her.

After answering all those questions, in true Jessica style, Jess demanded to know what was happening. By the time that they were halfway to the forest preserve, Jessica grabbed her necklace, closing her eyes. "We need to hurry! Bane's in trouble!"

"I know that! He's riding around with someone that took on the appearance of his best friend and could very well be the serial killer," Pamela spat back.

"No, I can feel his fear and pain," Jessica said sternly. "It's been that way ever since he gave me this pendant. Carrie and Bane saw this at a medieval renaissance fair and felt compelled to buy it for me."

"Great . . . just great, more hocus-pocus crap—exactly what we need on this case," Pamela groaned in exasperation. "Since you seem to have all the answers, you can tell me what's wrong with him?"

"Well, it isn't like I can see him. I can sense his feelings."

"If that's true, then the pain could be over losing his wife this morning. What makes you think that means he's in trouble?"

"I've never known anything to scare Bane." Jessica fixed Agent Phillips with a somber stare. "Not ever."

"Why does that not surprise me? I hope his luck holds out until we get there."

"I've got complete faith in Bane Bloodworth; he's unlike any other person I know. What makes you think that you and I can save him? He's a better survivor than both of us combined."

"We may provide the magician with multiple targets, and you might be able to dispel his illusions since you know a great deal about that type of thing."

"Doesn't this thing go any faster? It is a cop car, isn't it?" Jessica complained.

***

Spinning clockwise, Bane swung his wakizashi downward, forcing the demon to dodge to its right. Meanwhile, he brought his katana upward to slash Xanithsabar on the shoulder. The howl of pain that was released from the demon was bestial, making Bane feel as if his internal organs were merging. It brought images of dragons being pierced with arrows in a movie that was set in medieval times. Spurts of blood spewed out of the wound; instead of the natural red color it was blue, showing that even the open air wasn't affecting the blood. Blood without being touched by oxygen, is, in fact, blue; upon reaching open air, it comes out red. The sight was startling. Bane had caused plenty of blood to be spilled; never once had he seen it any color other than red. Xanithsabar didn't look at all phased by the slash wound; instead, it barreled Bane backward ten feet with the injured arm. A

188

long gash along the left side of Bane's ribs appeared. Whether it was from the demon's talon or one of the tree branches he had crashed through, he wasn't sure.

Pausing briefly to shake off the pain, Bane rolled back onto his shoulders, flinging his feet in the air and propelling himself to his feet. He yanked the rubber band from his hair, letting it flow freely, thinking of Samson and his legend. Besides, something about feeling completely free made him feel far more invincible. Once more, he stood defiant of the demon, swords defensively positioned.

"Is that the best you got?" Bane laughed, hiding his fear and pain behind arrogance.

"Puny insect, you will be squashed and devoured!"

"Ouch, calling me names . . . good come back, you mentally bankrupt asshole," Bane snarled pitching three ninja throwing stars silently at the demon, who batted them aside like he would gnats. Bane then mumbled, "Oh crap."

Xanithsabar engaged Bane, first by batting the katana from his right hand. Bane stabbed the demon through the right leg, as he was lifted off the ground by his neck. He had to escape the grasp of the mighty talon for fear that it might snap shut and pop his head off like a cork. Bane kicked down frantically, only to discover the demon didn't appear to have testicles for him to strike. At least, Xanithsabar didn't have them in the form he had chosen to fight in.

Five bullets slammed into the demon's spine, forcing him to release Bane, at which point, Bane fell to the ground and rolled out of the way. Bane rubbed his eyes to be certain they were clear because he thought he saw Pamela standing in a professional firing stance. Jessica was right beside her, holding a necklace in her left hand. She was dressed in a red sequined leotard, with a small black cape whipping in the wind.

Obviously, Jess had been taken directly from stage to this location, although Bane wasn't taking anything for granted anymore. For all he knew, it was another illusion from the demon, who had many tricks up his sleeve. Both of the ladies looked utterly stunned at the sight of Xanithsabar; neither had expected to encounter a demon; instead, they were prepared for a magician utilizing his illusions to gain an advantage over Bane. Pamela still believed that the demon form was just a trick, but was still taken aback by the sight.

189

As Bane crawled to his feet, a fit of coughing took over him. He wasn't even aware that he held no weapons until he rubbed his inflamed neck. He couldn't see where his katana had landed, and his wakizashi was still lodged in the demon's leg. His only silver bladed weapon left from the set was a tanto knife.

Xanithsabar turned slowly to glare at Pamela; his mouth carved into a vicious sneer. She fired again, hitting the demon in the chest, causing him to pause with each blast. Yet he approached her confidently, knowing she was no match for his power. Bane was still gasping for air, so he posed no threat at that moment. However, he sensed a potent source of power from the woman whose form he had stolen. It was something he hadn't encountered in a long time, though he couldn't remember where or when.

Pamela reloaded her weapon and opened up with a rapid barrage of bullets at the demon. Just as he got within melee range of her, Bane shot the demon's horns off his head. A bright flash of blue light and he was standing inches from Bane.

"Bad move," Xanithsabar stated flatly as he punched Bane in the stomach, once again launching him into the air. Bane's breath left his lungs in a painful whoosh before he slammed into a tree trunk, splitting the back of his scalp open. The demon rushed at Bane, talons aimed at his heart, preparing to shred it to small chunks.

Bane's heart pounded painfully against his broken ribs, and each breath he sucked through his teeth shot flaming agony throughout both lungs. The nicks and cuts on his face and arms were easily ignored compared to his more serious injuries. Every second Bane took to recover brought the demon ten feet closer to ripping out his heart.

Just as the demon's talons were millimeters from Bane's chest, a yellow colored hand gripped Xanithsabar's wrist, stopping him dead in his tracks. Even with his massive inertia, he couldn't manage to move forward to impale Bane. Both Bane and the demon looked up in awe to see who had saved Bane's life. Standing there, surrounded by a beautiful mystical aura, stood Jessica. She wore white robes and had dove-like wings protruding from her shoulder blades.

"You!" snarled Xanithsabar, frothing at the mouth, dark oozing spittle spraying outward. "That's why my amulet didn't function right; you're the reason my plans were thwarted in the hotel room! You're one of the guardians!"

Xanithsabar moved back from both Bane and Jessica the moment she released her grip. Bane nearly passed out. The entire scene was far too much for his mind to handle. Jessica stepped in front of Bane protectively, squaring off against the demon.

"I was sent to keep this man fighting for the side of light. We saw the danger of his soul being lost to us after he rescued his family. He saw his potential and began to fulfill it with all the skills he needed to enhance himself," Jessica explained. "You cannot touch him, without going through me."

"You're too late; his hatred has consumed him. He has swung back into our grasp, and with his death, hell will be waiting," Xanithsabar argued. "His willpower will work for us now!"

"No, his capacity to love can set him free. If he dies now with only hatred in his heart, he may proceed you to hell, but I'm not about to let that happen," Jessica countered. "He is loved by me, his guardian angel, and loves without hesitation or doubt. Saving him is as simple as destroying you."

Angel and demon locked arms, each grappling for a better hold over the other. Suddenly, Bane leaped from behind Jessica and plunged his silver-plated tanto into the demon's left eye, while pulling his wakizashi free. Weakened by the blow, Xanithsabar fell to one knee, still clutching Jessica, trying to utilize her body as a shield. Jessica began to sing, and instantly, Bane and Pamela started to cry. It was the most beautiful sound they had ever encountered in their lives. Xanithsabar was forced to revert from his gargoyle form into that of a fallen angel.

Xanithsabar's appearance was that of a cherub, with wings dark as a raven's. Yet they weren't leathery like before; they were feathered as Jessica's wings. Bane made a running leap onto a tall tree stump, from there, he launched over Jess's head, bringing his wakizashi down into the demon's right eye.

Flames burst from the damaged eye sockets, singeing Bane's face and hands. Bane fell to the ground, his lack of energy and wounds not allowing him the luxury of getting up again. He had put all of his strength, willpower, hopes, and ebbing energy into that last attack. All Bane could manage to do was lie on the soaked leaves, with his mouth open to keep his mouth moist. He couldn't feel his body; it went numb the moment he hit the drenched earth.

With Xanithsabar dying, Jessica produced a bowl of water from within her robes. Dipping her index finger in the water, she wiped a cross along the demon's forehead. Her finger came away red with the demon's blood, its immunity to oxygen nullified. Xanithsabar fell next to Bane, twitching violently in body-wracking spasms. Jessica finished the job by sanctifying the ground surrounding the demon.

Pamela approached gun aimed at the demon's head, eyes as wide as saucers. She had never been a religious person, but after what she had seen, she was quickly reconsidering her position. Xanithsabar regurgitated as his life shriveled in an ever-increasing rate; the putrescence ate through Pamela's ankles and feet like hydro-caloric acid. Everything that touched the vomit was instantly disintegrated, like a last-ditch attack by a dying demon.

At last Xanithsabar was dead, his body withered like a plucked rose in the sun at noon in July. Bane groaned softly, his eyes starting to roll into his head. Jessica bent over him with deep concern in her heart.

"Bane, can you hear me? It's Jess; please look at me!" she pleaded.

From the depths of his confusion and haze of pain, Bane groggily said, "You're an actual angel?"

His voice was nothing more than a gargled whisper, but Jessica understood exactly what he said. She wasn't ever supposed to reveal her true identity, so she was hard pressed to find something to say. Jessica had been prepared for every situation but this one. Bane had a hard time accepting that she was the reason he led such a charmed existence.

"Try to rest. Help is on the way. I'll make sure the doctors have good fortune today."

"Was our friendship part of the job, or did it actually mean something to you?" Bane rasped, trying to maintain his stand against unconsciousness.

"No, it was very real to me. Once you give a person a chance to get to know you, you're really a good man and a terrific friend," Jessica confided.

"What happens now? I mean now that I know the truth about you?" Bane managed to utter aloud.

"You won't remember that I'm not mortal. We'll talk more when you are feeling better. I've got to check on Pamela—" were the last words that Bane heard before the stars and blackness filled his vision.

Special Agent Pamela Phillips was losing blood quickly—her legs splashing it out like an open faucet. Her gray pallor, shallow breathing, and shivering body proved that she had only moments left to live. Seeing that she could do nothing more for her, Jessica bent over the body and performed last rites for agent Phillips. Jessica used one hand to close Pamela's eyelids and whispered softly, "Rest now. Your final assignment will not go unnoticed dear lady."

Epilogue

B eeps, chimes, and soft whispers filled his ears; he was warm and comfortable but didn't know how. His last memory was of being in a forest preserve in the cold wet torrents of rain. Bane was about to face off against the demon, and now he was in a hospital, from the smell and sound of it. His right eye was swollen shut, which had turned a deep ugly combination of purple, yellow and blue. He felt no pain but knew that something very bad had happened to him in that forest preserve.

Forced to squint when he opened his left eye, Bane tried to ascertain what was wrong with him. A fiberglass cast-encased his left arm from his wrist to the shoulder. Bane could feel the tape pull from various bandages across his body. His head throbbed abysmally. When he reached up with his good arm, Bane discovered a bandage around his head as well. It was an easy conclusion to draw that he was heavily medicated.

For hours at a time, he drifted in and out of consciousness; time having no meaning to him. When he awoke a few days later, Jessica Braun was sitting at his bedside. His body tensed since he didn't recall what happened. He still believed that Jess was the demon, Xanithsabar. That time he felt considerable pain, which must have shown on his face because Jessica leaned in closer. She smoothed the little hair that was showing from beneath the bandage.

"Can I get you some ice chips, another blanket, more pain killers?" Jessica asked.

"I want a nurse," he said coolly.

"Bane, listen to me." Jessica dropped her voice to a whisper, her breath tickling his ear. "I'm not the demon. You fought him. It's really me, Bane. When we are alone, I will tell you everything. Right now, just tell the local police you fought the serial killer and destroyed him by fire. That will explain your condition and the charred remains of Xanithsabar. You're a hero to the law enforcement community— Pamela is as well; she gave her life to stop the killer, and you nearly ended up the same way."

"How can I be sure, it's really you?" Bane asked thickly.

"Feel my pendant, hold it in your hand. You'll know that our bond has never been broken. Please, Bane, you must trust me," Jessica pleaded.

When Bane grasped her pendant, a flood of memories came rushing through his mind. All the places they had been and the entertaining times they had spent together, feelings of camaraderie, love, and happiness filled his heart. He knew she was the friend he had known for so many years.

"So we won? I killed a demon?" he whispered urgently. "No more kids are gonna die?"

"You did wonderfully. Don't you remember any of it?" Jessica probed.

"Just waiting for Xanithsabar to show up. The rest is a complete fog, like a vault sealed to protect the memories, and me without the combination."

"Don't worry. It's probably temporary. You had a severe concussion when you were brought in. Your lungs were punctured, your left arm broken in three places, and you needed two hundred and fifteen stitches or staples," Jessica consoled. "Considering what you were up against, I'd say you were damn lucky to be alive. You'll be in the intensive care unit for another week at least, but you're going to recover nicely."

"Will you come to visit me every day?" Bane asked, sliding rapidly back into a dreamless sleep.

"I will be here, Bane, as I have always been here," Jessica answered her sleeping friend, kissing him on his forehead.

The news media had caught wind that Pamela Phillips had died subduing the serial killer. No mention of Bane had hit the airwaves since his involvement in the case was classified material from the CIA. Jessica's role in this had also been kept from the news; she explained to a man named Tom, the friend of Bane's who gave him a phony position in the CIA, that she was drafted as Bane's assistant. Reporters were dying to discover how the killer was immolated during the shootout with authorities. However, no one was talking, not even the coroner's office, who had many questions for Bane when he was feeling better.

As she promised, Jessica was at Bane's bedside during visiting hours every day, performing little magic tricks to keep him entertained while stuck in the hospital. While he was still heavily medicated, Jessica was able to weasel out of him how he came to have so much money. As it turned out, he wrote love poetry under a pseudonym, and the sales from his first twelve anthologies made him wealthier than he had ever dreamed. Jessica found it incredibly ironic that a strong warrior like Bane chose love poetry for his genre.

Though she thought it ironic, Jessica wasn't really surprised. She had always known what a hopeless romantic Bane was deep under his gruff appearance. Despite the rules about jewelry in the hospital, Jessica placed a golden cross around his neck, saying a silent prayer. None of the doctors or nurses ever noticed the crucifix, but every day Jessica was at the hospital, she would take Bane's good hand to grasp it and pray with him.

It would take several months of rehabilitation before Bane was able to do things for himself again. Jessica planned to take Bane into her home and nurse him back to health. He had the money to support them while she was on hiatus from her work. She withheld the information that his wife's body turned up missing from the morgue. He could deal with that news when he was better. Bane would make a full recovery under Jessica's care. He'd have gone straight through hell to help her. She owed him no less. . . After all, what were friends for?

The End?

The Author

Born and raised primarily in Illinois, Slate R. Raven started his writing career after attempting several other means of artistic expression. However, after a debilitating injury to his spine, Slate was left with the option of watching daytime television or finding something that proved to be more productive. So with that, Slate chose writing as a means of purging the turbulent emotions that coursed through his veins over being a prisoner of one's own body.

The first of many novels emerged while sitting under a Laptop computer, a generous gift from his father. To pass the time during the long months of surgery and physical therapy Slate continued to write finishing his second novel, *Fresh Start,* which is where he was offered a contract with a publishing company along with several other of his books. After several years, Slate has made the decision to go the Indie route and has recently re-written all of his novels and hired an editor to bring out the best in his work.

Doctors had embedded a morphine pump in Slate's abdomen, allowing a drop of morphine to hit the nerve directly once per hour. This allows Slate a great deal more movement and less pain than prior to the injury; as an added bonus since the amount of the morphine is so slight since delivered directly to the source, Slate isn't forced to walk through life in a perpetual fog that oral painkillers bring about. Life has started to look a whole lot better!

At this time Slate has already re-written several of his older novels and each are waiting their turn at the editor, while new work is underway. Keep an Eye out for his all updates at www.SlateRaven.net. This guy has got his battery tuned up and you can expect some super-charged up stories coming your way soon!

***

Thanks for reading! If you enjoyed this book, I'd be very grateful if you'd post a short review on Amazon. Your support really does make a difference. I read all the reviews personally, so I can get your feedback and make these books even better for your entertainment.

Thanks again for your support!

Acknowledgement

Enormous thanks to you, my editor and friend, Lorraine Kolmacic Carey! A talented author in your own right, you took time to not only clean up my mistakes, but lend me an arm on my journey back to the world of Publishing! You are a truly remarkable woman!

Huge thank you goes out to Erika M. Szabo for your efforts on cover artistry and all the publishing help a man could ask for, you're one of a kind.

Thank you Anthane "Bug" Paterek for being a solid friend, brother and man that I could call on anytime of day or night. You bring honor to all you give your friendship! I appreciate you hanging in there throughout my "Slate Style Thinking!"

To Robert and Kathe Slater, without your help I wouldn't be here to create new worlds for others to enter! Thank you for joining me in the decent into madness, and for having the fortitude to lead me back out!

To Gretta Raven you were there for me during the darkest times, when no one could possibly know how dangerous things really were, and still you leaned against my shoulder and said, "Don't worry, we've got this handled!" You were taken too soon!

Thank you to Cyndie Kresge-Todd for being such a die-hard friend, and fan for so many years! (*No dear, I won't say how many.*)

A very special nod to Breanna Hayse whose assistance was invaluable to me exactly when I needed it the most. Wherever did you disappear to, my kind friend?

Thank you to Stevie Nicks "the Goddess of Rock and Roll" for your ever enchanting music!

Thank you to Fleetwood Mac for your lifelong dedication to our musical delight!

Thank You to all the local music bands in the Chicago area playing live and living your dream!

Contents